Awakening The Moon Goddess

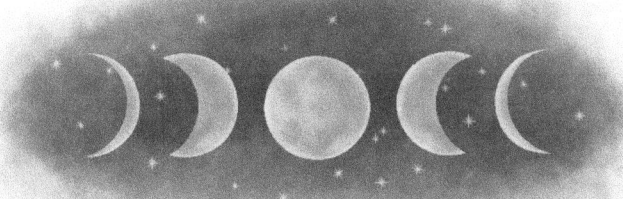

M.C. Grail

Author Note: all names, characters, businesses, events, and incidents are the production of the author's imagination. Any resemblance to actual persons, living or dead or actual events is purely coincidental.

ISNB : 979-8-9907871-0-0

Cover Art by: Every Moment Matters Photography LLC

Editing by: Reedsy

For my husband who always supports me and all my crazy ideas,

and

for sixteen-year-old me, look at what we did!

CONTENT WARNINGS

Hand to hand combat, Blood, Abuse, Violence, Death, Murder,

Torture, Graphic language, Adult graphic sexual content, Parent loss,

Talk about Sexual assault, suicide, alcohol use, child abuse

Chapter 1: Let It Begin

Mazzy

BEEP, BEEP, BEEP.

Loud beeping of the alarm echoes in my head, waking me. I reach for

the annoying box making my head throb with every beep with my

hand blindly searching the bedside table. *There it is*, I think as I finally

find it. Slamming my hand on the top, the incessant beeping is finally

silenced. Ugh, no way it's morning already. I haven't lifted my head

off my pillow and don't want to. I'm too hungover for it to be morning.

Groaning, I settle back into a comfortable potion and lay there. I can't believe it is already eight in the morning. That's the last time I let my coworkers/roommates/friends talk me into going out for my birthday, especially if it's on a Sunday night. Turns out, Sunday is still a pretty busy night for a bar. I didn't care for the crowd, but hey, it had a decent DJ playing. Rolling in my bed, I wince and groan as the light peeking through a crack in the closed curtains hits me in the eyes.

Ahh, bright light.

Seriously though, I don't know why I drank so much. I don't care for it, but for some reason, I kept drinking. I think I was so uncomfortable with how crowded the bar was, and I'm weak and totally caved to peer pressure. My friend and roommate Serafina was egging me on to keep up with her. She's the party girl out of the four of us. We invited more, but the others chose the smarter option. I should have said no, but did I? Nope. I let Serafina's words get into my head. *You only turn twenty-five once, girly, so why not have some fun? Plus, for a single, decently attractive woman, you act more like a granny with twelve cats.* I'm not a huge cat person. I'm more of a dog person.

More like a wolf person. Literally.

Rolling over again, I fight what I know I need to do. I need to get up, but gods, I don't want to. Closing my eyes, I try not to move. I'm hoping a few more minutes of rest will help the throbbing in my head, and the room will stop feeling like it's spinning. Serafina knows me. She knows I act like an extrovert when in public, but I'm actually a closet introvert. It's a mask I put on, and it's exhausting to keep up with. Maybe, I drank so much hoping the mask would become who I really was.

Great logic there, Mazzy. Eye roll.

I should have known I was going to overdo it trying to "fit in." I would have much rather stayed in my bed reading a good spicy romance or fantasy novel. Instead, I let loose for once in my life. I know she means well, but I don't care to be around all those people.

Two-faced humans, fae, and shifters.

Serafina can be a bit much at times. She will keep pestering you until you give in. She is the Whitlock Police chief's daughter and a literal princess; she takes that role seriously. Her father, Archer Whitlock, is half-fae, half-human. He is the son of one of the High Fae lords, making Serafina part of that royal family. The fact that she is more human than fae makes her chances of being accepted as queen one day unlikely, but none of that stops her from acting like a real princess—and the chief certainly spoils her. I think he is trying to make up for Serafina's mother not being around.

Get your hungover ass out of bed, Mazzy.

BEEP, BEEP, BEEP.

Fuck.

I sit up way too fast, causing the room to spin again. Closing my eyes, I bring my knees to my chest as I run my hands through my messy hair, massaging my scalp and using my knees as a table for my elbows. Groaning, I try to ignore the beeping from the alarm clock. I hit the snooze button by accident, and the beeping is pounding through my head like it's a jackhammer.

Ugh, make it stop.

Slamming my right hand onto the stupid alarm clock again, I hit it just right to launch it from under my hand and off the bedside table. It beeps its final pathetic beep as it hits the floor and breaks into pieces. Sighing, I stretch and realize at this point I need to get my hungover ass out of bed and get to work. After getting out of my warm bed, I head to the bathroom. I love having a bathroom in my bedroom. I don't love that my roommates tend to use up all the hot water, but that's what you get when you share a three-bedroom two-bathroom apartment with four people.

That reminds me, I need to make a mental note for later. I need to talk to Harper and Clay again about switching rooms. I think it makes more sense for them to have my room with the attached bathroom now that they are officially a married couple. That way, they have their privacy and keep their married people's things out of the only other bathroom in the apartment. I don't know how many times Serafina or I have walked in on something we didn't need or want to see because they forgot to lock the door or didn't even close it before getting lost in each other.

Honestly, good for them for having mind-blowing sex with someone they love, but not everyone has that or wants to see it when all they want to do is go pee or do a load of laundry. They love each other, and it's super cute—most of the time. Sometimes, it makes me a little angry and admittedly a little jealous.

Don't go there right now, Mazzy.

Right now, I need to focus on getting my ass to work before I end up sitting in a two-hour lecture about the importance of showing up on time by my boss. *Shower. Get in the shower*, I say to myself.

Yeah, just keep repeating that to yourself. That will help keep yourself on track.

Rolling my eyes, I take a deep breath as I continue to the bathroom. I step into my bathroom and the cold tile sends a shiver up my spine. The rest of the apartment might be boiling hot—our AC unit is broken, and the landlord said he would "get right on that" when we told him three weeks ago—but somehow, the tile in the bathrooms is cold no matter what time of year. It doesn't make sense to me at all, but it's always a bit of a wake-up when your warm toes touch the cold tiles. I grab a clean towel from the cabinet under the sink and catch a glimpse of myself in the mirror as I stand up.

Yikes, you look rough!

It's a coffee day for sure and maybe some makeup. Trying to ignore my reflection in the large mirror, I head to the shower. I can't wait to feel the hot water hit my skin, the hotter the better. Is it just me or does every woman in the world take hell-worthy hot showers?

While stepping into the shower, I catch a hint of an odd but pleasant smell. I can't pinpoint exactly what it smells like. It's far too faint, but it smells nice.

Serafina has a lot of different perfumes. I'm sure it's one of those, and if you're thinking how I could smell her perfume in my bathroom, well, her bedroom is on the other side of the bathroom. She probably sprayed so much that it seeped through the walls. I wouldn't put it past her. She practically bathes in her body sprays and perfumes.

Grabbing my body wash, I wash my body first, saving my hair for last. I hate washing my hair. It's long, almost too long, but I don't have the time right now to get a haircut. My hair is slightly curly, like relaxed ringlets, and goes down to my hips. I have a love-hate relationship with my hair—mainly with how much it draws attention to me. If I go out to the store or anywhere besides work, I will often put it in a ponytail or braid. I have worn baseball caps and winter hats to hide it, too.

Yeah, it's your hair you hate… Sure.

Okay, it's not my hair. It's all the eyes that it draws from strangers who feel the need to comment on my hair whether it's a nice comment or a nasty one. I have had people tell me how much they love it, how it's so healthy looking for how long it is, or that the color is neat. I smile and say thank you. What else am I supposed to say? I don't want them staring at me or pointing it out, but it's rude to say nothing. Body washed, I shave my legs and underarms, and by quickly, I probably missed some hair on my legs. But that's no biggie at least not right now. While shaving, I drift back into my thoughts about people making comments on my hair, rolling my eyes.

I remember what happened yesterday at the club before I got so intoxicated I didn't care. A group of men were whispering, yelling actually, negative comments back and forth about me. They were at the table next to us, so it was hard not to hear them. It's not like their comments were anything I haven't heard from people before, but fuck, they could have at least tried not to make it loud enough for me to hear it. Harsh comments about the color—how I'm ruining my hair by bleaching it, and how they would never go out with a girl like that. I can usually brush those comments off.

The ones I hate the most are the men that have no issue saying to my face that I would be much prettier if it was darker, or I'll never find a guy who will date me because of my hair. Such dicks. I try to walk past people whose opinions really shouldn't matter to me, but I would be lying if I said they didn't get to me sometimes.

Placing the razor back, I stand under the water for a moment, letting the hot stream flow over my body. I don't bleach my hair; I don't need to. I was born with silver grey hair with nearly white highlights. My roots are a little darker grey. I have had people assume I'm part fae because of my eyes and hair. There are a few fae bloodlines where white hair and light-colored eyes are common, but not eyes like mine. My eyes are a nice mix of Caribbean blue and turquoise. They stand out against my pale skin. I have had people assume I am related in some way to Serafina, like a half sister or distant cousin. But while she has light hair, it's not silver in color; it's blonde. Another difference between us is our skin tone. Well, that and the fact that she's a fucking model and beyond stunning. The fae side certainly shows in Serafina's beauty. Serafina is like six feet tall and super skinny. I am nowhere near that tall. While I'm fairer skinned, Serafina has beautiful caramel skin that she gets from her fae side.

Also from her fae side are her eyes. They are a bright silver grey, just like her father's.

Realizing I have stayed standing under the running water for far too long, I shampoo and condition my hair. I probably should have taken more time with it, but I'm definitely going to be late if I don't get moving. After rinsing out the conditioner, I run my fingers through it to gently detangle any knots. Then I tie it in a loose braid before getting out of the shower.

You're going to be late. Fuck.

I took a much longer shower than I intended. I grab the towel off the counter and fling my bathroom door open as I wrap the towel around myself. I need to get dressed and head out now.

Once I reach my closet, I take out a set of my typical workout clothes. A black sports bra that will squish the crap out of my chest, black leggings, and a teal crop top tank top. I grab the duffle bag off the closet floor before turning to my bed. I can't forget it. My officer uniform, badge, and gun are in it. After a nice long lecture, I have been making sure I have it with me. If I don't, I avoid the chief like the plague.

Reaching my bed, I toss the duffle gently onto it and my clothes next to it. I start to towel dry as I get myself ready for the day. I don't need my gun for my job, but as a cop, I shouldn't leave it at home in my apartment, my bad. The Whitlock Police Department runs a combat seminar for new police academy graduates. It began a while back and was intended as a competition, giving the chiefs the chance to get the best graduates in their departments. This caused fighting between the different department's chiefs, so it slowly turned into something far more useful. I'm a combat instructor. Today starts the first day of a new session with the newest graduates, day one of a ninety-day combat session.

Day one of dealing with massive alpha holes.

I'm not looking forward to the hot-headed men with god complexes that I will be forced to deal with. Fuck, there are a lot of them, and I often wonder how some didn't get booted from the academy. When I took over as the combat instructor in Archer's place, our department became known for giving those guys a nice reality check. I don't put up with men who think they are god's gift to the world, let alone god's gift to women.

The female officers coming in are trying too hard to prove themselves. They can be a bit bitchy or snide to each other, but when they realize they don't need to prove themselves to anyone or compete, they do just fine. The main goal of the seminar is to find their weak skills and improve them, hopefully making them more comfortable and capable of handling hard situations when they move on to their assigned departments.

Today will be good. Just keep telling yourself that.

I catch my reflection in the tall mirror I have in my bedroom while getting dressed, and instantly, negative thoughts start popping into my mind. I'm not super skinny. I have some jiggly bits like large hips and a C nearly D-size chest. I have an hourglass figure I try to hide in my tight sports bras and baggy tops. My "crop top" I work out in is a men's medium tank top that I cut to shorten a little. I'm fit, but I can't help but focus on areas that I see as flaws or ugly.

Lose a few pounds in your ass and thighs. You aren't working out enough. Work out more.

I need to stop thinking like that. Our department general fitness instructor tells me he thinks I'm good. That for someone who is not even five foot three, my BMI is good. I'm not happy though. I had to throw away my scale a few weeks ago when I got upset that it dared to read my weight at one hundred and forty-five pounds—ten pounds over the weight I want to be at.

Trying to take my mind off the body image issues, I start getting my workout clothes on. I leave my hair in the loose braid for now, no point in making it look good when it will just get messy on the ride to work. I contemplated makeup after catching my reflection in the mirror before my shower but remembered I'd just be getting sweaty today. These trainees don't care what I look like. They all come in calling me the Ice Queen, and my appearance other than maybe the color of my hair plays no role in that name.

They all know I'm a hard ass on people and "ice cold," in other words. I don't care if I hurt their feelings or break a bone or two to prove my point or knock the assholes down a few pegs. It's the side of me I have to show. They can't see the real me. I put my sneakers in my duffle bag and put on my black lace-up flat leather boots, almost ready to head out. The shower helped. I feel a little more awake than before, hungover but a smidge more alert.

I grab my duffle and fling it over my shoulder as I spin around in search of my phone. I usually sleep with it in my hand or on my bed so the beeping and vibrations from the alarms will wake me, but it wasn't in my hand or on my bed when I got up. I thought I put it on the charger last night. I find the cord with my fingers and give it a tug. Crap, it comes up too easily, almost smacking me in the face with no phone attached. Fuck, where did I put that thing? I must have left it in the kitchen with my keys last night, which means I'll have to hope it's charged enough for the ride to work.

Double-checking that I have everything, I head out my bedroom door into the hallway. I hope my roommates are all up or still sound asleep. I do not want to talk to people this morning—even people I like and live with. I reach the end of the hall and freeze when I smell that scent again. In front of me is the other bathroom, the door is open, and I can tell it's not coming from there. To my left is the doorway to the living room/kitchen area of the apartment, not coming from there either. The scent is coming from my right. Serafina's bedroom door.

I take a few steps toward the door and reach for the handle. The smell is coming from her room. What in the world could it be coming from? Maybe a candle or new body spray she didn't tell us about yet? She loves showing off her new purchases.

More like rubbing it in our faces.

I go to turn the handle, forgetting to knock, but I stop when I hear a high-pitched giggle and a deep moan. Oh gods, did she bring someone home last night? *Oops.* I release the handle before it's able to unlatch and walk away as quickly as I can.

I didn't know for sure if she brought someone home from the bar last night, but I guess I do now. I hope this isn't another broken heart in the making. I turn to my left, pass the bathroom, and glance across the living room to the other bedroom door. The door is wide open. I can see from here that the bed is made, so I can assume that means Harper and Clay are up. Trying not to focus on that scent, I keep walking until I reach the island.

There it is.

Smack dab in the middle of the faux butcher block countertop island is my phone right next to my bike keys. Shaking my head, I place my duffle at the foot of one of the stools and plop myself down on it. Sighing, I grab my phone and peer at the screen. It's nearly dead, and it's 9:00 a.m. I need to get going. I place my phone and keys in my duffle bag. My back is still facing the living room when I hear some movement from behind me.

"Good morning, sunshine," a female voice says from behind me.

"Morning, Harper," I say without looking in her direction. "Serafina is having some fun this morning, huh?" I ask.

Spinning on the stool to face the living room, I find Harper lying on the lap of her husband, Clay, who is making a face, clearly trying to hold back his signature booming laugh. Rolling my eyes at him dramatically, I try not to laugh.

"Don't hurt yourself, big boy," I tease and bring my pointer finger to my mouth. "Shh, she might hear you." I laugh. I love that we can tease each other even when we are hungover. I don't mind their company, but I would have rather stayed in bed.

"You look like hell this morning. How much did you drink last night?" Harper asks while sitting up.

"Ouch. That hurts. I drank just as much as you," I say, hopping off the stool. I head to the coffee maker in the kitchen. I need coffee—lots, and lots of coffee. I hear the door of Serafina's bedroom open and try hard not to peek in that direction as I round the island headed for the coffee maker.

It's none of your business, Mazzy. Let her be.

"Seriously, how are you two so wide-eyed this morning? I know you both drank just as much as I did if not more," I say as I pull down a to-go mug from the cabinet.

I'm not a huge coffee person, especially the kind my roommates like, but I don't have the energy this morning to be picky. Caffeine is caffeine, and I need it. I make myself coffee, and as I'm putting the lid on the cup, I hear feet stop at the island behind me.

"Well, well, look who finally decided to get up," a sweet voice says teasingly. Turning to face her, I try to ignore her *just had the best morning sex of my life* afterglow. It must have been good to have her looking all hot and bothered still with a giant smile on her face.

Lucky fae.

"Well, good morning to you, too. Does your friend want some coffee, or was your pink kitty enough of a pick-me-up for him this morning?" I tease, taking a sip of my coffee.

She knows I'm picking on her, and she would for sure be doing the same to me if I had been the one who brought a guy home. Not that that has ever happened or will ever happen, but it's nice we have a good relationship like this. It wasn't always that way, but it's grown for the better. I know she won't take offense to it, and if she does, she will for sure let me know.

"Ha, ha, ha," she says mockingly. "Very funny, smart ass." That was a weak comeback from her, and she knows me better than that.

"Was his dick so good that it short-circuited your normal witty comebacks, darling?" I ask with a chuckle. I walk over to her and nudge her with my shoulder as I pass her, giving her a wink. "I'm kidding. Good for you, girly," I say.

As I bend down to pick up my duffle bag, I get another hit of that scent. This time it's a little stronger with a hint of honey to it that makes my stomach sour. I normally like the smell of honey but not right now. That scent is coming off Serafina as anger starts to boil inside me.

Chill, Mazzy. What is your problem?

"Hey, did you get a new body spray?" I ask while standing and swinging my bag over my shoulder.

"Nope, why?" Serafina answers, a puzzled expression on her face.

"No reason. I keep getting a hint of something that smells good that I can't figure out. I thought it was coming off you," I say. I head for the door of the apartment, taking a quick glance at the two love birds on the couch. "Are you guys planning on coming to work today or am I the only one not calling out hungover today?" I joked.

Just as I take a step backward and grab the apartment door handle, something over Serafina's shoulder catches my eye coming out of the bathroom.

More like someone. Holy shit. Look at those muscles.

One-Night Stand Guy is coming out of the bathroom with his back facing toward the living room. The muscles on his back are…impressive to say the least. Tilting my head a little more to peek around Serafina trying to get a better view. My eyes go a little wide when I notice he only has a towel around his waist.

Bet he has a nice ass.

Okay, judge me all you want, but I know a fine ass man when I see one. Serafina must have noticed me staring. She glances over her shoulder then turns back to me with a huge smile and her sweet high-pitched giggle. Still smiling, she walks to me, picks up my black bike helmet from the coat rack on the wall next to my head, and places it directly in my face, breaking my line of sight to the god-like man walking into her room.

Hey, get that out of the way.

"Here, you don't want to forget this," she says, shoving the helmet into my hands. "Seriously girl, you need to get laid." She giggles.

There it is.

I was waiting for that to come out of her mouth. She couldn't help herself. Why does she think I need to get laid to be happy or "less grumpy" as she puts it? Have we regressed in our "we don't need no man, we are women, hear us roar" movement? No, I didn't think so. I don't need a man to make me happy. Plus, I can't.

"Oh...thanks. I'll get right on that," I say sarcastically as I grab my helmet from her. I tilt my head to catch another glimpse of the man, hoping for a small glimpse at his face before he disappears into her room. No such luck.

"Seriously, Sera, how did you manage that one?" I say jokingly. Placing my helmet under my arm, I turn the apartment door handle and get ready to head out the door.

"I'm just that beautiful. What do you expect?" Serafina says with her normal pretty girl attitude as she flips her hair and reaches for the door so she can close it behind me.

Nothing like being yourself, Serafina. Eye roll.

I want to call her out on it, but I don't want to hurt her feelings...too badly. I know her well. We have known each other since we were fifteen years old. I know the truth. Behind that perfect fae Barbie facade is an insecure girl just wanting people to accept her.

Same, girl, same.

Serafina's main insecurity is the human side of her and how that drastically affects her fae magic. She barely has any, and when she does try a spell, it backfires or only lasts a few minutes. Laughing, I remember the one spell she did that ended with her and the bathroom looking like a glitter bomb went off. She was cleaning up glitter for weeks. She's good at hiding how insecure that makes her feel. I have to give her credit for that. I'm not as good at hiding my insecurities unless I give everyone the cold shoulder. I start down the hall with one thing replaying in my head over and over.

Why did that scent mixed with Serafina's make me so angry?

The apartment building halls are sweltering, but I can't help but be excited. Why? You might be asking. Well, it's sunny with zero chance of rain today, which means it's a bike day. Hell, most days are bike-to-work days for me. I don't own a car. If the weather is nasty, I will walk or ask my roommates for a ride. It helps that three out of the four of us work at the police station anyway.

We live in a somewhat big city, so the commute to the station isn't that far from the apartment. Think a tad smaller than New York

City. On nice days, I try to leave early, so I can take the long way but not today. I'm running late. I would much rather be on my bike than a stuffy car.

Plus, who doesn't like a biker girl in black leather.

By the time I reach the elevator, I hear rushing footsteps coming up from behind me. With a laugh, I pause in the elevator doorway and hold the elevator door open without turning around. I already know who it is, and they know I'll wait for them. Tapping my foot a few times, I make a *tisk, tisk* sound as they reach me.

"Okay, okay, we get it," Harper says as she ducks under the arm I have holding the elevator door. She laughs as she rights herself and turns around, making a face at her husband who comes up behind me panting, like a dog.

"You know, Clay, for a fit-looking man and police officer you sure get easily winded," I joke, letting go of the door so we can both walk into the elevator.

"Funny," he responds as his eyes darken, and he stalks toward his wife, backing her to the wall of the elevator with his body. I turn away dramatically, holding my helmet up in front of my face. They just can't help themselves either apparently.

Get a room.

"Not in here, guys. I don't want to have to bleach my eyes," I tease.

By the time the elevator door opens on the ground floor, we are all laughing and joking about random shit. Passing through the lobby of the apartment complex, we check the mail then head out to the parking lot. The happy couple plays grab ass the entire way to their black SUV. Harper is giggling up a storm.

"See you guys at work," I yell, waving at them as I continue to my bike a few parking spots down from their SUV.

"Hello, beautiful," I say as I place my hand on the gas tank of my sports motorcycle. Gosh, I love this bike. This all black, sleek looking, and hella-fast bike is one of the few real joys in my life. The other, well, that's something I won't be sharing—at least not right now.

I look forward to this part of my day and taking my time on the ride home later. Sunset rides going the long way home are stunning. I'm not a photographer, and my crap cell phone camera doesn't do the sunsets any justice. But it's stunning, and I feel at peace when I'm biking through the roads surrounded by trees versus buildings. I'm not a huge city girl, but I make it work. Maybe I'll leave work and take a nice ride around the surrounding towns since I can't do it this morning.

Chapter 2: Anxiety, Take a Chill Pill

Mazzy

Walking in the doors of the police department after parking my bike

always causes a little bit of anxiety. You would think I would be used

to it by now. I have been walking through these doors since I was

fifteen. This was like a second home to me. The chief knew my

mother, and when she died, he took me and my sister in.

No matter how much I trust the chief, I can't silence that

nagging little voice in my head. *He knows. He figured it out.* I try to

silence that thought as I walk in the first set of double doors to the station. As I reach for the second set of doors, a little panic starts to rise in my chest. I try to push that down, but that voice is still there. Man, I'm struggling with my anxiety today.

You should run.

That's just a thought inside my anxiety-ridden brain, but it's the truth. If they find out what I'm hiding, no matter how much they say they care about me, I know they will turn on me. They will have no choice unless they too want to join me in a death sentence.

And you chose to become a police officer because that's not upping your risk of being found out at all.

"Go to work, test the newcomer's combat skills, and train them more before their final assigned departments and partners. That's it. That's all you have to do," I whisper as I force myself through the final set of doors. I blame my hangover for this relentless anxiety.

The double doors open to a decently sized lobby with a large reception desk in the middle. There are metal benches on either side against the walls. No one is sitting on them yet, but I'm sure they will be full by lunch. This is a somewhat large city in our state, and well, people do stupid shit all the time. I reach the desk in the middle of the room and tap on the countertop like I'm annoyed and have been waiting here for hours. I'm waiting to see if she notices.

"Good morning," says the sweet receptionist as she shifts her glance my way, realizing it is just little old me standing there. I'm smirking at her as she drops her fake customer service smile. Her grin reaches her eyes. She's probably thankful she doesn't have to repeat her normal customer service-sounding greeting.

"Good morning, welcome to Whitlock Police Department. What can I assist you with today?"

Poor woman. I would get so tired of saying that repeatedly to every single person who walks in these doors or calls the reception desk.

"Mazzy, hey, you look a little tired this morning. How was the ride in?" she asks.

"I can't confirm or deny that I may have had a little too much to drink with everyone last night," I joke.

Lori is great. She's a sweet and sassy woman in her late fifties. We asked her to come out for drinks for my birthday, but she said she was way too old for that party scene. I call BS because this woman is stunning for her age. To me, she looks no older than her early forties with little grey hair and the body of a fitness instructor. She's human, so it's good genetics. And she takes amazing care of herself. I have seen her let loose at work holiday parties in the past, so she could have easily kept up with us if not showed us up. I think only Serafina would have given her a run for her money.

"Like always, the ride was great. You missed a good time last night. You should have come out with us. Are the new graduates here yet?" I ask, hoping she says no so I can get a small workout beforehand. Lori shakes her head no and points to the clock. "They will be here at ten," she says, completely choosing to ignore my comment about last night.

It's only 9:20 a.m. Sweet, I have time for a workout.

"Chief wants to see you first," Lori yells as the phone rings. I turn around to see her answer the phone while silently gesturing to her left.

Plans squashed like a bug, ugh.

I want to throw a few punches on the punching bag but nope. A meeting with the chief usually means I'll be there for a bit or there's a problem. I need that workout time before dealing with the newcomers.

Spinning on my heels, I head in the opposite direction, tapping a hand on the reception desk as I pass it. I mouth *Thank you* to Lori and head to the police chief's office at the end of a long hall. Knocking on the door, my heart is beating so fast as I feel like I'm about to throw up.

Seriously, anxiety, can you take a chill pill please, for like two seconds?

I take a few deep breaths while waiting for the chief to respond to my knock. He can answer any minute now. That would be fantastic.

"Come in," the Chiefs gruff voice bellows from behind the door, and I slowly turn the handle.

I need time to work out. It helps calm my anxiety, and it's going to be a bad day if I don't get a few minutes in. The last time I was in desperate need of a punch session and didn't get it, I had three incident reports for breaking the noses of the trainees. And my mouth got me in a massive amount of trouble when I sassed the wrong chief and almost got Archer reamed out by the council. Yes, I have anger issues. I know. I'm working on it.

"Chief, Lori said you wanted to speak with me," I say, walking in and stopping a few steps inside the office.

"Come have a seat, Mazelynn," his scratchy voice says. He sounds a little tired and annoyed. Shit. He called me Mazelynn. He only calls me that when the talk is truly serious, or I'm in some kind of trouble, usually incident reports.

Heading to the chair in front of his desk, I set my bag and helmet down by the foot of it and take a seat. The chief is sitting in his chair behind his laptop on a cluttered desk.

His desk makes me more anxious. I don't think I have OCD, but his desk makes me twitch. It's a huge mess with papers everywhere and a million coffee cups. Okay, that might be an exaggeration, but he does drink a lot of coffee. His office always smells like stale coffee. I don't know how he finds anything in that mess.

"Is everything okay this morning, Chief?" I ask. The man who took me and my sister in when we were fifteen could at least give me a slight sign that I'm not in for a huge shock but nope, nothing. Archer is a tall, mocha-skinned fae. He, like all the other fae, even half-fae, is decently attractive. His normal soft expression is replaced with a hardened expression. His jaw is clenched, his eyes are squinting, and his brows are a little furrowed. That expression and his tone make me nervous. I start to feel uncomfortable in the chair and fidget a little.

Staring down at my lap, I tap my hands on my thighs trying to regulate a little. It's not helping. I start to bite the inside of my cheek.

Any time now, Archer.

"I want you prepared for who will be here assisting you with this combat session," he says, still not taking his eyes off his computer.

"And who would that be?" I ask with a little bit of annoyance in my tone. I don't want assistance, especially at the last minute.

Why such short notice?

Clay and Gage help, and sometimes, I pull Harper and Bex. I don't need more help. The new trainees will be here shortly, and I had already planned how I was going to handle it today with Clay to assist. If I were told a day or so ahead of time, I would be a little less annoyed, still annoyed, but not nearly as bad as I am right now. Staring at Archer, I'm at a loss for words—respectful words.

"You know my friend and fellow police chief, Alpha Colak Dolton?" he asks.

I nod in response, clenching my jaw and dreading his next words.

Please don't say what I think you're about to say.

"His sons," he says, finally raising his head to look up at me.

Fuck, fuck, fuck.

"WHAT? Are you fucking kidding me, Archer?" I yell, it comes out a lot louder than I intended, and I instantly regret my choice of words. If anyone was walking outside his office from the break room or the other office, they for sure heard it.

Oops.

Archer stares at me like he knows I didn't mean to yell. We agreed when I graduated from the police academy and got assigned here that I would call him "chief" or "sir" in the station while on duty.

Growing up, my sister and I called him Archer, so sometimes, I slip up, especially if my emotions are high.

"Loen, as in the future alpha, the hot-headed wolf shifter with probably the biggest god complex in the world? Not to mention the reputation of being the biggest playboy who fucks anyone with a vagina between their legs. Half the female officers in town talk about him," I say.

I don't even feel bad now. I do not want to deal with this man. He is the dick of all dicks, and if his younger brothers are anything like him, I'll probably lose my shit on them too. I squeeze my fists on my lap and clench my jaw tighter—a little too tight, making me feel an instant headache forming.

Unclench your jaw, dumbass.

Just what I ordered—crippling anxiety mixed with a side of migraine. Today of all days, I don't need this. Not on day one of a new combat seminar session. Trying to calm myself down, I remind myself that it's not Archer's fault. I have no right to snap at him. Taking a few breaths while trying to relax, my jaw makes a loud popping noise when I force it to unclench. Yeah, that's how tight I was clenching it. My dentist *loves* me. Did you get the sarcasm there?

"Why do you think they are here?" Archer asks. A smirk on his now relaxed face tells me there is something else. He grabs his phone from his desk. How he found it under all those papers and cups I have no idea. Unlocking his phone, he tosses it to me. I stare at him with a puzzled expression as I catch the phone.

"Sir?" I ask.

"Look at the texts from Chief Dolton," he says and turns his attention back to his laptop. I don't even know if I truly want to know. But at least it will give me some kind of context. Sighing, I start reading the texts between Archer and Chief/Alpha Dolton.

Dolton:
Hey buddy old pal.
I need to ask a favor.

Archer:
What did you do, old friend?

Dolton:
Funny, it's about my son, well sons.
I want them to aid this upcoming training session.
Can we make that happen?

Archer:

What did they do?

You know that starts today, right?

Dolton:

I prefer not to say.

Archer:

Prefer not to say or won't?

Dolton:

....

Archer:

Fine!

But I'll be calling to discuss this later,

old friend.

Dolton:

 Thanks, old friend.

They will be there within the hour.

Sent them your way yesterday.

Archer:

before talking to me?

a little cocky, aren't we?

I don't need to read anymore. Checking the time-stamped from the start of the texts, I notice it came in about an hour and a half ago. That's all the notice he felt like giving us.

Cocky asshole.

I guess it shouldn't be that big of a shocker. He is an alpha shifter after all. If he's sending his sons here for a reality check, that means they have probably done something insanely stupid, and this is their attempt at saving face and his reputation. I hesitate to ask at first, but something tells me there is more to this.

"You think there is more to it than that," I say as I sigh and toss the phone gently back on Archer's desk.

"Yes," he agrees, leaning back in his chair with a somewhat mischievous smirk. He knows me too well. I'll have fun with this either way. I'm not one to back down from a challenge, so if Archer wants me to have them "assist" me, then they will assist me. They won't like what I have them help with, but I'll get a kick out of it. Plus, how great would it be to see a high alpha's sons get pinned on a mat by little old me?

"Okay, fine, but no promises this time," I say as I pick up my helmet and duffle bag before I stand up from the chair. Now I desperately need to punch something before I come face-to-face with

Chief Alpha Dalton's sons. I don't need my first incident report of this seminar to be that I said something "disrespectful" to the alphas' sons.

"I wouldn't expect anything less, Mazelynn. Last thing, the bus with the new graduates is running late. It's expected to be here at 10:10 a.m.," he says, laughing as he gets back to whatever he is doing on his laptop.

Smiling, I shake my head as I head out of his office, closing the door behind me. He suspects something is up, and I do too. An hour and a half notice that they will be here is rude and too sudden for there not to be a hidden agenda of some kind. As I pass the reception desk, Lori is giving me a *ready or not* expression as she points to the front door with her pen while talking to someone on the phone. I turn my head to see a tall man in a bike helmet with a black leather jacket and black jeans walk into the lobby followed by two handsome dark-haired men dressed in grey sweats and t-shirts. I roll my eyes at Lori as I walk past the desk down the hall to the girls' locker room. My phone was nearly dead when I found it on the island this morning. That's what I get for forgetting to charge it. When I reach the locker room, the first thing I do is throw it on the charger we keep by the door.

9:45 a.m. Let's hope it charges enough while I change.

I always listen to music while working out, and today feels like an angry playlist kind of day. Finding my locker, I undo the lock, get my sneakers out of my duffle bag, and set them on the wooden bench that runs in the middle of this row of lockers. After sitting on the bench, I change my shoes and stash my duffle bag and boots in my locker. Making sure it's locked, I start down the row of lockers to where I plugged my phone in. I took the phone off the charger and checked the battery, 15 percent. Well, that's better than the 5 percent it was at. I'm messing with my phone, trying to get the playlist I want as I head out. Without paying attention, I push through the locker room doors and down the hall eyes on my phone and walk right into a wall—or at least that's how it felt. Ouch, I rub my nose after smashing into this boulder of a man's chest, the hard chest of the man in black leather.

Shit, shit, shit.

Taking a tiny step back, I slowly gaze up, and I meet the same tall man I saw walking in a few minutes ago. The one in all black with a black motorcycle helmet on, the tinted visor still down. Hearing chatter at the reception desk, I shift to my right to peer past the boulder standing in front of me. The two men in sweats at the desk are chatting it up with Lori and one of the other female officers. They appear nearly identical, meaning the one standing in front of me, the one I ran into with the chest built like a brick shit house, is the oldest Dolton. Loen. Seriously, though, how the hell is his chest so hard?

Leave it to you to run face to chest into Loen Dolton.

"You should watch where you're going instead of playing on your phone, Princess," says the tall mountain of a man in front of me. The way his gravelly voice said "princess" catches my attention, and not just my attention but my vagina's attention too. *Easy, girl.* Now I'm standing here, hoping my facial expression doesn't reveal my utter shock and hope to the gods that helmet will mask any scent I'm giving off.

Holy fuck.

His voice sends shivers down my spine and heats a part of my body that now desperately wants attention and not from my little buzzy friend on my bedside table. I don't know if I'm more thrown off by the sound of his voice or my body's involuntary reaction to it. He's a dick and a fuck boy, but his voice nearly made my legs give out. Trying to get my head out of my vagina, I compose myself.

Without saying a word, I put my earbuds into my ears while glaring right at the dark blackened visor of his helmet where his eyes should be. Giving a somewhat sarcastic smile, I take a step to the right and walk past him. I'll deal with him and my body's odd reaction to him after I punch the bag a few times.

I can hear the guy's locker room door open and close as I continue into the gym headed for my favorite bag. Yes, I have a favorite. It might be weird, but it helps me with my anxiety. It's the only bag that even with my back turned to the door allows me to see the entire gym. I don't like being snuck up on.

Once at the bag, I do a big no, no and forgo stretching. I'll probably regret it later, but I don't have a lot of time. As I'm fixing my wraps, I check the mirror to see the two men in sweats pass the gym door and head for the locker room. Yup, those are the twins. I ran square into Loen, just fucking peachy.

Pressing play on my music app, I get right to my workout, and by workout, I mean punching the ever-living shit out of the poor punching bag. I could easily get lost in thought during this time, especially on days like today. Instead, I hyperfocus on my breathing and check the mirror constantly as I'm throwing punch after punch at the bag. *Today is just another day*, I repeat over and over.

Just another day.

I'm getting lost in my head again. I should take up a hobby other than beating a punching bag or agree to see a counselor again like Archer wants me to. I don't care for that last option. Don't get me wrong. Counselors are good, and I think everyone should go. But the ones who I have had the pleasure of going to always call me on holding back information or that I'm hiding something they feel I should talk about. Getting ready to throw another punch, I glance in the mirror to see two men walking in. Clay and fuck...

THUD.

Ouch. That was smooth, Mazzy!

Way to miss that punch, I think. I'm practically hugging the bag at this point. I'm hoping no one heard or saw that. Pushing myself off the bag, I scan the mirror. Nothing indicates that anyone saw that blunder, and if they did, they knew better than to keep staring at me.

My eyes land back on Loen. He's the guy walking in with Clay. The one who literally made me kiss the punching bag with my face. They're laughing it up like they have been friends for years. Clay must think Loen is hilarious because even with my headphones blaring, I can hear his laugh. In Clay's defense, he has one of those loud laughs that gets everyone going. You know that kind of laugh that triggers everyone else to laugh but not in a teasing way. You can't help but laugh with him. Taking a few deep breaths, I go back to punching the bag for ten minutes, which is not long enough for how I'm feeling right now.

Loen, fucking hell. He is attractive.

I need to focus, not on Loen, but on getting some stress relief. I shouldn't be so distracted by Loen. You would think our paths would have crossed before now, but they never have. I may have talked to him on the phone a few times, but we have shockingly never met in person. I know he has two younger brothers who are twins. They're my age, and Loen is a few years older. Their father runs one of the bigger police academies in the state, and a lot of people try to attend his academy. Who wouldn't if it's run by a *"well-respected"* alpha who has a reputation for putting out strong cops?

Eye roll.

Chief Dolton's son isn't the only one with rumors about him. The alpha himself has one that's been circling for a while. It said that Chief Dolton dismisses a high number of female officers from his academy for idiotic reasons. To this day, there has been no record of him dismissing any of the males.

Sexist much?

Archer cringed at the thought of me at Dalton's academy. He never would have let me go there. Not that I wanted to. In hindsight, I probably would not have been better off there. Any time Archer went to see his "old friend," he never took me or my sister. He would always be giving us vague excuses, not that we actually cared much. I wasn't big on being social after our mother died. I didn't trust people. Let alone shifters. I didn't care that we never met his friend or his friends' kids. Living with Serafina wasn't pleasant, but eventually, we got along. The times I did talk to Loen on the phone, he was rude and condescending.

Taking another glance in the mirror, I realize how tall he is, towering over Clay. Clay is nearly six feet tall, so Loen must be well over six feet.

Stop staring at him before he notices I'm checking out every inch of him.

Loen has perfectly tanned caramel skin. His eyes are a shade of amber that I haven't seen before. They are so bright that even from across the gym hall I can see how beautiful they are. There is a hint of a five o'clock shadow on his face. I'm fine with that because it shows off his defined jawline. His hair is black. It resembles a slightly grown-out military cut. The one where the top is slightly longer than it is on the sides. Okay, I guess I should admit he is somewhat attractive.

Who are you kidding? He's fucking hot.

That's so not helping. I try pulling myself from my thoughts again. I start punching the bag again, trying hard not to stare in the mirror at Loen on the sparring mat. I release my next punch, and a shock wave runs up my arm from the impact. Fuck, I knew before it touched the bag this was a bad punch. I wasn't paying attention. I rub my right arm and then stretch it out a little, rolling my shoulder. The pain will go away, but that still sucked. Not how I wanted to end my stress relief time. Sighing as I start taking the wraps off my hands, I turn to face the sparring area. Loen and Clay are doing some light stretching while they wait for the new trainees to arrive.

Reaching down, I grab my phone and water bottle before walking toward the bleachers just in front of the sparring mat. Once I reach the edge of the bleachers, I toss the hand wraps down on the bottom row and then place my phone on top. My back is to the mat and more importantly Loen. Maybe Serafina is right, and I do need to get laid because why else would I be this distracted by a man? Taking a much-needed drink from my water, I'm trying not to focus on the laughter I'm hearing. My earbuds are still in my ears playing kind of loudly, but I can hear Clay's laugh over the music. I place my water bottle next to my phone and pop out the earbuds.

Placing them on my phone, I stand up ready to head onto the sparring mat. I do a few leg stretches by the bleachers, but I'm hit with a familiar scent—the one I smelled earlier in my apartment. The one that was on Serafina made me want to throw up and punch her in the face at the same time. It's so much stronger now—an earthy smell with a hint of eucalyptus. Distracted, yet again, I turn to walk onto the sparring mat and run into a familiar mountain…

Klutz.

"You know, you should work on this 'running into me' thing," Loen says in his smooth deep voice. I barely register what he just said. I'm too overwhelmed with his scent, the sound of his voice, and what I realize this means. Fuck. It's him. The scent is 100 percent coming from him. The longer he stands near me, the more of his scent I can smell, and the more I can smell Serafina. My blood starts to boil at the thought of him with her. Mate.

Fuck. Not him. Not now!

This isn't supposed to happen. I'm not supposed to be able to scent him, and he isn't supposed to be able to scent me. I never wanted to find my mate. That's why I did what I did.

So much for that spell working. FUCK!

"Did you hear me?" he asks. I turn back around to grab my stuff. I need space and air that isn't full of his scent mixed with my friend's. Loen, the tall dickhead with the reputation of fucking a ton of girls is, fuck...my mate.

The thought of him with Serafina last night and this morning has me fuming. Shifters by no means need to be celibate. They have fated mates, but they aren't expected to save themselves for their mate. It shouldn't make me this mad, but I was in the next room while they fucked, and he is said to have slept with half the women in his pack. That's infuriating. I can smell a hint of honey which is for sure Serafina. Serafina's horizontal tango partner last night and this morning was Loen, my... No, not my anything. I need to walk away right now.

She didn't know. You can't be mad at either of them.

"Oh, my gods," I say. That wasn't supposed to be out loud, but I'm struggling to keep my composure. I'm screwed.

"You good, Mazzy?" Clays asks as he walks toward me.

No, Clay, I'm not good.

"What did you say, Clay?" I ask, pretending I didn't hear him. Let's hope he believes I didn't hear him. I already took my earbuds out, so I have no real excuse not to hear what he said.

"I asked if you are good," he says while giving me a cheeky smile. He's a sweet guy. I know he is asking because he can tell something is off with me, and he cares. But fuck, dude, let me be. "You look red in the cheeks. Are you blushing?" he teases.

"No," I snap. "Yes… I mean no. I'm not blushing, and yes, I'm good," I say.

I feel so stupid. This is not what I needed today or any day for that matter. I'm about to run to the locker room when Archer walks in with sixteen people holding big black duffle bags in black gym shorts and grey t-shirts with the word *Police* across the chest in bright white letters. The new trainees are finally here, and that means no escaping for me.

Ugh, this is not happening!

"Mazelynn," Archer yells and waves to me to come cover.

So much for getting some air that isn't full of Loen's scent. I can't go to my locker now. Placing my stuff back on the bleachers, checking the time on my phone. 10:10 a.m. They are right on time, well late but on time. You get what I'm saying. Heading to Archer, I stop a few feet away from them. All the trainees have their eyes on me, and I can feel my heart rate increase as panic starts to settle in my chest.

Run, need to get away, need to run.

Ignoring my instinct to run, I plant my feet in place ready to speak to the new trainees. I can't run, but I do need to breathe and get control over my thoughts and body. The less control I have over my emotions, the higher the risk that I'll lose control. Losing control would mean exposing myself, and that can't happen. Now more than ever.

Shit.

"Hello everyone," I announce, taking a deep breath. "I'm Mazelynn. I'll be your instructor. We will be testing your skills today to help determine areas that need improvement. Over the next ninety days, we will help each of you improve on your weaker skills," I say.

staring at them. I hope they see the confident combat instructor they have heard about and not the ball of nerves I am right this second.

"What weaker skills?" one of the male trainees says in a cocky tone.

There's one. Eye roll.

"Please go to the locker rooms, get your stuff situated, and come back in here. We will start in ten minutes," I add, ignoring the arrogant man's comment.

Let's hope they believe that façade.

I need to work on my negative self-talk. I can be a real bitch to myself sometimes. They all turn and hurry off to the locker rooms. Now I'm left standing face-to-face with Archer, who has a confused but knowing look on his face.

"Everything all right?" he asked.

"Yup," I mutter, lying. I hope he believes me. I doubt it, but if he doesn't, I'm hoping he won't call me out right now.

"Great. I'm going to pretend you didn't just lie to my face, Mazelynn. Get to work, and I'll check in later," Archer says as he turns. "Try not to break too many bones today, okay?" he shouts over his shoulder with a deep booming voice that has a hint of laughter in it.

Archer gets a kick out of my anger issues most days. I guess today is one of those days. If I'm off enough for him to pick up on it, there will be a few incidents reported today. I tend not to hold back on my off days. The first day means I'll be holding back to see what the trainees can do. How no one has figured out my secret, I have no idea. A tiny, "human" girl like me shouldn't be able to take down full-grown male shifters or fae, let alone break their bones in the process.

You have issues.

I need to get a grip on myself. Clay laughs behind me and that brings my attention back to the mat and…Loen. Turning around to face them, Loen is standing there with his arms crossed looking hot as hell.

Stop thinking that. You need to keep your distance.

Clay has a smirk on his face. What is he smirking at?

"Clay, wipe that smirk off your face before I do it for you," I tease, walking toward him.

"I would if I could, Mazzy," Clay says, letting out his booming laugh as he quickly blocks his junk with his hands as I walk by him.

That was a smart move, Clay.

"You are safe…for now," I whisper, patting him on the shoulder.

The wide-eyed expression he has now tells me he knows I'll get him for that later when he least expects it. I know where he lives. Not all my revenge is violence, I swear. I also love pranking him. Besides, my focus isn't on that right now. It's on one thing and one thing only. I need to avoid being too close to Loen.

My mate.

Chapter 3: God Complex

Mazzy

"Asshole. Why are so many of them assholes, Archer?" I ask. I'm

venting, and poor Archer is on the receiving end. To be fair, he called

me into his office to ask me how today went, so he had to have been

expecting it. Right? The moment the question came out of his mouth, I

had to bite my tongue. Of course, my first thoughts about how today

went were something I could not tell him. I wanted to shout,

"Hey Archer, today was just fucking peachy. You know, woke up hungover as fuck. Got to work anxious as hell for something I can't tell you about, and oh, the spell that was supposed to forever keep my mate from finding me and our bond from forming failed. Now, I have to break the bond, which is going to fucking suck. Oh, and my mate is Loen. You know the man who slept with your daughter? I'm about two seconds away from punching both of them in the face."

But *no*, I couldn't tell him that, so I lied. It was a shit day just like I expected. Not only was I trying to avoid being too close to Loen, but a lot of these males have such horrible god complexes that they wouldn't follow one direction I gave them without turning to Loen, Clay, or the twins to give them the instructions. I'm the one in charge, damn it.

"There are a few who need reality checks badly. They are so full of themselves, and they don't respect me or any of the other female officers. Hot-headed, pig-headed alpha holes," I blurt out as I pace his cluttered office.

The clutter isn't helping calm me down, and neither is he. I'm sure it's driving him crazy at this point. He hates it when I pace, but I can't sit down. Archer chuckles a low crackle of a laugh and closes his laptop as he pushes himself back on his chair so he can recline it back. He crosses his arms over his large barrel chest and continues to laugh.

"I don't think it's funny, Arch—" I shout but stop myself

Shit.

"Sir," I murmur. I'm trying to be respectful. My mouth sometimes speaks before I want it to.

"That's why they send them here," he says, pausing for a second, likely hoping I'll stop pacing. That's not happening anytime soon, sorry. "You and the rest of our combat training team are great at knocking sense into those who need it," he adds with pride.

I slow my pacing a little, but only a little. He's not wrong. Out of all the departments in this state, we are the best at taking the dick out of the dickheads that come out of the academies. But these guys are bad, or it's something I don't want to admit. I might have been too distracted to handle today well.

"Chief, I know, and I usually enjoy it. But I'm…" I try to come up with the right words, but they aren't coming to me.

"Hungover and extra distracted," Archer says. His tone isn't annoyed or angry. It's actually soft and kind. He feels bad for me. Great, just what I need today—pity.

"Yes, sir," I whisper in agreement as I stop pacing. Archer stands from his chair and walks over to me. The chief is a nice and caring guy but can be a real hard ass. He hates when officers come to work not at their best. So I'm preparing for a lecture as he starts toward me. I think he is nicer to me because we have a history, and by history, I mean he was my legal guardian starting at fifteen.

When I turned eighteen he backed off a little on the guardian role but never stopped acting like a father figure when he knew I needed it. He stops next to me, close enough I can smell he just finished yet another coffee of the day.

"How was your birthday celebration last night?" he asks nicely.

"What?" I ask. Did I hear him right? Did he really ask how my birthday outing went? Staring at him, I don't respond.

"How was your night out for your birthday?" he asks again, this time making eye contact with me. His eyes are a silver color similar to my hair but a few shades darker. They reflect compassion right now.

"It was good other than being far too crowded. It was nice to be out. Plus the music was good," I say. I can admit it was nice, even if I would have rather been at home reading a book.

"I'm glad. I knew Serafina would win you over. I did, however, remind her you had obligations in the morning and not to get you too plastered," he says with a hint of a smirk. Walking toward his office door, he walks close by until we reach the door. Before opening it, he pauses, and I know what that means.

There's more.

"Oh, Chief Dolton called and asked how his sons did today," he says slowly. I was hoping that wouldn't come up. I didn't want to talk about them, especially Loen. Giving him an eye roll and a little glare, I prepare myself to fill him in.

Get it done and over with, Mazzy.

"The twins were nice. I expected them to be huge dicks like their brother, but compared to a handful of the trainees, they weren't bad. Loen wasn't as big of a jerk as I expected him to be either. His reputation seems to be worse than the reality…unless he was playing me," I say. "Archer…ugh I mean, Chief." I pause and try to think of what I want to say.

"Mazzy, it's fine," he says, placing his hand on my shoulder. "I don't like seeing my niece overwhelmed with anxiety like this. If there is anything you need, all you have to do is ask."

"I know," I squeak out, quietly.

"I would like you to start seeing one of our counselors again. We shouldn't have stopped after you went to the academy just assuming you were good. My sister would be disappointed in how I handled that," Archer says.

Giving me a supportive glance and a slight squeeze of my shoulder, he smiles softly. I'm sure he wants to hug me, but he doesn't. I appreciate him giving me some space. He is wrong, though. Mother would not be disappointed in him. Mother would be so grateful for all the support and everything else he did for me and V. If there was anyone she would be disappointed in, it would be me.

"I'll think about it," I say, nodding my head at him. He might be right on the counseling part. I probably should have kept going, but it's not like I could tell them the full truth anyway. I didn't see a point in it. Not when they could tell I was still keeping something major to myself.

"Go home. Go to bed, and we will talk more later. Okay?" he says, letting go of my shoulder and opening the office door.

As I go to walk out of the door, I run face-to-face into Serafina, who isn't exactly the person I want to run into at the moment.

The smell of stale coffee and dusty stacks of paper leaves my nose and is replaced with the scent of honey and Loen. I hold back confronting her, clenching my jaw and fists as I walk past her, keeping my eyes on my door and not saying a word to her. I can't right now. A few days from now when her scent is no longer mixed with his, I will be able to handle the idea of those two sleeping together, right?

Probably not. Fuck.

I have to remind myself that she didn't know. Hell, I didn't even know he was in our apartment, let alone that the stupid spells in place weren't going to work. Maybe they did work at first. Was that why I didn't smell him right off when he entered the apartment or why his scent was so faint in the morning? Who knows.

As I continue down the hallway away from the office, I take a quick glance back. They didn't enter the office, talking just outside of it. I can see the smile on her face, and her being giddy over something she is telling him. My guess is she wanted to tell her dad about a model gig or Loen. As I start to head through the lobby, I hear Serafina's high-pitched giggle getting closer. Must have been a quick talk. Walking down the steps of the station, I scan the parking lot. Fuck, he waited. Next to my bike is Loen, sitting on his bike next to mine, just waiting.

You're screwed.

I don't want to talk to him right now. I get lucky, or unlucky, depending on how you look at it. The moment she reached the bottom of the station steps, Serafina runs past me and leaps into Loen's arms, nearly knocking him and his bike over. I start to feel my blood boil again, watching her hang on him.

Don't lose your shit. Don't lose your shit.

Taking in a deep angry breath, I shove my helmet on my head and flip my tinted visor down. It's nighttime, I don't need it, but it's at least blocking the sight of Serafina locking lips with Loen on his bike. Not wanting to see much more, I jump on my bike and get the fuck out of there.

I should stick around and see how this plays out with Archer and Loen. But I don't think watching that drama will do me any good right now. I don't want to think about Loen or what I'm feeling. I want to feel the rumble of the road under the tires of my bike as buildings turn into a blur instead of seeing Serafina anywhere near Loen—let alone hanging all over him or kissing him. I should go directly home, lock myself in my room, and fall asleep reading one of my books.

As I'm pulling out of the parking lot, I take a quick glance back. Loen is going somewhat unwillingly with Archer and Serafina back toward the station. I was shocked that Loen waited next to my bike for over an hour after being released for the night.

The talk with Archer took longer than I thought it would. Like he said, he is my uncle, my adoptive uncle, but still my uncle. Archer wasn't too happy about his sister's choice to take me in, but I guess I grew on him. He treats me just as well as he treats Verena. After our mother died, I honestly expected him to take in his biological niece, Verena, and send me away, but he didn't. When I told him I wanted to be a police officer, he fought for me to be assigned to his station and wouldn't take no for an answer.

After pulling out of the parking lot and getting a few stop lights away from the station, I decided to take the long way home. Being out on the bike under the night sky usually helps calm me down, and I need to clear my head some. It should have been only a twenty to thirty-minute ride. I'm tired, so I went slower.

Near home, I realize this ride has taken me closer to forty-five minutes. I nearly fell asleep a few times. I need sleep. Finally home, I park my bike as fast as I can and head up to the apartment. If the elevator lights weren't so bright, I could have fallen asleep on the floor.

Grabbing my keys, I can hear laughter from inside the apartment as I unlock the door and open it. Not surprised by the sight, I see my roommates eating dinner and chatting in the living room. Serafina is bragging about her one-night stand, saying she genuinely likes him ,and that she's seeing him again. How she can't wait to see him naked and—

La, la, la. I don't want to hear it. I don't want to hear it.

Like hell that will happen, Serafina, I think as I drop my duffle on the floor by the door and toss my helmet on it. Not feeling like talking to them or risking interacting with Serafina, I try to head to my bedroom, hoping no one tries to talk to me.

"Mazzy, how was day one of the combat seminar? Was it fantastic as usual?" Serafina's annoying voice carries through the apartment.

Letting out a grumble only loud enough for me to hear, I continue walking toward my bedroom. *Not now, Serafina, shut up and let me be*, I think. I'm too tired for this.

"Any cute guys you think want to hook up with you?" she tries to ask, but this one makes me snap. She can't help herself, and I'm not dealing with it tonight.

"Fucking stop," I say loudly. "I'm tired and have a headache from hell. I need you to shut up and leave me alone so I can go to bed."

I snapped. I didn't mean for it to come out as angry as it did, but it did. I glare at her as her soft smiling features turn to shock. Her grey eyes go wide, as she turns to Clay and Harper. Those two wordlessly glance at each other and then look my direction. An apologetic expression slides over both of their faces.

"Are you hungry, Mazzy?" Harper peeps softly, trying to break the tension in the room.

"NO," I blurt coldly.

Harper didn't do anything wrong. She didn't deserve that at all. Reaching my room, I go in and close the door. I change as quickly as I can and practically face plant my bed. I can hear the three of them talking out there. Clay is trying to explain to Serafina and Harper that today was a long day, and the hangover didn't help matters. I can hear Harper asking what happened.

I take my pillow and shove it over my head, trying to muffle their voices more with the pillow. I scream into my mattress before releasing a few held-back sobs. I have never snapped at Harper like that before. I needed Serafina to stop talking. She still smells like Loen, and I can't help how mad it makes me no matter how many times I tell myself she didn't know. I'll have to say sorry at some point, but for now, I need space and sleep.

Removing the pillow from my head and sitting up, I take my phone out of my pants pocket and reach for the charger. I won't forget to plug it in this time. Plugging my phone in, I triple-check that I have all the alarms set before curling up and pulling the covers over myself. It's only 7:30 p.m. Normally way too early for me to go to bed, but not today. I'm so looking forward to sleeping.

"Day one of our combat seminar done, only eighty-nine more to go," I mumble before letting my heavy eyelids shut as I drift off to sleep.

Chapter 4: Welcome to the Shit Show Day One

Loen

Well, my father is going to kill me. He is going to be seeing red when

he finds out I slept with the police chief's daughter last night and this

morning. In my defense, Serafina is a fae model, so she's an attractive

woman. I feel no real emotional connection with her, but hell, it was a

good time and a much-needed distraction. I can practically hear my

father's voice in my head, ripping me a new one after I tell him the reason Chief Whitlock beat the crap out of me and kicked my ass all the way back home.

Way to live up to the Playboy name.

Rolling my eyes, I am kind of mad at myself for it if I'm being honest. I normally don't go for a one-night stand kind of thing, but last night, I let loose. My brothers are going to have a field day with this when they find out the girl I went home with last night is our temporary boss's spoiled daughter.

You're so fucked.

The muffled chatter of Serafina's roommates reminds me this is not a large apartment. If I can hear them then they can probably hear us. The kitchen and living room are maybe ten feet by ten feet each. I think the biggest rooms in this entire apartment are the bedrooms.

Taking in the room, I notice there are only two doors in this entire bedroom. Fuck, that means there is no bathroom but the one in the common area. I wish I didn't have to walk into the hall to use the bathroom, but I have got to piss. There is pink everywhere, and I mean everywhere. A pink lace canopy hangs from the bed with greenery and fairy lights. The fairy lights are strung up around the room with way too many fake flowers. All the artwork on the wall are photographs of her at modeling gigs or photoshoots.

Self-centered much?

Expensive outfits, bags, and jewelry litter the floor and walls in every corner. This chick is seriously giving spoiled princess vibes—so not my kind of girl. My eyes finally land on a thin tall blonde-haired girl on a baby pink comforter. She is sprawled out naked, laying on her belly and taking up the entire queen size bed. Which ironically takes up most of the floor space in this room.

"Pants?" I say, glaring at her.

Way to be a dick, Loen.

Serafina picks her head up and props herself up on her elbows. Giggling, she smiles at me with a big toothy smile and starts lazily scanning her room. Shrugging her shoulders, she tilts her cute heart-shaped face to the side and then points to the floor.

"Somewhere down there," she says with another giggle and a flirty expression.

So not helpful, I think. What did I find attractive about her last night other than her face? Oh yeah, I was drunk, like capital D.R.U.N.K. kind of drunk. It's been a rough few years for our pack and family. Last night, I just kind of let it all go. A night of drinking sounded like a great idea at the time.

"How about a towel to cover myself? I need to use the bathroom," I asked, crossing my arms across my chest.

I'm standing naked in this girl's room. We're done fucking—again. She flops on the bed the moment we finish, so I start looking for my clothes. I only manage to find one of my black socks in this mess.

Do fae have ADHD or are they hoarders? The fae I have seen outside of a fae realm are all masters of clutter. Their spaces are always full of stuff, mostly shiny things. Maybe fae are part dragon? I chuckle to myself at that joke. Dragons aren't real, but I think the fae are probably a close comparison to dragon hoarding. Checking at my watch, I know I need to get my ass in gear. I'm going to be late on my first day of work and that won't look good.

Yeah, because sleeping with the chief's daughter is going to look so much better.

Fuck, this is going to make things interesting. That's for sure. I need to find my shit and make it to the police department before the Ice Queen herself gets in. Luckily, if I'm late, the shit reputation I have will come in handy. The Chef and the Ice Queen will hopefully think I'm being my normal dick self. I will admit that I'm interested in meeting this girl. The Ice Queen is known for being extremely cold and calculated and isn't afraid to break a bone or two without a second thought. That's my kind of woman though. One who can kick some ass but others, not mine.

I have never met the instructor in person, but Mazelynn has a reputation that is like mine. It's well-known. Everyone talks about her and how incredible she is. I know other county chiefs want to send troublesome new officers to her to knock some sense into them. From what I have been told, she's young, a few years younger than me. Somehow, despite her age, she has managed to make a good name for herself.

Another rumor I'm interested in confirming is that she's hot and feisty as hell. It was going around one of the academies a while back that one of the new girls was feisty as fuck and knocking all the guys on their asses. I'm sure I can use my charm to get on her good side. I have not met a girl yet who can resist me when I put the charm on. Yes, I know I sound full of myself, but that's the role I must play now—so I'm going all in.

All or nothing.

Serafina sits up, swinging her thin long legs over the side to stand. I guess drunk me doesn't mind that this fae with a heart-shaped face is missing the wholesome curves I'm normally drawn to. I had no idea she was the police chief's daughter 'til this morning when she mentioned her father. Yes, it was before our morning workout. I should have walked away then, but I was already screwed. So why not get a release before a stressful day?

Serafina walks catlike across the room passing me and fetching a towel from the back of her closet door. She throws it over my head, and I grab the towel as she laughs.

"Thanks," I groan. Wrapping the towel around my waist, I start toward her bedroom door.

"Hold up."

I turn to see her frantically grabbing a robe from her closet. Turning back to the door and shaking my head, I wait for her to get her shit together before heading out of the bedroom. As soon as I see her standing next to me, I take that as my cue and open the door. She passes me and walks into the kitchen, standing in front of the island.

I head right to the bathroom, glancing to my left for a few seconds before entering the bathroom. I didn't see anyone at the island other than Serafina, but there is a familiar black duffle bag at the foot of the island stool. It's like the ones the academy hands out to the cadets.

Taking care of my business in the bathroom took a little longer than planned. When I was walking into the bathroom, I got a hint of a sweet-smelling scent. It was faint but nice—a sweet citrus, juniper smell with a hint of what smells like lilacs. I had to pause for a second when I closed the door.

I thought the smell was coming from there, but it wasn't. I bet it's one of the fae's many perfumes. After relieving myself, I stand at the cheap vanity to wash my hands. The walls in this apartment aren't very thick. I can hear Serafina talking to one of her female roommates. Trying not to eavesdrop too much, I listen in just a tad.

Okay, you got me. I was eavesdropping. Sue me.

These two are practically roasting each other. Something about drinking at the club last night and, oh fuck, what about my dick? Huh. Well, at least they get along. I don't get along with my roommates, but my roommates right now are my younger brothers. And they are dumb as fuck sometimes. Noticing they are still busy chatting, I decide to head back to Serafina's room to find my clothes. I have somewhere I need to be. As I step into the doorway of her bedroom, I get a slight hint of that sweet scent again.

Focus, Loen. You have somewhere you need to be.

Serafina mumbles a comment about someone needing to get laid as I head into her bedroom, closing the bedroom door behind me. I start the search for my clothes, phone, and keys. I can't wait to get to my temporary apartment and change out of these walk-of-shame clothes. Finally finding my clothes on the floor of Serafina's room, I get dressed quickly.

I can hear the other two roommates rush to get out the door behind the first roommate. Clay, the only male roommate, poor guy, is nice. I had a chat with him earlier this morning when I was getting a drink of water from the kitchen before I lost my clothes again. He wasn't shocked to see a strange guy in his place. That was slightly concerning. He also gave me a *you poor bastard* kind of glance.

When Serafina walks back in, I'm already dressed and picking up my phone to text my brothers to let them know I'm on my way to the station. Instead of running home, I'll have them grab my duffle on their way out.

Serafina unties her robe, dropping it by her feet as she stalks toward me. I think she has plans for us, and I don't have the time or the desire anymore. The idea of touching her actually makes my skin crawl all of a sudden. Why? I have no idea, but I'll trust my gut and get my ass out of here.

"This has been fun, but if I don't head out, I'll be late. I can't be late on my first day," I say. After a quick goodbye, I head out of the apartment. It's nearly 9:25 a.m. I will need to rush to get to the station before ten.

In the apartment parking lot, I notice my bike. I guess I can thank my brothers for bringing my bike here last night before they went home for the night. Serafina had a little too much to drink to drive, so we walked. It wasn't that far, so it was all good. Hopping on my black and blue sports bike, I put my helmet on and start her up.

Gosh, I love the sound of this bike. It's a bigger city than my hometown, so I'm keeping my fingers crossed that I don't hit traffic. Heading out of the parking lot, I get a text notification that will have to wait until I reach the station.

I have the worst luck. I knew traffic was going to be an issue, but I didn't factor in hitting every fucking red light in the city. The gods are against me today. After parking my bike next to the only other bike in the parking lot, I head inside not even removing my helmet or riding gear. I want to get inside before Chief Whitlock notices I'm late. As I head up the steps, I hear a horn honk behind me, spinning around. I notice my dumb brothers pulling in like they are in the *Dukes of Hazzard.*

Dumbasses.

Grabbing my duffle from Jayce as we start through the station door, I focus on getting inside. Walking through the doors, I notice a silver-haired woman walk by shaking her head. She appears annoyed, and I think I know who that is. After a quick hello with the lovely Lori, the receptionist, she let us know the trainees' bus was running late, and they were set to arrive ten after ten. She had to answer the phone for the third time in less than five minutes and pointed us to the locker rooms so we could get changed. I don't wait for my brothers who got easily distracted by two young female cops that came into the lobby. They are flirting it up at the reception desk.

Heading down the hall to the locker rooms, I admire my surroundings. I'm impressed by the way this station is set up. The offices and desks are to the left side of the building, and to the right, they have a large training area and gym along with the equipment vaults and locker rooms. The training area is huge. I see a ton of different workout machines, weights, punching bags, and a large sparring area with bleachers. We don't have this kind of setup at home. It's nice, but this is genuinely nicer than ours.

Too distracted to notice someone walking out of the ladies locker room, I run right into her with a solid thud. Peering down I am met with silver hair and the delicate face of a stunning woman, I nearly stumble to get words out.

Fuck, she's gorgeous.

"You should watch where you're going instead of playing on your phone, Princess," I say with a snarky tone. The way "princess" comes out is far more gravely and deeper than the rest.

I wasn't paying attention either, but I also won't admit I was also at fault here. I need to play up this alpha-hole thing. So much for trying to charm the Ice Queen... Guess we are going with snarky. The rumors do not do this girl justice. Her silver-white hair is in a relaxed braid hanging over her shoulder, and those eyes have me drowning in them. She looks a little shocked at first then leans to her right and gazes down the hallway.

What is she looking for?

My head is telling me to say something or move, but I can't do either. I keep staring at her. She's breathtaking. Her eyes are a stunning mix of ocean blue and turquoise. They are mesmerizing. Tilting my head to the side a little, I squint my eyes. Yes, I could take my helmet off to get a better look, but then, she'll know I'm studying her sweet face. She is a fair-skinned beauty. There is the slightest hint of freckles on her pale face running across her cheeks and nose. Glaring back at me without even a word, she stares right at me through my own blackened helmet visor.

Fuck me.

Popping her earbuds in her ears with a sarcastic smirk, she passes me. Turning to watch her for a second, I can't help but notice how tight her leggings are. Wow, look at that ass.

Head out of your pants, dumbass.

Heading into the locker room, I find an empty locker and try to get my head on straight. Putting my duffle bag into the locker, I hear the door open and close.

"Hey, man," a familiar voice says. Turning, I see Clay, one of Serafina's roommates.

"Hey, didn't you leave before me?" I tease.

"No comment," he jokes with a loud booming laugh. Wow, this guy has one hell of a laugh.

Chatting while we get ready, I learn that Clay and Harper just got married a little bit ago. They want to get their own apartment but can't afford it just yet. I can see why that would be an issue, the apartments in this place are crazy expensive.

We were lucky our father had lined one up for us. I asked him how he did that so fast, but he told me not to ask questions. I let it go. Clay and I chat for a few more minutes before heading out. Instead of waiting for my brothers to get ready, I head out to the gym with Clay.

We are chatting away as we walk and end up on the topic of Mazelynn. Clay warned me that Mazelynn can be a hard ass even to those helping her, but not to take it personally. He also says she's actually caring but doesn't like when people see that side of her. Before walking through the open gym doors, I notice the silver-haired Ice Queen beating the crap out of a punching bag directly across the room from the door. She has some powerful punches and clearly has some anger issues. I can't help but wonder what her body looks like under that baggy men's tank top.

Nope. Can't think that way, Loen.

***

The number of times I bit my tongue today has me shocked I still have one. The new trainees showed up right at 10:10 a.m., carrying their duffels. Some were scowling, clearly not thrilled to be here. The way a few of the men looked at Mazelynn before training even started made me want to punch them in their faces. When the skills testing started, Mazelynn sparred with all the trainees. She took a lot of them down quickly, a few took a little longer, but I could tell she was holding back. I was impressed at how equally Mazelynn treated the females and male trainees until they started pissing her off. Wow, does this girl have a short fuse.

In all fairness, I do as well, and a few of them had me ready to snap. They don't want to respect the fact that she was in charge and keep looking to the male instructions for the instructions. I can see the rage in Mazelynn's face every time a few of the men intentionally ignore her. The females are not bad, but a few are way too catty for their own good.

More than half of these guys don't deserve to be here. They deserve to get kicked out on their asses and not just from this combat seminar. How some of the guys passed the academy is beyond me. They are so disrespectful. A number of times, they are a little too handsy with the female trainees and Mazelynn as well. It has my blood boiling. Thinking about it makes me see red. Tomorrow better be different.

Training has been done for a little over ten minutes. The trainees are all changing and heading to their hotel or other living arrangements. I am sitting on this bench, listening to some of these men talk about the women and Mazelynn like they are eye candy for them. Shaking my head, I try to remind myself that I have the dickhead reputation to live up to. These guys are over-the-top even for me. I have a few who are now on my beat-them-senseless list.

"But did you see her ass in those leggings?" one of the trainees jokes with another in the row of lockers behind where I am. I hope they are not talking about Mazelynn. For their sake, they better not be.

"Right, dude, like holy fuck. Did you see her tank top slip up when she was sparring with Loen? You can tell she is hiding tempting curves under that baggy top," another says.

Fuck, they are talking about Mazelynn. I stand from the bench, throw my stuff inside, and slam the locker door shut. The loud clanging noise echoed in the locker room. It goes silent for a few moments before they start talking about a few of the other women. At least they aren't talking about Mazelynn anymore.

Locking the locker with my padlock, I grab my helmet and key. I need to get out of here before I take the heads off one or more of these smartasses.

Passing the gym, I hear a few of the girls still sitting on the mat chatting away. Half are chatting about how they love that Mazelynn is treating them all the same, and the other half are pissed that the guys refuse to spar with them unless Mazelynn orders it.

Shaking my head, I keep walking but at a slow pace. I have to admit I don't like having the shifter or fae males paired up testing their skills with the female trainees. They could hurt them, especially the female officers who are human. The shifters and fae are stronger than the humans, but miss Ice Queen insists they spar with each other. When they refused, they had to spar with her again. She would hold back less and less during those matches.

The anger that came up in me when a few of the guys' hands touched Mazelynn during their sparring was hard to hold back. I wanted to rip them off her, but I knew she was fine. She could hold her own. If I intervened, it would only show the men that I don't respect her as the instructor either. I do. I really do.

Chucking to myself, I text my brothers making sure they made it to the apartment okay. They both respond, and I quickly let them know I'll be there as soon as I can. I want to chat with the chief before I head out. That's a big fat lie, but they don't need to know the real reason I want to stay behind, not yet at least. It took me far too long for me to realize why I was getting so angry over those guys touching her during sparring.

Mazelynn wanted to demonstrate something and reluctantly had to use me to spar with to demonstrate. I think she would have rather used Clay, but Clay had taken his lunch break. My brothers are rusty on the skill she wanted to show. It hit me like a truck.

The first hit she landed near my face, her scent blew into my face—citrus, juniper, and lilacs. The sweet smell was coming from her, and I wanted to be closer to her. Shockingly, at one point, I was able to pin her to the ground. She wasn't entirely ready for it. I could tell by the shocked look on her face when her eyes met mine. It took me all of two seconds of deep eye contact with her for her soul to light something in mine.

My mate.

Pulling myself from my thoughts, I head to the reception desk where the lovely Lori is telling her shift replacement the details of the day. The new girl is much younger than Lori with long black hair, glasses, and deep brown eyes. She's a heavier-set woman with a round face and rosy cheeks. She seems cheerful for someone working the night shift at the police station reception desk.

Godspeed to this lady.

Lori swivels her head in my direction and gives me a soft smile and a tiny wave. Instead of waving, I walk up to the desk to introduce myself to the new receptionist and say goodnight to Lori. I have a feeling this lady doesn't get a lot of out-of-office attention.

"Hello, I'm Loen," I say, reaching my hand out to the cheery new face.

"Hi, I'm Susie. Are you one of the trainees?" she replies.

Ouch.

"No, he is one of Mazelynn's assistants. The one I was telling you about," Lori says. She gives a wink to Susie and then turns her mischievous eyes on me. I don't even want to ask what all that was about.

"Anyway, I wanted to introduce myself since I'm sure I'll be seeing you around from time to time. I like to know the people I work with," I explained.

Susie nods her head as the phone rings. She holds up a pointer finger, answering the phone in a shockingly deep voice. I try to hold back a laugh as I see Lori pull her hands up to her mouth. I squint my eyes and give her a confused expression.

She points to the phone mouthing *caller ID*. I lean over the desk to read the screen. *Jackon and Jackson Law.* Okay, there is some kind of inside joke I don't know about just yet cause Lori is practically turning purple as she tries to hold back her laughter.

"Hey, Lori, can I ask you something over here?" I ask, hoping she will agree. She nods and heads with me over to the benches not even ten feet away from the desk.

"What's up, buttercup?" she says sweetly.

"Mazelynn, did she leave already?" I ask.

She gives me a questioning glance for a few moments and then scans the lobby. She looks as though she is trying to decide if she wants to answer that question or not. I need to talk to Mazelynn. She didn't seem affected when our eyes met like I was. If she was, she did an exceptional job at hiding it. She freed herself from the pin I had her in, turning the tables on me. I honestly didn't mind, and I was impressed with how fast and strong she was.

"Lori, I have a few things to ask her about the seminar. That's all," I say. I really don't but she doesn't need to know that.

Lori takes a deep breath and finally answers my question. She explains that Mazelynn is in the chief's office, going over how the day went. Knowing the chief, she says Mazelynn could be in there for an hour or two, but that if I want to wait for her, I could probably wait by her bike outside. Mazelynn rides the black sports motorcycle I parked next to. This girl was made for me.

I thank Lori and wave to Susie who is still on the phone. This time she has a cheery tone instead of the deep one she just used. I'll wait here for her as long as I need to. I need to talk to my mate. As a human, she is unlikely to feel the pull, but part of me hopes she feels it.

Relaxing with my feet up on the gas tank of my bike and laying back, I could probably fall asleep like this if I wait much longer. It's been nearly an hour of waiting for her. I hope she didn't get in trouble for anything. I sit up so I don't fall asleep and then see her. Coming down the steps in a black leather jacket, black riding pants, boots, and her helmet under her arm is a jaw-dropping woman. I stare at her as I lean forward on my bike. I am so focused on her that I don't notice someone coming at me until it's too late. She throws herself at me, pulling my face to hers and planting a kiss directly on my lips.

What the hell?

Pulling away from the kiss, I take a second to figure out what just happened. Serafina. Serafina happened. Fucking girl came out of nowhere. Peeking past Serafina's head, I try to find Mazelynn. I catch a glimpse of her for a second as she shoves her head into her helmet kind of hard. Before I have a chance to push Serafina away and get Mazelynn's attention, she is on her bike and pulling away.

Fuck, worst luck ever.

"Hey," Serafina says with a high-pitched overly excited tone.

"Hey, back," I say. I am not thrilled to see this woman. Not one bit.

"Daddy wants to chat with you," she says. I almost choke on the air. *Daddy?* Really, she is a grown-ass woman still calling her father "daddy." I really need to have a chat with drunk me and tell myself to raise my standards.

Fuck.

"Why?" I ask, scowling back at Serafina with a confused expression and trying, but failing, to hide my annoyance.

"I told him I met an awesome guy, and he wants to meet my new boyfriend," she squeals as she claps her hands rapidly. *Oh, for the love of the gods, why do you hate me?* I ask myself as Serafina grabs my hand, trying to pull me to walk with her.

"Hold up." I break my hand free and stop walking. "Last night was fun, but I thought we were on the same—" I'm interrupted by a booming, somewhat intimidating voice.

"Mr. Dolton," yells the police chief.

Shit, shit, shit.

I'm dead, like buried six feet under dead. The no one is finding your body kind of dead. *Okay*, that might be exaggerating things a tad, but judging by the look on the man's face as he approaches and the pit I now have in my stomach, I am in a massive amount of T.R.O.U.B.L.E…TROUBLE.

And not with just him, stud.

Fuck!

Chapter 5: What Are You Up To?

Mazzy

BEEP, BEEP, BEEP.

Opening my eyes, I sit up quickly and grab my phone from next to my pillow. I set the phone alarms to make sure I got up at seven, but I must have been over-tired. It's been going off for thirty minutes. That never happens. Picking my phone up, I hit the stop button and place it on the bedside table. The others must not be home.

If they were, I'm sure they would have come in and stopped my alarm from going off. Instead of getting up, I sit for a few minutes. I had to fight every instinct in my body not to run to Loen and yank Serafina away from him when I saw her kiss him last night.

Mate, my mate, mine.

He can't be. I have to push him away. Shaking my head a few times, I place my head in my hands. I can't help but feel defeated. The idea of pushing him away, the one person that was made specifically for me, hurts. But it's what needs to be done. I can't have him, or it will change everything—and not for the better. How am I going to convince him that what he feels is one-sided when it's not?

Rubbing my hands over my face and into my hair, I sit up and examine my room. The one place it's okay to be myself. Well, as long as the door is locked and my privacy curtains are closed. I hate that I can't be myself around anyone. I have to keep myself hidden, only letting the world see what I know they will accept of me.

This is going to hurt.

Hurt is an understatement. It's going to feel like my heart is being ripped from my chest, but the worst part is that I'm going to have to hide that pain from everyone. Other shifters know that rejecting a fated mate bond is insanely painful for both involved as long as both feel the pull.

A tight pain starts in my chest. I know it's my heart starting to break already. Why do I feel so strongly already? I hardly know him, and he doesn't know me—not the real me.

I'm surprised Loen didn't notice I felt something. I had to close my eyes tight while breaking free of the pin to hide it. Huffing, a thought comes to me. What did I do to deserve this? Why the hell did the gods give me a mate that's a player and a major dickhead?

A hot dickhead.

Resting my head in my hands again, I take a few deep breaths before pulling myself together and getting myself out of bed. I can't let this show. I need to keep up with hiding everything, and he will move on. Hell, maybe he will stay with Serafina. She's attractive. I clench my fists and jaw at that thought and let out the breath I didn't know I was holding. This is going to suck.

I throw extra clothes in a backup mini backpack. I head to the kitchen all while processing the situation. When I reach the kitchen island, there is a bright pink sticky note on it. Serafina loves pink, so it's easy to assume the note is from her. I have a feeling I'll need coffee before I read this note. Picking up the sticky note, I read while walking to the coffee pot.

Mazzy, I hope you're not mad at me for something. I noticed the way you sped off last night after seeing me talking to Loen. And you snapped at me last night. Daddy mentioned you were off all day. I hope today is better for you. I love you.

Forever your bestie, Serafina!

P.S. I think I like Loen; I hope that isn't why you're mad at me.

Yes, that's exactly why, you spoiled brat.

Dropping the note back on the island, I take a seat on the stool. Not only do I have to figure out what to do about Loen, but I also need to think about how I'm going to handle this situation with Serafina. As I start to get lost in thought, my phone goes off. Grabbing it, I check the notification. It's from Harper.

Harper:
Hey, heads up, Chief is pissed!

Me:

Why??

Harper:

He is fuming in his office about Loen and Serafina

Me:

That's going to make today fun now, isn't it?

Harper:

See you when you get in.

Taking a sip of my coffee, I can't think of a reason why Archer would be that angry about Loen and Serafina. Some fae, depending on the bloodline, aren't always okay with mixing the species, but Archer is half-human so that doesn't make a lot of sense to me.

Unless he was trying to push Serafina toward a full-blood fae partner. I guess that would make sense. Since her magic is weak from being more than half-human, it's possible Archer wants her to be with a full-blood fae. The fae don't have mates like the shifters do. They haven't in hundreds of years. Most of the time, they have arranged marriages to grow their magic.

Shaking my head, I can't spend forever thinking about why Archer is pissed. Loen is in for a hell of a surprise if he breaks

Serafina's heart though. Archer has more magic than his daughter, and he will for sure use it.

A thought crosses my mind. Loen is a shifter, and shifters have fated mates unless they are broken wolves, shifters born with no wolf. Archer is probably angry because he knows Loen will leave Serafina possibly heartbroken when he finds his fated mate. Ironic isn't it? That I'm his fated mate? Either way, Loen is screwed. You don't want to get cursed by a fae, especially one that has your full name and can make your life a living hell.

Setting my coffee down on the island, the glass mug makes a soft thud as it touches the countertop. The silence in the rest of the apartment is uncomfortable. This place is rarely this quiet in the morning. My life wasn't complicated enough before this mate thing. Now I have to deal with this shit on top of it. Staring into my coffee cup, I zone out, lost in my thoughts.

A loud knock on the apartment door catches my attention. Startling, I look around the apartment before glancing at the door. *Who in the world would be knocking on the door this early?* Still sitting at the island, I'm tempted not to answer it in hopes whoever it is will just go away. Another knock rings through the apartment, this time much harder than before. Fucking hell. Are they trying to break down the door?

"Okay, okay, hold your horses," I shout.

Getting up from the island, I head to the door. As soon as the door opens, I am met by two large men with sinister-looking faces. I regret not taking the time to peek through the peephole first. These two don't look like they are here to sell cookies. An uneasy feeling fills my body. This isn't good.

"Can I help you?" I ask.

They don't answer at first. Instead, they both stare at me oddly. The one standing a few feet behind the first man tilts his head down, and I see the corner of his mouth tick up in the start of an evil grin. Yup, this is bad.

"Are you the only one home, miss?" the first guy asks and turns his head to his buddy behind him then back to me. He now has a similar grin on his face as his buddy.

That's not suspicious or anything, boys.

Do these two buffoons think I'm dumb enough to answer that question? I start to close the door a little, not wanting to give them a clear view into the apartment. They don't know if I'm alone, and I sure as hell don't want them to see for themselves that I am. I shake my head, studying their faces for a second.

"Nope. My very large, very protective boyfriend is inside, so unless you can tell me what you want, we were in the middle of something that I very much would like to continue," I say. Please let them believe that lie. I doubt they will, but I need to stall.

Examining the faces of these two closely, I can tell they are not from around here. The moment I opened the door, their stench hit my nose. They smell horrible and that for sure matches their appearance. They both could use clean clothes, haircuts, and a fucking shower with tons of bleach. Yes, they smell that bad.

Both men are dressed in dingy jackets and jeans. Their jeans are severely stained with gods know what. I can't tell what color their jackets used to be, but now they are so stained they are a grungy brown, blackish color.

Their faces are somewhat hidden behind unruly beards and long greasy hair. The one in front of me must be older than the other. A good ten years or so is my guess. He has more wrinkles around his eyes and forehead. His hair, while similar in greasiness, is a salt and pepper color unlike his buddy with his dark brown hair, I think. It's so greasy that it could be light brown or even a dirty blond and I wouldn't know.

Close the door, close the door, close the fucking door.

My gut is practically screaming at me. These two give me the creeps. Looking past them into the hall, I hope to see others passing by, but it's a bit early in the morning for a lot of people in this building. Fuck. Reaching for my back pocket, I remember my phone is on the island. That's a good fucking place for it.

"Okay, well this was fun, but I have something much more enjoyable to get back to. So unless you have something else, I hope you two have a good day," I say loudly.

They step closer to the door as I try not to step away. Fuck, the size of these guys means they are likely shifters. They tower over me, easily. I reach my right hand behind my back into the bottom pocket of my mini backpack. Trying to move as little as possible so I don't alert them, I search the bag with my fingers, hoping to land on the small blade hidden inside. I always have some kind of blade on me, whether it's a small one or a large one.

"Wait a minute, pretty lady. We aren't done here," the salt-and-pepper-haired man says, placing a hand on the door frame.

"We were sent here for Loen, Jayce, and Zyon by the alpha," the second man says.

I can tell by the way they are standing and talking to me that they are trying to intimidate me. I don't like how some wolves think they can intimidate whoever they deem weaker than them. When they do, they try to be sneaky by leaving out the true reason or hiding who actually sent them. The moment they hear that they were sent by an alpha, most humans will start answering their questions.

Try harder, boys.

"Huh, I'm not sure who you are talking about and why you think they are here in this apartment, but there is no one here by any of those names," I say. The cold sharp feeling of my blade grazes my fingertip.

"The alpha sent us," the first man says quickly. Liar. Seriously, this is just sad at this point.

"Well, I hate to ruin your day, boys, but I think you have the wrong apartment," I say sternly.

Grabbing the door with my left hand, I start to close it, but it meets a sudden resistance. *Fuck me.* A large, black booted foot blocks the door from closing the rest of the way. The man lets out an angry snarl as he throws his shoulder into the door, knocking me back a few steps as it swings up. That stumble caused me to lose the grip I had on the blade in my backpack.

Shit, shit, shit.

I don't like my odds here. Even as one of the best combat instructors, the odds are not quite stacking in my favor against these two large buffoons. Stepping backward, I give them some space. I need to think of a plan that doesn't involve revealing what I have been fighting like hell to keep hidden. The man who threw his weight into the door closes the door as his buddy quickly gets in front of me and backs me to the living room wall, caging me in with his body. Gods, this man needs a shower and a mint. Turning my face away from him, I try not to gag.

"We saw Loen here, so don't play like you don't know," the older man says as he starts searching through the apartment. I guess my bluff that a large protective boyfriend was inside didn't fool them one bit, or they thought they could take him on too. There is no one, but if there was, these two have some balls.

He goes down the hall toward the back bedrooms. The thud of a thick boot on a cheap hollow core door echoes through the apartment as the man kicks open one of the bedroom doors. The man pinning me is gawking at me with a slimy smile. I try not to make eye contact. His sewer scent and filthy body make me want to throw up.

"Pretty," he whispers near my ear as he runs his right hand down the side of my cheek. Resisting the urge to throw up in my mouth, I try to focus on how the fuck I'm going to get out of this.

"You need a mint and a bath," I say. Trying to push him back, I place both my hands against his chest and give him a shove. He pushes back against me and pins me to the wall again. This time, his body is flush with mine, making my skin crawl.

"Careful, pretty lady. I have some ideas on how to make you squirm that you won't enjoy, but I sure will," he says. His eyes dart to the hall archway and then back to me. Angry heavy footsteps are coming this way. His buddy must be done searching the rooms.

"You don't get to play with her yet, Axel," the man in the hallway says as he walks back into the common area. Crossing the apartment to Harper and Clay's room, he searches and turns back around. "You lied. That's not very nice," he snarls.

The man pinning me lets out a low chuckle then pushes his body harder into mine. A slightly painful-sounding groan comes out of my mouth. Staring at the man I now know as Axel with the same creepy expression on his face, I can't wait to wipe that look off his face. I can tell the thoughts behind his eyes are vile.

"They aren't here. You have the wrong apartment," I shout.

There are about forty apartments in this building. How did they know it was this specific apartment that Loen was in last night? However, that does confirm that they are not with Alpha Dolton.

"I bet this was a booty call for the future alpha, huh?" Axel snickers as brings his face closer to mine again.

Keep that up, perv, and you won't be seeing out of those eyes for much longer. I try a little harder to wiggle free, getting my right arm behind me to help give me leverage off the wall. Of course, it would backfire, leaving me now pinned between the man and the wall with my right arm behind me. The man lets out a throaty growl as he puts his face closer to my neck. Closing my eyes, I take a breath as I feel his hand run down my side landing on my hip.

Please stop.

I shouldn't have closed my eyes. My heart rate starts to race as my breathing gets harder. Tingles start in my fingers and toes working their way up my arms and legs. Fuck, panic attack. *Dang it.* I thought I worked through this shit. Shaking my head, I open my eyes not that the view of this man touching me is much better, but at least I know it isn't someone else. This panic isn't going to go away. If it gets worse, I'll lose control. If my secret is revealed, that will be the end for me.

"Why are you here?" I holler as loudly as I can. Please someone hear that. Axel snarls, glancing toward his buddy who is now rummaging through the kitchen. "I'm not your leverage."

Fucking jerk is making a mess of this place.

"Switch with me, Faris, and shut her up. As much as I want to toy with her, her voice is getting annoying. If Loen was here with this one, he'll be back," Axel says as he runs his dirty hand down my cheek and neck, heading for my chest again. This man needs to keep his slimy hands to himself.

"Stop touching me," I yell, trying to push myself off the wall even a little bit. The man moves his feet, trying to make it harder for me to move his large frame, but what he doesn't notice, I pick up on right away. I may not be able to move my upper body but his shift in stance has placed one of my legs between his leaving me a clear way out of this.

"Seriously, Faris. Come check her out. We could have some fun while we wait," Axel says and turns his head to face Faris again. "I'm bored."

I don't want to be held here any longer. Feeling unable to move has feelings coming back that I have tried to lock away. Instead of taking my arm out from behind me, I use the little space I have to wiggle my hand into the backpack to grab the blade.

Axel adjusts his shoulders, and his dingy jacket moves enough that I notice something around his neck. Squinting, I see a pack crest. I have a leg free. Not wasting any more time, I act, bringing my knee up on the leg that's free between the man's legs with as much momentum as I can get behind it. As soon as my knee connects to his body, the man drops to the ground, grabbing his crotch and writhing in pain. I hope that fucking hurt, perv.

"You bitch," Axel says, groaning in pain before attempting to stand.

I move my body so I'm not backed to the wall again. As he turns and lunges toward me, I raise my left arm with my hand pointing at Axel as it comes up. I flick my hand up, palm flat toward him. His eyes go wide as the magic in my hands flashes bright blue-white light as it leaves my hand and heads toward him.

The moment the concentrated magic hits him, he is blown backward off his feet. His seemingly weightless body flies over the armchair and lands hard on the floor. Not moving. I can tell he is out cold. Taking a hit like that to the chest that close most definitely hurts. I am somewhat surprised it didn't stop his heart though.

Allowing the magic I was holding back to flow through every inch of my body, I roll my shoulders as I straighten my posture. Standing taller and stronger, I always feel stronger when the magic is coursing through me and not suppressed away.

"What the fuck," Faris shouts, rushing off the island stool toward me.

I cock my head to the side. Then without hesitation, I bring my right arm from behind me. I quickly throw the blade in the direction of the second shifter, watching it as it soars through the air to find its target. It lodges into the stinky shifter's throat.

I wasn't quite aiming for his neck, but if he hadn't rushed me, it would have hit him in the chest or stomach instead. So that's honestly on him. Chuckling as I shake my head, I watch Faris fall to the hardwood floor with his hands around his neck. Rushing over to him before he has a chance to pull the blade out, I place my hand on it and grip his greasy hair. I gag at the feel of it in my hands.

"Now, now, I wouldn't take that out just yet," I warn. "It's a silver blade. I'm sure you don't want to bleed out."

He still goes to remove the blade, placing his other hand on mine to try to pull it away. There is a look of shock on his face as his eyes catch mine, but he quickly fixes his expression to one of anger.

"Bitch," Faris says as blood starts to fill his mouth.

"Fine, have it your way," I say. Letting go of the blade handle and taking a few steps back, I wait. He isn't reaching for it yet. Interesting. Guess he doesn't want to die after all.

"Not possible. You are… You are a Nova" he says, a gurgling sound follows as more blood fills his mouth. I can see the wheels in his brain turning as he registers what he is seeing.

"Quiet now. I can help you, but I need answers first. Why does your alpha want Loen or his brothers?" I ask, squatting down in front of him. Making sure his eyes are staring into mine, I say, "I would think twice about lying to me."

"Fuck you."

Blood from his wound sprays all over the place as he grips the blade and yanks it from his throat. Attempting to swing at me, he lunges. Standing, I take a few large steps backward. I am only a few feet away as he continues to rush at me, leaving a blood trail. I give him an eye roll and wait.

A loud echoing thud fills the apartment when the man falls to the floor. The force of his own body combined with blood loss from his neck was too much for him, so the moment he slammed into a nearly invisible barrier I placed in front of me, he collapsed. His impact sent ripples of white light through the barrier before it faded.

What a fucking disaster.

Letting out an audible sigh, I have two shifters knocked out on the cheap hardwood floor. One is bleeding. This is going to be a pain to explain to the landlord.

Even though it's morning and light shines through the windows, the apartment looks as though all the lights are on. That isn't the case. That glow is from me. As I calm down, the glow starts to fade, leaving only the natural sunlight to light the apartment. Walking toward the Island, I step over Faris. That idiot needs medical treatment or a fae healer until his own natural shifter healing returns. Silver slows that ability down for a few hours. More if the silver is injected into the bloodstream.

Grabbing my phone from the island and a small kitchen towel from one of the drawers, I head back toward the two men. Staring at the man in the living room, a thought comes to mind. If he had the pack crest necklace on, he could have something else that might give me a few clues. I search him. He is still out cold and probably will be for a little while. After the quick pat down, I mumble to myself.

Well, fuck.

Finding nothing in his pockets other than a few beef stick wrappers, one half-eaten, I stand, grabbing the towel and my phone. I go over to the other guy with the neck wound and put pressure on his wound with the towel. Using one hand to put pressure on his neck, I use the other to search his pockets.

The first few pockets have nothing in them, but as I reach into one of his jacket pockets I feel something. Pulling it out, I'm pleasantly surprised. A burner phone. I wake the screen up and slide to try and unlock the phone. I expect it to be passcode locked, but it isn't. I'll go through it later.

Placing the burner phone on the ground next to me, I go back to his jacket pockets. In another pocket, I find something else—a few of the same beef stick wrappers and what I think is a credit card at first turns out to be a hotel card key to one of our local hotels, Under the Sun Hotel. The last pocket has the same crest in it as the other dude.

No fucking way.

I know this crest. There are two packs I never want to deal with. Dolton's is one of them, and this crest represents the other. Bex's old pack. The pack she jumped at the chance to leave the second she was able, and I don't blame her. It's a horrible pack run by a twisted alpha who makes money using his men as bounty hunters. They have been connected with kidnapping girls for trafficking.

Placing the items I found on this guy on the floor with the burner phone, I pick up my phone and dial the station. Archer is going to want to hear about this. I'm hoping Archer can't use his fae magic to detect lies over the phone because I'll be telling a few.

"Thank you for calling Whitlock—" Loris voice comes through the phone, but I interrupt her.

"Hey, patch me to the chief, now," I say. Making sure she can hear the sense of urgency in my tone.

"Mazzy?" she asks. Gods, I don't have time for this.

"Yes, Lori, I need the chief, NOW," I nearly shout into the phone.

She patches me through to his office. Archer answers in an annoyed tone. I've either caught him at a bad time, or he's still in a pissy mood about Loen and Serafina.

Let me make your day that much better, Chief.

I start filling Archer in on everything and explain that one of the two men here needs medical attention. I leave out exactly how I was able to take them both out by myself of course. After making sure I'm okay, he informs me that help is on the way.

Ending the phone call, I keep pressure on the man's neck. My mind is racing. These two somehow knew Loen had stayed here last night. This exact apartment. Why are they after them in the first place? Last I heard, these two packs were in an agreement to be friendly with each other.

It didn't take long for help to show up. After the EMTs checked the two men out, they loaded them up on stretchers, cuffing them to the stretcher before taking them away for medical treatment. The officers left in the apartment are taking photographs and gathering up what evidence they can. I gave my statements already. I'm sure I'll have to go over it a few more times in the next few days.

I can hear the other officers knocking on the surrounding apartment doors. Our apartment door is wide open as people come in and out. I doubt any of our neighbors are going to give them anything useful. Either they heard and ignored, or they didn't hear anything. Trying to stay out of the way while my coworkers do their jobs, I stand back, leaning against the wall outside the bathroom, where the kitchen and bathroom meet. With my back against the wall, I cross my arms and watch.

"Nearly done here, Mazzy," one of the officers taking photographs says from the kitchen.

"All good. I know this is a process," I say softly, waving a hand at him.

I'm not annoyed with my coworkers. I'm annoyed because I got caught in the crossfire between the Dolton and Blackheart packs. A lot of people are aware that Colak Dolton has enemies, but we were not aware that any of them were stupid enough to try to kidnap his grown sons. Anger grows as I think about things more. The stench of the guy who put his hands on me still fills my nose. It likely seeped into my clothes when he pinned me to the wall. His touch triggers me, making things so much worse.

I fucking knew there was some kind of hidden agenda to the Dolton sons being here. Archer and I both suspected it. I guess this is confirmation. I already had a small confirmation when I overheard Jayce and Zyon complaining while they were watching the skills testing. Enhanced hearing can be a real bitch sometimes—especially when I have to pretend I don't hear anything. I hate having to pretend I'm something I'm not.

A lot of people think I'm human—no magic, no shifting abilities, no enhanced abilities. I am anything but human, but that's what I have to show people. No wolf shifter has magic besides the stereotypical shifter abilities. Things like enhanced senses, healing more rapidly, telepathic abilities with their pack members, and of course, shifting into a giant wolf. I have all those abilities as well as the magic of a fae and witch combined. If my abilities are found out that would be a death sentence for me. Closing my eyes and resting my head against the wall, I try to stop my mind from spiraling.

A familiar deep voice reaches my ears, and my eyes snap open. Lowering my head, I scan the room, only to see Loen and his brothers standing in the apartment doorway searching around taking in the mess that is now my apartment. They were talking to one of the officers taking photographs of the living room. Loen turns to me. His eyes struggle to stay on mine. Clearly, he feels guilty for something.

This fucker.

My skin is still crawling from that creep, Axel, touching me when he had me pinned to the wall. The expression on the faces of the twins standing next to Loen tells me they know something. Not an ounce of shock about the attack. They expected something like this to happen. If they knew they were being followed, Loen knew he led them here and said nothing. He didn't even warn us that we might be in danger. I push off the wall and cross the apartment toward them. When I nearly reach them, Loen takes a few steps toward me.

"Are you okay?" he asks.

I can't look at him. I'm so angry at him. The fact that he knows I'm his mate and still didn't say a word, not even a hint, pisses me off more. Ignoring him, I glare at his brothers instead. Stopping in front of Jayce and Zyon, I cross my arms and give them a harsh glare.

"Yeah," I say sharply. "Either of you want to fill me in on why these two morons from Blackheart tried to use me as bait for you three?" Jayce lowers his gaze to the floor then darts his eyes to his twin Zyon who glances at Loen next. "Don't all start talking at once,"

"May, back off," Loen snaps, grabbing my upper arm tightly.

May? Big fucking mistake, Loen.

Taking a deep breath, I uncross my arms. With my opposite hand, I grab Loen's hand on my arm and pull it off me. He releases quickly, but I don't let go of his hand. Instead, I grip his hand harder and give it a twist. He gives into it. His elbow bends, and I'm able to bend his arm behind his back. Kneeing the back of one of his knees, he falls to the ground, and I use my weight to push him flat on the floor, using both of my arms now to contort his bent arm more. His face hits the ground harder than I expect, and a crunching sound is followed by a groan and a pained, "Fuck."

"Do not call me May. You have sure as hell not earned using a nickname, especially that one," I say. When I put a little more pressure on his bent arm, Loen lets out another strangled groan. "They attacked me trying to get to you. You led them here, knowing this could happen and you said nothing. He had his hands on me, touching me, so I would appreciate some fucking honesty."

There is not a single sound from them or anyone else in the room. Someone behind me clears their throat. Letting the breath I was holding out, I slowly release Loen's arm and stand. That was not super professional. Guess I'm living up to the Ice Queen's reputation right now.

Taking a few steps away from Loen, I put up the mask. My, "I have no emotions" mask. I can't show how scared I am, or how hurt I am. Most of all, I can't show how much hearing Loen call me May nearly broke me down. Loen stands and puts his hand on his now broken nose. A slight pain in my chest tweaks at the sight of him hurt.

I never wanted to feel this. Fucking fated mate bonds.

Taking a step back to give Loen room to get up, I turn my attention back to Jayce and Zyon, who are standing there dumbstruck.

"Why are they hunting the three of you?" I demand, but before either of the twins can get a word out, Loen stands and turns to me with anger in his eyes. Without saying a word, he steps out of my apartment, dragging his brothers with him.

Chapter 6: What the Chief Says Goes

Mazzy

Fuck my life.

Today has been a long day, starting with the bounty hunter kidnap attempt. Those two bounty hunters are in a cell here at the station, and I'm restraining myself from going down to see if they remember anything about me. I don't want them to. The one with the neck wound is finally healed, and so far, he says he remembers nothing. But he could also be lying.

Loen made a complaint against me for the takedown in the apartment, and that resulted in a long psych eval. I got out of that an hour or so ago. Now I have weekly counseling sessions to work on my anger issues and trauma. Oh, they also took my gun and badge away. Archer has benched me until my next psych eval in a few months.

Thank you, trauma and Loen for that.

Luckily, being benched doesn't take me out of doing the combat seminar. I'm not a typical drinker when I have days like this. But fuck, I think I need a drink tonight.

"But Daddy," Serafina whines.

Archer called the four of us here to discuss what happened at the apartment earlier this morning. Harper is sitting on Clay's lap on the chair in front of the chief's desk while I stand, leaning on the wall near the door. Serafina is standing next to her father, who is sitting in his big office chair, trying hard not to cave to his daughter's puppy dog eyes.

Good luck, Archer. She's laying it on thick.

"Sweetheart, this is for your safety," he says to his daughter, and she huffs as she sits on the edge of his desk.

"Chief, do you think the alpha of the Blackheart pack would be stupid enough to send more bounty hunters after them now that Mazzy has taken two of them out by herself?" Clay asks while softly rubbing his hand up and down Harper's back. She seems anxious, or maybe that's me.

"I do. According to the hotel, the key card belonged to a room rented by four occupants not just two," he says.

"Shit," I say loudly. The chief gazes up at me, and I think he's thinking the same thing I am.

"They have two hidden and probably a lot closer than we would like," he says, confirming we are on the same page. "Mazzy, keep a close eye on the trainees. I would hate to be caught off guard if it's one of them." I nod in agreement.

"Now, back to the living arrangements," he says, earning a whining sound from Serafina.

The chief doesn't want us staying at the apartment until we know for sure the bounty hunters are not coming back. I don't like the idea, but I get where he is coming from. The plan is for us to stay here in the gym or the bunks. Three of us don't have an issue with that, but Serafina is throwing a princess-worthy hissy fit. Archer is trying hard not to cave to her, but we all know it will happen. It's only a matter of how much longer he can hold out.

Clay and Harper turn to me, and we all crack a smile. It's betting time. Harper holds up ten fingers and laughs softly. Archer is pretending not to notice what we are doing, failing as he gives me the stink eye as I show three on one and a zero on the other. I give him another thirty minutes before he caves to Serafina. Clay shakes his head and holds up five fingers. The three of us are trying hard not to crack up.

This is a serious thing. We are not going to be staying in our own apartment for who knows how long, but at this point, we can't help but joke. Serafina always gets her way.

***

I win.

Thirty minutes. That's how long it takes Archer to finally cave, but not in the way Serafina wanted. It's decided that Harper, Clay, and I will stay here in the station. I'm giving them the bunk room, and I'm crashing on the mats in the gym. Serafina will go stay with the chief. She fought that idea at first until she realized he wasn't going to fully cave and rent her a super fancy hotel room.

Spoiled much?

This is one of the reasons we didn't get along at first. I hated how spoiled she acted. Archer was raising three teen girls at the same time. Two that were not his. Serafina was not used to having to share anything, so we fought a lot over stupid shit. We eventually worked it out, but her spoiled attitude still gets on my nerves sometimes.

I'm also happy to have her as far away from me right now as possible. It's been twenty-four hours. His scent isn't as noticeable on her anymore, but every time I see her, all I can think about is that she had sex with my mate in the room next to me. The other issue is she wants to go out with him again, and she's so pushy that I'm sure he will cave to her like everyone else does.

After leaving the chief's office, I have about an hour or so before the trainees are dismissed for the day. All because of the chaos that was this morning, the original plan for today went out the window. Clay, Bex, and Gage ran day two of the seminar, which from the looks of it went okay. I have enough time to watch them work on a few skills and do their end-of-day run.

Loen and his brothers are supposed to be here pairing them up, but because of this morning, they aren't here either. This is going to be a long combat seminar.

Chapter 7: Reality of a Night Terror

Mazzy

Everything feels funny. My hands and feet are tingling. My body is heavy as I try to walk around and figure out where I am.

What is happening?

I try to yell, "Hello," but nothing comes out.

What happened to my voice? Why can't I talk?

Peering around, I recognize the room I'm in. It's the only part of the training academy that doesn't have cameras besides the bathroom and locker rooms. The equipment storage closet. The camera that is normally in the hall pointing this way has been broken for about three weeks.

Why am I here? How did I get here? I collapse on a stack of folded-up gym mats. My body continues to feel heavier. It's like I'm losing control over my limbs, like my entire body is falling asleep. A light shines from across the decently sized room, revealing all the extra gym and training equipment and a man's silhouette in the open doorway. Whoever it is walks in and lets the door close behind them, and it gets dark again. My vision is a little fuzzy. What was I doing earlier today?

Come on, Mazzy, think.

"Mazzy, what are you doing here?" a familiar voice says, and my heart rate starts to race, not out of excitement, but out of fear.

A soft cast light from a cell phone reveals the face behind that voice, and my heart nearly stops. This can't be happening. When did he… How did he…

"Oh Mazzy, Mazzy, my little Ice Queen, what seems to be the matter?" he asks.

Tristen.

Sophie didn't lie about what happened. She said she had a dream and went into great detail about it. This is her dream, but this time it stars me. I try to fight my tired body, but it fails me. Walking closer to me, Tristen sets his phone down on a stack of weights and closes the gap between us. I want to run to fight, but I can't move.

Why can't I move?

"Can't run away from me anymore, Mazzy. Can't say no. You can't stop me, Mazzy," Tristen says as he scoops me off the folded mats and puts me on the floor.

I can't help but panic. The magic I have should be working for me to undo whatever this is. But nothing is working. Why isn't my magic working? Why can't I counter whatever spell or potion is causing me to be paralyzed and speechless?

"Don't touch me," I try to scream as Tristen starts placing his hands all over my body. *"Please stop."*

He can't hear me because nothing comes out. He knows I'm trying to tell him to stop. I have been for weeks. I can't stand him. He thinks he's the god's gift to this earth and that all women want him. He's a pompous jerk who sees women as sex toys. I have turned him down so many times over the last three weeks.

"You are mine now, Mazzy," he says with a cocky grin as he reaches into his pocket and pulls out a pocketknife. Flipping it open, he cuts off all my clothes starting with my top. I need to fight for control. I want to close my eyes, but it's like they are frozen open, a literal frozen spell.

Who would help him do this?

"All mine," he says as he stands to take his clothes off. He's ogling my now naked body. I want to do anything and everything to get away, but I can't. After he's undressed, he positions himself over me. This can't be happening. I try to focus on my magic more, but again there is nothing, not a twitch or even the smallest sensation of magic.

"Please stop," is still nothing but silence....

***

"STOP."

I sit up suddenly, panting, sweating, and on the verge of tears. It takes me a second to ground myself as I take in the room around me. *Where am I?* I can still feel the panic running through my body. I'm shaking. It's hard to breathe, and my heart is beating way too fast. I need to try to calm myself. I am so worked up that my vision is foggy, making the room around me hard to make out at first. This doesn't look like the academy equipment closet. I don't see Tristen anywhere.

Blinking a few times, the fog over my vision finally starts to clear, and I remember where I am. I'm at Whitlock Police Station, sleeping on the floor of the gym. I let out a relieved sigh,

"You're not in that closet. You are safe. He isn't here," I whisper, trying to take a few deep breaths. I hate that dream. It sucks. It's not a dream. Call it for what it is—a night terror.

Shit. Take a breath, Mazzy.

The normally dark room has a glow of light from the hallway but also surrounding me. It's faint, but it's there. Looking down, I see the faint glow of familiar tiny star-like shapes on my skin. I quickly grab the blanket on my lap and throw it over my body, concealing all of me and more importantly the glowing stars. No one can see them. They will give away what I have hidden. I hope no one on the night shift saw it.

Searching around for my phone, I find it under my pillow. I try to keep it in my hand while I sleep, but apparently, I let go of it at some point. I'm temporarily blinded by the screen when I unlock it. Squinting at the screen, I see that it's only three in the morning. I don't need to be up until seven, but I won't be going back to sleep any time soon—not after I lost control of my magic.

Sighing, I try to remember the coping skills I learned from counseling sessions. I never told anyone the details of the night terrors or that I have a few different ones. I told them that I have trouble sleeping and have these night terror-like dreams. They assumed it was past trauma from my mother's sudden death and showed me coping skills to help ground myself after I had one.

"Breath in, breathe out," I say. "You are safe. He is not here. You are in control." The lights from the stars on my skin start to fade. I hated counseling. It was hard to talk about my issues without giving too much detail. I don't trust people. Even those I do trust don't know about my inner turmoil or the magic I have hidden.

When the lights have faded, I take one more deep breath and uncover myself. Slowly sitting up, I need to double check that no one was around to see that. From the looks of it, no one is in here, and the halls are quiet.

I should have slept in the locker room or maybe one of the unused offices, but Archer thought the mats in the gym would be better than a hard bench or floor. Hanging my head, I try to think of anything but that dream as I set an alarm for ten minutes that will repeat until 7 a.m. Just in case I do fall back asleep, I'm not taking any chances. I'll keep waking myself up if that means I stay in control of my dreams and the magic.

It's day five of the combat session. Three days since the attack at my apartment. Loen has been giving me and everyone else the cold shoulder the last couple of days, and I'm hoping he comes in today with a better attitude.

Chapter 8: Her Secret

Loen

I can't sleep. I haven't been able to get a full night's sleep since those

stupid bounty hunters attacked Mazelynn at her apartment thinking I

would be there or show up.

Morons.

They weren't stealthy or effective in their attempt to kidnap my

brothers and me, and that's a little insulting. I was fuming when the call came about an attack on Mazelynn that morning. I had gotten to the station early to do a workout but dropped everything to get to her apartment the moment my brothers came to tell me about it. She was so mad, but I didn't care. She appeared unharmed, and she's hot as hell when she's mad. I didn't care for her snapping at my brothers and refusing to ask me. They aren't to blame for any of this.

You're not to blame either, remember?

Sighing, I shake my head. Rolling over so I'm lying on my back, I put my arms behind my head and lace my fingers together. This entire situation is becoming one big shitstorm after another. I fucked up by calling her May and grabbing her arm suddenly.

Clay told me about her hot buttons—nicknames and sudden touch are the biggest ones. I don't understand the sudden touch unless she had something traumatic happen to her. Clay explained he didn't know why that's a thing either. They have asked, but she refuses to talk about it. The sudden touch aside, I have heard Clay and Harper call her "Mazzy" and "Mazz." I think I have heard, maybe three other people call her "Mazzy." Everyone else calls her by her full name. Why is she so picky about nicknames?

I can't lie here staring at the ceiling expecting it to give me any answers or solutions to this cluster fuck. Unlacing my hands and sitting up, I reach toward my bedside table and tap the small touch lamp to give my darkened room a little bit of light. Running my left hand through my hair, I tap my head with my finger a couple times.

I can't stop thinking about Mazzy and her reaction to the name I called her. I don't know why I called her May, but it felt right when I said it until I saw her eyes. I could see the hurt in her eyes when she turned to me. She masked it quickly. I was not expecting her to take me down though. Her takedown was impressive. It hurt too, or it could have been just how my nose kissed the hardwood floor with the force of my own body weight. Fucking hell, the crunching noise it made and the pain. I could smell and taste my own blood. I wanted to answer her, but to keep my pack safe, I couldn't—at least not yet.

Standing from my bed, I walk over to one of the two windows, pulling the curtain back and gazing out the window at the night sky. The street is somewhat quiet with only a few cars passing by every few minutes. The streetlights are bright, hence the blackout curtains.

Resting my head against the window, a wave of guilt hits me like a smack to the face. Maybe I shouldn't have put in the report. It caused her a lot of trouble. It was my stupid father's idea, and me being me, I could not think for myself in that moment and did what dear old dad asked. Fuck, that was stupid. I should have told my idiot brothers to leave our self-obsessed father out of anything that happens here.

Pushing myself away from the window, the curtain drops over the window, darkening the room once more. The only light is coming from the small lamp on my bedside table. I contemplate trying to go back to sleep even though my mind is racing. Should I go for a ride and maybe get an intense workout in? Walking to my bed, I sit on the end of it, placing my hands on my face as I rest my elbows on my thighs.

You got her badge and gun taken away from her.

I should have let it go, told my father I put the report in, and not actually done it. She had every right to be angry after I read her statement. Okay, I had my brother Zyon hack into the file so I could read it, but they wouldn't let us read it since they are not entirely sure how we are involved or whatnot.

She had every right to lose her shit. Hell, it took everything in me not to go to the station and beat the shit out of the man who kept groping her. I'm still a little confused about how she managed to take them both down, but I'm more thankful that she is for the most part okay.

Yeah, there is no way I'm going back to sleep. How about a nice workout to kick my own ass? Sounds like a great plan, right? I deserve to feel like shit for a few days after treating everyone, especially Mazelynn, like shit the last three days.

I head to the closet to change before grabbing my duffle bag and helmet. Trying to be as quiet as I can, I head out of the apartment to my bike.

***

The ride to the station is good. I need that time to think about everything. Finding Mazelynn's bike in the parking lot is a shock.

Until I remember, duh, she is staying here until the chief feels it is safe for them to go back to their apartment. Fuck, I don't blame him.

The Chief cares a great deal about his officers. You can see it in the way he talks about Mazelynn, and that he cares for her more like a father figure cares for his daughter than a boss for his employees.

Parking my bike next to Mazelynn's, I turn it off and sit here for a couple minutes. What am I going to say to her if I run into her? Or should I try to cold-shoulder her like I have been and ask for forgiveness later when she has had a few more days to cool down? I think I'm in a lose-lose kind of situation here.

Walking toward the station, Susie is at the reception desk. She gives me a soft smile and a quick wave before going back to whatever she is doing. As I go to walk down the hallway to the locker rooms, I notice the gym lights are off. Fuck, that's right. The Chief told everyone that the use of the large gym would be closed at night because he was letting Harper, Clay, and Mazelynn crash in there. So much for my workout. The smaller gym in the basement has shit for equipment, a few treadmills, and one weight machine.

With the plan to work out down the drain, I decide to do some digging into Daren Blackheart. I probably should have let the officers assigned to the case do their jobs, but he sent those idiots after me so I'll do my own digging. It's nearly three in the morning when I start down the hallway to the locker rooms.

The hall lights only light up the gym a little bit. As I pass a few of the windows, I can see a dark lump of blankets. Only one though, and there should be three. Stopping for a moment by the door, I hear a shaky female voice coming from the far end of the gym. Whoever is sleeping in there is talking to themselves. Moving in the door a little, I get the scent of Mazelynn, and no one else. She's in here alone, and she's talking to herself.

"Please stop," she whimpers. Muffled pained whimpers follow. She thrashes around while saying "please stop" a few more times.

I want to go wake her, but she's made it clear she doesn't like me near her. I'm hoping to change her mind. I don't want to give up on the mate fate gave me. My feet are frozen in place even though I want to go in there and comfort her.

"Please stop," she cries again a little louder. She is not talking to herself. She's dreaming. What is she dreaming about?

As my feet finally agree with the rest of me to start walking over to her, I notice a faint whitish-blue glow start. Did she wake up and pick up her phone? When she rolls over, the blanket that was covering her body from view reveals the faint glow now brighter. That's not her phone. Little stars... Am I having a stroke?

"STOP!" Mazelynn screams. Sitting up suddenly, the blanket falls from the rest of her.

Holy fuck.

Mazelynn is scanning around the room panicked. She is acting like she has no idea where she is. It's like she's in a fog, frantically trying to figure out her surroundings. I can see more of her now. The glow from her skin allows me to see she is wearing a thin-strapped tank top. Her silver hair is down and frizzy from her tossing and turning.

The glowing stars on her fair skin trail up her from her hand, across her shoulders, up her neck, and onto her face to her hairline. There is also a small cluster on her chest. I can't take my eyes off her.

The entire night's sky of stars is right there on her skin, and it's breathtaking.

A Nova!

The moment her eyes shift toward the door, I jump to the side out of sight. Why did I hide? Would it have been that big of a deal if she realized I saw what she was hiding? Something in my gut tells me now is not the right time.

Glancing into the gym, I notice she has curled herself up into a ball with the blanket covering herself. I can hear her muffled voice as she tries to calm herself down. No wonder this girl keeps people at arm's length. She knows if she's found out, she will be killed, and anyone who helped hide her would join her in that fate.

Instead of going to a desk to do digging into Blackheart, I have a new agenda. I need to refresh my knowledge on the Nova and see what new information I can gather. Maybe that one fae from high school wasn't as crazy as we thought she was. She insisted the Nova were a gift, and that our ancestors made a huge mistake killing them and cursing the moon soul. Maybe she was right after all.

We were taught some stuff in school—mostly how they are a danger to our world and way of life. They were hunted down, eventually removing every one of them from this world by our ancestors many, many years ago. It's been so long that no one alive now can tell us for sure what is true and what isn't.

Even though they have been removed from our world, our governments and the magical councils still have a law in place for them. Any Nova discovered is to be turned over to them immediately for execution. I always thought that was odd. If those on the councils and in our governments knew the Novas were long gone, then why keep the law in place?

The articles coming up on my screen after I searched "Novas and their history" have said the same thing over and over. It's everything I remember from school—nothing new or useful.

The glow from my laptop screen lights the dark corner of the locker room I'm sitting in. Luckily for me, it's quiet, and no one else is around to ask me what I'm doing. Finding another page on the internet about the Novas, I start to scan through hoping for new information, but it's just like the last few articles. Nothing but the same old story. Ugh, this is getting me nowhere!

Looking up from my screen, I think back to grade school. We were young when we started learning about the Nova. In fourth grade, we started to get into how the government handled them. Nine-year-olds learned that infants were murdered on sight if they showed the markings of a Nova. Talk about traumatizing. In high school, I had a classmate who was a fae. She thought it was so odd that in our world—a world full of shifters, witches, fae, and humans—all those beings came together to rid the world of the Novas. I didn't question things. We all thought that girl was crazy and were told by our parents to stay clear of her and her off-kilter thinking.

Still nothing new in this article, the same old stuff. The part I'm on now is how to tell who a Nova is. Novas are born with markings that resemble tiny glowing stars all over their body. Parents rumored to either hand their child over to the councils without question or kill the child themselves if they bore the marking of the Nova. How could parents do such a thing to their own child?

I couldn't imagine handing my newborn child over to someone knowing they were going to kill them. Let alone being the one to do it. Novas are always born to shifters but were far more powerful than a normal shifter. The Novas are said to be children of the gods sent here to destroy us. Their magic is nearly as powerful as the gods themselves.

The fae girl in high school was so determined to learn everything she could about the Novas. She insisted they were shifters gifted the magic of a fae and witch as well, making the Novas one of every being in our world, tying them to us all. Maybe that meant they were supposed to protect us all.

To see the Nova markings on my mate has me both amazed by how beautiful they are and worried. It also has me questioning everything I was taught about the Nova. If Mazzy holds that much power, she isn't using it. She isn't hurting anyone. Well, not the way our ancestors feared. She is actually trying to help people. Hell, she became a cop despite knowing no one would accept the real her.

I need to talk to her and let her know she can trust me—that I won't turn her in. I wish I could say the same for others in my pack, but honestly, I know a good handful who would feel very differently about that, even with her being their luna. My father would turn on her in a heartbeat. He is so focused on himself and how he appears to the world that he wouldn't care if it hurt me or our pack to lose our destined luna.

However, her pushing me away makes sense now. I will show her she can trust me, and that I will do whatever I need to, to keep her safe. I hope I can before she finds the courage to break the bond.

No one will harm her. That's a promise.

Chapter 9: Make Me Jealous

Loen

Serafina invited my brothers and me out to a club with her, Mazzy,

Harper, and Clay tonight. I'm not a big nightclub person. The night I

met Serafina at the bar nearly two weeks ago was just a drunken night

to let loose and not think about the stupid Blackheart pack situation. It

was a small bar with a decent DJ. This is a full-on nightclub. My brothers thought it would be fun, so we agreed to meet them at the club.

Scarlet Floor is owned by a scarlet realm fae with some kind of agreement with Archer Whitlock. Not only is Archer Whitlock the police chief, but this city is what he considers equivalent to a fae lords' realm. Since he is half-human, he was passed over as ruler of his blood-right fae realm, so he made this city a close equivalent. Fae are weird creatures when it comes to their realms and bloodlines. I figure that's why Chief Whitlock was so pissed about me and his daughter. He wants her with another fae, not a shifter. I don't blame him for that one bit. I'm not even interested in Serafina like that anyway. I have my mate to win over.

After getting ready and heading out in the twins' car, all I can do is hope this doesn't turn into another shit show. I have tried a few times over the last week or so to talk to Mazelynn, but she's been a real bitch. Constantly being rude to me, making me do grunt-worthily jobs, and ignoring me when I try to give her suggestions on how to improve parts of the combat seminar. Anything she could think of to make me miserable, she did. She even sent me a photo of herself in her motorcycle gear during one of her rides, flipping me off when I texted her asking if we could chat. That girl is doing everything she can to try and piss me off. She looked hot as fuck in that photo though. I think she blocked my number after that.

I can't take her avoiding me and pushing me away anymore. I want my mate. I need her. I know she feels the bond too, but her keeping her secret has her pretending she doesn't feel a thing. I know she is pushing me away, hoping the mate bond will go away or maybe I will reject her. I have no plan to reject her. I need to show her she can trust me.

Walking through the Scarlet Flood front doors, it's like we step into a club from a dark romance book. Red velvet curtains line the walls near the entry, and the floors are a shiny black marble of some kind with gold flakes. The bouncers are dark and menacing. The only white lights are the lights above the bar. The lights at all the tables are red light fancy lamps surrounded by a few red LED candles. There are a good twenty tall high-top tables with black velvet tablecloths. Those are near the bar.

On either side of the giant dance floor are about six large booths with black metal tables. Not bad. The DJ booth is elevated nearly above the dance floor which is kind of neat. Scanning the tables and bar, I don't see Mazelynn or any of the others. We continue in as we find a table to sit at near the bar. As I'm sitting down, I see her.

Mazelynn is on the dance floor with Serafina and Harper nearly smack dab in the middle of the dance floor. She looks amazing in the outfit she has on. It's far from her normal get-up, workout clothes, or her bike gear. No, tonight she wears what appears to be black sheer lace bodysuit with a black tank top underneath it, making it less sheer. She has on light blue high-rise jeans with a premade worn-out hole in one knee and black knee-high flat boots.

Look at those curves!

I have noticed her slight curves while watching her during the combat sparring and runs. She wears tight sports bras and baggy T-shirts or tank tops in what I can only assume is her way of hiding her body but still allowing her the movement to do what she needs to. I don't understand why she is so determined to hide her body. She is in great shape. I want to see more of hers. I won't lie. She must still be trying to hide some of her body in this outfit because to me her chest appears a little squished like she's wearing her typical tight as fuck sports bra.

I bet Serafina talked her into this outfit. It seems more her vibe without how revealing it could be if worn without a tank top under it. I start to picture what Mazzy might look like wearing it with nothing under it—nothing hiding her beautiful body. *Fuck me.* I'm thrown back into this reality the moment Mazzy makes eye contact with me from the dance floor because if looks could kill, the one she shot my way would have put me six feet under.

Hot as fuck, but yikes, she hates me.

From the somewhat shocked and irritated expression on her face, I gather Serafina did not tell her she invited us out tonight. The moment Serafina sees me, she starts waving at me with over-the-top excitement. If she waves her hand any faster, she might levitate herself off the floor.

Rolling my eyes, I wave back. She smiles and points to her right near the bathroom sign where Clay is sitting at a booth with the girl's drinks. He is scowling but also scanning the room, clearly bored as fuck keeping an eye on the girls' drinks. Maybe we should go sit with him, keep him some company. I decide, for now, I'll give Mazzy a tiny bit of space and stay here at the table with my brothers.

Speaking of my brothers, those two are already at the bar ordering drinks. They wasted no time getting over there. I already told them before we got in here to get me any kind of beer. I'm not picky and didn't plan to drink much tonight. I'm trying to formulate a plan for how to talk to Mazzy. Nothing has come to mind yet that doesn't result in a slap to the face or her turning her back on me and walking away. So while my brothers grab the drinks and likely flirt with girls at the bar, I'm sitting here brainstorming and watching the people on the dance floor.

More like watching Mazzy.

"Loen, here, man," Jayce says, setting a glass in front of me. Jayce takes a seat to my left, and Zyon comes up and sits to my right. "Earth to Loen. Here's your drink," he echoed, this time pulling my attention back to him.

"That's not a beer, Jayce," I mutter.

He gives me one of his *so what* kind of responses and laughs. Picking up the glass, I go to bring it to my lips, eyes still on Mazzy on the dance floor. I lower the drink back to the table. She's smiling, a semi-genuine smile, not her sassy smirk or forced fake smile. This smile nearly reaches her eyes. I need to find a way to make this girl smile more, because fuck, she is stunning.

"Go talk to her, dude," Zyon says. His words pull my eyes away from Mazzy. I have not come up with a plan yet. Instead of responding to him, I take a sip of my drink. A Jack Daniels and Coke, one of my favorites, but also one they know I'll keep going back for more of.

Smart fuckers.

"Down your drink, get your alpha ass up, and go talk to her. You have been looking at her nonstop since we got here." Zyon takes a drink of his beer. Of course, they got me this drink on purpose.

"Shut up," I snarl.

Downing the drink, I slam the glass down. I give them both an *I hate you* glare as I stand and slowly head toward the dance floor.

"Or don't. That's your problem, not mine," Zyon mutters.

Ignoring my soon-to-be-dead brother's comment, I continue toward the dance floor. Weaving my way through the dance floor, I suddenly get surrounded by a group of drunk and overly touchy women. They are giggling and pretending they didn't intentionally surround me. Glancing at each one, I notice they are dressed in similar pink sequin mini-shirt dresses. One has on a white version and is wearing a white sash over her shoulder with the word, *Bride*, written on it.

Rolling my eyes at the drunk bachelorette party girls, I try to push by them, but a few of them move to stand in front of me again, still drunk and giggling. Giggling her head off, the bride tries to whisper to her girlfriends, but it comes out more of a yell than a whisper.

"He's hot. Let's see if we can get him to take one of you home," the drunk bride whisper-yells to her friends.

Rolling my eyes again, I try to take a few steps, but again they are in my way. Over their game, I give them all a nasty glare and a growl loud enough for them to hear. A few of the girls' eyes go wide then drop to the floor. Shifters. Giving them another glare and a lower warning growl, the few shifters in the group start to slowly back away from me, the bride being one of them.

"Sorry, Alpha," the now sober bride says as she ushers her friends away from me.

Good choice, ladies.

With the drunk bachelorette girls out of my way, I set my focus back on Mazzy and instantly notice a man approach them. Harper keeps glancing over at Clay every few minutes then back to Mazzy and Serafina. Mazzy seems just as uncomfortable with this man's suddenly close proximity as Harper, but Serafina remains clueless as she giggles and dances around.

"Hey sexy, care to dance," the drunk man says as he stumbles all over Mazzy and tries to grab her closer to him. I know she handles herself well in the combat seminars, but there is a slight hint of fear in her eyes. What could she be afraid of? The man? Or is she afraid she could get in trouble for defending herself from a pervert?

Crossing the rest of the dance floor in seconds, I walk up behind Mazzy. I know she hates sudden touch. I try to warn her by placing a gentle tap on her shoulder before fully placing my arm around her while simultaneously giving her a slight tug away from him and into the nook of my arm. The moment her body touches mine, I feel my heart rate increase. Her touch feels like heaven.

"Hey man, keep your hands off my girl," I say. Mr. Drunk Guy puts both hands up and starts to back away slowly, eyeing me, then Mazzy, and then back at me. I unintentionally tighten my hold around Mazzy's shoulders, bringing her body closer to mine. I want her as close as I can get until she stops running away from me.

"Sor...sorry, man. I didn't know she was here with anyone. That's my bad," he says. The man turns on his heels and practically runs away.

"You're welcome," I say with a smirk, still not letting her go yet.

"I didn't say thank you," she snaps back. Using her left hand to throw my arm off her shoulders, she moves her body away from mine. "I didn't need your help."

"That's not what it looked like to me," I say. Should I have said that? Probably not. But if she wants to be sassy, I'll give it right back. The hardened expression on her face softens for a second before she goes to turn away from me.

Fuck.

"Mazelynn, can we talk?" I ask. She continues to turn away from me.

"No," she says, walking across the dance floor back to the table she and the others were sitting at.

Dang it.

No, she's not walking away from me. She's talking to me whether she likes it or not. Moving across the club, I quickly catch up with her. The moment I reach her, I do what I know I shouldn't.

Grabbing her by the upper arm, gently squeezing her, and tugging her with me as I continue to walk. I know for a fact Mazzy can put me on my ass in two seconds if I'm not somewhat prepared for it. I don't want to be embarrassed in front of the entire nightclub, but at the same time, this talk needs to happen. With my large hand on her somewhat small upper arm, I guide her toward the hallway to the right of her table. Clay gives me a strange look as we pass him.

"Let go of me," she yells.

She isn't resisting me other than her words. At least some part of her is okay with me touching her and bringing her with me. I'll take what I can get for now. We continue down the hallway, and she glances over her left shoulder and then to me with an angry glare on her still beautiful face. Her cute nose wrinkles, her eyebrows pinch, and her jaw clenches. *Nice try, Princess*. That look isn't going to work on me right now.

"Give me that look all you want, Princess. We need to talk," I say.

Just as she's about to yell at me, her mouth instantly closes again, and she looks forward as we reach the back door at the end of the hallway. Pushing the door that says for employees only open, I pull her out into the alley behind the club.

After the door shuts, I let go of her arm. She stumbles ahead of me a few steps then turns to face me. She is angry but *fuck me*. That look is hot. This may have been the wrong way to go about this. She is visibly upset, but she isn't moving around me to get back inside.

"What the fuck is wrong with you?" she shouts in a hot but pissed-off tone.

"You have been avoiding me. When you're not avoiding me, you're intentionally trying to piss me off. Do you get off on pissing me off?" I ask her and step closer to her.

She backs away with each step I take until her back hits the wall on the other side of the alley. Her eyes have gone wide with my question. I take another step closer. She frantically starts to search around, down the alley to her right first. I glance as well. It's a dead-end—nothing but a brick wall. She quickly looks to her left. Down that way would be an exit if it wasn't for a closed and padlocked metal gate and a large dumpster. Lucky for me; not so lucky for her.

She has no choice but to talk to me if she wants to go back inside through the doorway. Closing the gap between us before she could push off the wall and try to go around me, I position my large frame in front of her. I place my arms on either side of her small frame, caging her against the wall.

Careful, dumbass.

Trying to show her I have no intention of harming her and that I do not want her afraid of me, I raise one of my arms from her side and place it above her head. I'm still caging her with my body, but with my arm up, she should feel less trapped. If she wants to move, she can. She glances at the new opening I gave her but then back at me. She doesn't try to leave.

"Loen, you need to move," she whispers. Her tone isn't at all angry. It's soft and sweet. Her voice is counteracting the words coming out of her mouth.

"You feel it, don't you?" I ask. Leaning my body closer to her, my face is now only inches away from hers. She is trying hard not to make eye contact with me, but her eyes fall to my mouth. I see her bite the inside of her cheek. Her eyes dart from my mouth to my eyes then to the ground.

"I don't fee— I don't know what you're talking about Loen. Now move," she says. This time, I hear a little bit of her normal coldness in her tone.

"Are you sure about that? I think you know exactly what I'm talking about," I say in a deep voice. Taking the hand from above her off the wall, I gently grab her chin between my thumb and index finger slowly lifting her gaze so she is looking at me. Her blue turquoise eyes are trying to look everywhere but my eyes.

The moment her eyes connect with mine, I lean in claiming her mouth with mine. She doesn't push me away. She opens for me, and her arms sneak around my neck, pulling me closer to her. Lost in her touch, I'm expecting it when she pulls away and shoves me away.

"Mother fucker," she yells. Pushing me back more, she walks past me back to the back door of the club. Everything in those seconds tells me that she wants me just as much as I want her, but then she pushes me away. All I could feel coming from her was anger.

Fuck.

"May, wait," I say softly. "There's no way you didn't feel that. You feel the pull to me, the same one I feel to you. You are my mate, please," I say to her as I catch up to her. The moment I am standing directly behind her, I feel it. I feel her hate, her pain, and something else.

"STOP. Loen, I don't know what you're talking about. I'm going back inside. You need to back the fuck off. Don't call me May," she shouts. She tries to open the door, but it's locked. The door makes a loud noise when she tries again. She mutters "fuck" under her breath.

I might have fucked up here. She's angry, but I'm not wrong in what I'm feeling. She's my mate, and even if it was for a few seconds, she enjoyed that kiss. She was giving in. I felt it in my soul.

"May…" I catch myself. I need to show her I'm listening to her. "Mazelynn, please," I say as I reach for the door. She brings a hand to her lips and drops it quickly when she seems to realize I can see her face. She turns her face away from me and places her forehead on the door, closing her eyes.

Oh, you really fucked this up.

"Please, let me in," she whispers softly, almost pleading. I was about to say something else when she let out a strangled sigh and pulled on the handle of the door again. Unlike before, the locked door unlocks, and she swings it open. She lets out a sigh of relief, turns to me for a second, and then back into the hall as she walks inside. Like a scolded puppy with his tail between his legs, I slowly follow several steps behind her.

That didn't go well.

Mazelynn is practically speed walking down the hallway. Once she reaches the main room, she heads directly to the bar. I debate going to the table with my brothers or following her to the bar. Since the table we are sitting at is close to the bar, I decide to go to the table and watch her from there. Dropping myself hard into my chair, I pick up the glass that had my drink in it. Remembering I downed that already, I slam it back down. Not facing the table, I turn my body to keep an eye on Mazelynn. Is she doing shots? Realizing my brothers are staring at me, I turn to them for a second.

"Take a picture. It will last longer, or mind your fucking business. Understood?" I snarl, making sure to lace my alpha tone into it. Which at the moment doesn't sound alpha-like.

The twins eye each other and then glance back at me before nodding their heads. They ordered a few more drinks while that whole situation played out with Mazelynn in the alley. Returning my attention back to Mazelynn, she is still in the same spot taking yet another shot. That must be like the third one at this point.

After she downs it, she slams it on the bar. The male bartender smiles a flirty smile at her then pours her another one. I doubt it will take too many more before she's utterly trashed. Maybe I should go up to her, but before I can stand, she does the last shot then pushes the glass back to the bartender. Turning around, she catches me watching her. Rolling her eyes, she starts walking away from the bar.

As she's walking past our table, I turn to continue to watch her. I think she's heading toward the dance floor where Serafina is still dancing this time surrounded by a lot of random men, but that's not where she goes. She crosses the bar and heads to a table in the far back. It's hard for me to see who's at the table at first, but as she heads to the dance floor, I notice she has someone with her.

You have got to be kidding me.

Mr. Drunk Guy is following along with her to the dance floor, wearing the biggest grin on his face. When they reach the dance floor, he pulls her close to him, their bodies touching. My anger is now boiling to the surface. At this point, I should go home. I should look away. I should leave. Fuck this shit, I stand, and instead of walking toward the exit like I should, I head to the dance floor.

Mine.

Rushing across the dance floor, I grab the drunk man by the neck of his shirt, pulling him away from my mate. I pull back with my right arm and slam my closed fist into the guy's nose. Feeling his nose crushed under the impact, I drop him. I shift my body to reach for the man again, not fully in control of my own body. It's like I'm lost in a rage and not able to calm myself down. I want to murder this guy for touching what's mine.

"Loen, STOP. What the fuck is wrong with you?" Mazelynn snaps at me, getting in between me and the guy. "Walk away," she says, placing a hand on my chest. Her touch pulls me from my murderous thoughts and moves my attention to her face. I can't describe the look on her face. It's a mixture of anger and concern.

"What the fuck kind of game are you two playing huh?" the man says.

Even though Mazelynn told me to go, I can't. Her hand is still on my chest, and it's calming me. I fear if she lets go right this second, I could hurt this man even more.

"No game," she grumbles. Her eyes drift from mine to off my right shoulder toward the front door. A slight widening of her eyes has me ready to turn around to see what's coming before I turn my head. She stands on her tippy toes and grabs my face with both her hands.

"Loen, you need to leave, NOW," she yells.

Once she releases my face, I turn toward the door. I'm passed by two large bouncers who I expected to be coming after me. They walk past me without a second glance. It's like they didn't see me. My brothers, having watched that event take place, follow me out of the club. I can tell they want to say something, but instead, we stay silent all the way to the car.

For once, my normally chatty brothers ready to rub my nose in my mistakes are quiet, shocked. As we head home, the only thing making any noise in the car is the car itself and the radio. I sit in the backseat staring out the window, while the twins are likely talking to each other through our mind link. I don't care if they talk. I need to find a way to fix this or maybe accept what I don't want to.

I'm slightly impressed with my brothers right now. I don't think they have gone this long without talking out loud—the entire car ride and now the elevator ride to our apartment. I should tell them, but I also don't want to talk yet. As an alpha, I don't often hang my head and lower my eyes, but that's all I can do.

The elevator reaches our floor, and the doors open. The sweet little girl from the apartment down the hall is standing there with her dad holding a brown teddy bear. She's a cute little thing. I normally smile at her, but not tonight, I have no energy to smile. I quietly pass the father and daughter pair and head down the hall to the apartment door. Jayce has the keys, jingling from his hand as he reaches me and unlocks the door.

"I hope tomorrow is better for you," the little girl calls.

I peek down the hall to see the neighbor girl and her father standing in the elevator. He is beaming at her proudly. She is smiling at me and trying to wave with the hand she has holding her stuffed animal. It's cute of her to try, so I give her a wave and force a smile at her as the elevator doors closed. That's sweet of that little girl. Her father is so proud of her for trying to cheer up someone, a stranger at that. I wish our father showed us that much pride when we did something like that.

"What the fuck was that man?' Jayce asks, closing the apartment door behind him. He is the last one in, and I have already tossed my wallet on the island and started toward my room.

"Loen! What the hell were you thinking?" Zyon asks.

Not in the mood to deal with either of them, I don't say anything and go right to my room, slamming my door behind me. Throwing my phone on the bedside table, it slides off and crashes to the floor. Whatever. I don't care. Tonight was a shit show. She had to have done that on purpose. What was she trying to prove?

Chapter 10: Change of Plans

Mazzy

"Aren't you glad I convinced Daddy to pay for a hotel?" Serafina asks

with pride.

"Thrilled, Sera, so thrilled," I say sarcastically and roll my

eyes.

Only Serefina was unhappy about the living arrangements. I

was fine with sleeping where I was on the gym floor. Even Harper and

Clay weren't complaining. I mean, a few grumbles every now and then that they were missing out on sexy time, but I know for a fact, they found a way to make it work.

That image is ingrained in my brain forever!

I had no idea Harper was that flexible. How her leg was that close to her head without dislocating her hip I have no idea. As for Clay, holy fuck, let's just say the gods blessed this human in more ways than one way. Harper's poor lady bits, but she definitely wasn't complaining. Jokes aside, she's one lucky girl. A loud overly excited scream pulls me from my thoughts.

Thank you gods.

I need to get my mind off my friend and her hubby banging in the closet. Grounding myself in reality, I scan the room. Serafina is still standing in front of the TV with the biggest grin on her face like she came up with the solution for world peace or something.

Cue major eye roll.

Since that night at the bar, Loen has brought back the arrogant dickhead attitude he had when he first showed up but has upped the ante some. He started undermining me in front of the trainees, refusing to do the work I assigned him, and showing up on a few of my bike rides out of the blue. One of those times is stuck in my head.

***

Few days ago

Grabbing my key and helmet I storm out of the locker room, ignoring all the people in the hallway. I need to get the fuck out of here before I punch Loen in the face, again. I can't stand how much of a dick he has been since the bar a few nights ago. Today was too much, he pushed the wrong buttons.

Fuck him.

Reaching my bike, I waste no time getting out of the parking lot. Rushing through the city, I need to get out to where I am no longer surrounded by nothing but tall buildings. Not even ten minutes into my ride, the tall buildings and busy streets are finally giving way to a more relaxing view but that view only lasts a few moments until a bike similar to mine cuts me off before accelerating at an unsafe rate. The black and blue bike looks familiar but not as familiar as the leather jacket and helmet of the rider.

Loen.

This fucking idiot is going to get himself killed if he doesn't slow down around the tight turns ahead. Instead of slowing down, I speed up to catch up to him. A few tight turns later, I spot his bike at a pull off a few feet ahead and make a somewhat stupid decision.

As soon as I pull over behind his bike, I storm over to him, not removing my helmet and get right in his face. I am livid that he would drive so recklessly, but that was the straw that broke the camel's back so to speak.

"Do you have a death wish?" I shout.

Saying nothing, he rises from the bike in my direction, causing me to take a few steps backward.

"Why do you care?" he says, now standing toe to toe with me.

I want to shout at him for being an idiot, for kissing me, for being here, for undermining me, and for flirting with the females in my face.

AHHHHH, this man

"If you're going to go home in a box, I want to be the one to put you in it, you asshole," I snap. This gets a gravelly chuckle from him. I have to resist the urge to stomp my feet like a toddler having a tantrum. I am not trying to be cute right now. I want him to take this seriously.

"You think you can hurt me? That's comical, Princess." He laughs. His husky voice, muffled through the helmet, is music to my ears even with his harsh comment.

"What is your problem? You have been undermining me in front of MY trainees and flirting with MY trainees. Do you understand how doing so can change what these people are getting out of my semina—" I start saying as Loen cuts me off.

"Chief Whitlock's seminar, not yours," Loen grumbles crossing his arms. "Don't forget you are just an instructor."

Don't punch him. Don't do it.

"Just an instructor? Fuck you and your alpha-hole attitude," I yell, stepping closer. My helmet nearly touches his as he looks down at me. This would be more intimidating if I wasn't so much shorter than him. "Undermine me again and I promise you I will find a way to make your days here hell. Flirt with another female trainee, and I will make sure you get a sexual harassment report on your record," I say.

I'm trying hard not to let him hear any hurt in my tone. If he could see my face, he would know I am far more hurt by his flirting than him undermining me. He says nothing as we stand toe to toe, waiting for the other to break

Why did he have to kiss me? He is such a dick. Even fuming mad at him for his stupidity, the pull of the mate bond has me wanting to kiss him.

Fuck.

***

Present day

"It got you off the floor, Mazzy. I thought you would be happy," Serafina says.

Shit.

I got so lost in my thoughts I forgot Serafina was talking to us about the whole living arrangements thing. I knew it was only a matter of time before Archer grew tired of Serafina's whining about staying with him, and I think Harper and Clay voiced they were not getting a restful sleep in the sleep bunks. But I know it's more like they wanted space to fuck that wasn't at the station.

I have been okay, sleeping on the sparring mats. They aren't that uncomfortable, but Archer caved, like caved hard. He moved us all to a hotel close to the station. I told him I would stay in the bunks, but he insisted it was only fair that we all got to stay in a hotel. Serafina, of course, has her own room with a king-size bed and a kitchen. It's honestly nicer than our apartment. Harper, Clay, and I are in a small room with one queen bed and a pull-out couch that doesn't pull out.

Yeah, lucky us.

I can't help but shake my head, sitting on the bed next to Harper. Does she think this is better? Well, for her it is, but for us, not so much. I know Harper and Clay didn't get what they wanted. Hard to fuck when you have to share a one-bed hotel room with your roommate.

"Girl, I was happier on the sparring mats," I say with a chuckle.

"Oh, come on. This is way better," she says smiling and flipping her hair.

"Clay, sweetheart, can you get my phone, please? I think I left it in the bathroom," Harper asks. She has been oddly quiet during this conversation. Honestly, she's been quiet the last two weeks.

"You good?" I ask, leaning over to her. She hasn't been feeling well the last couple days. I have my suspicions, but I have kept them to myself. I mean I can smell something is off with her. Thank you, enhanced sense of smell. Her normal scent is just a tad off. It could be for only a few reasons, and I'm hoping it's the one I'm thinking of.

"Yeah, I need to check something on my phone. I thought it was in my pocket, but my ADHD brain probably left it in the bathroom," she says and puts her hand out as Clay walks the phone over and places it in her hands then kisses her on the forehead.

"Mazzy, any chance I can share the bed with my wife tonight?" Clay asks with a somewhat joking tone. I know he said it jokingly, but he truly wants me to say yes. I get it. I would want to sleep next to my spouse too if I were married.

"No," I teasingly say and smile at him. "The first time I catch you two doing the horizontal tango or any gymnastic positions with me on the couch next to the bed, you will be sleeping in the tub or in your car." I point at him, trying to keep a straight face for as long as I can, but I can't help but laugh. Harper and Clay laugh with me. I love these two. We get along so well. They know I'm picking on them, and I know they are respectful and wouldn't even think of doing anything like that with me in the same room—let alone on the couch not even five feet away.

The phone in Harper's hand starts beeping, and she smiles, getting up she rushes to the bathroom without saying a word.

A loud high-pitched excited screech comes from the bathroom, and Clay rushes to the door before he can open the door himself. It flies open, and Harper leaps into his arms hugging him. I can see a huge smile on her face and a little white stick with a pink lid in her hand.

I KNEW IT!

She's pregnant. I had a feeling the change in her scent was that she was pregnant because the only other reason would be that she cheated on her husband, and I know that's not something she would do. Shifters can usually pick up on pregnant women because they smell slightly different. It's weird but kind of handy too. I can pick up on a little bit more than a typical shifter. Clay can't smell the change in her because he is human.

They have been talking about a baby for a while and were worried with Harper being fae and Clay being human that it would be much harder for them to get pregnant. There is little time for celebration though. The three of us are due at the station in about twenty minutes, so we should get going.

You could be happy like them if you just accept it.

Chapter 11: Might Be My Last Chance

Loen

I know Mazzy doesn't trust me with her secret. I truly believe if she knew that I saw her that night she would panic and run away. I don't think she will ever accept our fated bond out of pure fear of what she is.

How do I prove to her that I won't tell a soul about her, not even my brothers unless her life depends on it? As far as this world is concerned, the Novas only exist in our history books, and I have no intention of changing that. Mazzy will not be found out if I have anything to say about it.

I have been second-guessing myself ever since that night at Scarlet Floor. I thought for sure she felt our bond. Knowing she was a Nova gave me hope that she felt it, but something was still off. Her reaction and the emotions I felt from her after that kiss in the alley and then the way she was dancing with that guy made me second guess myself.

I should never have kissed her like that.

Instead of sleeping, I am lying here thinking about Mazzy and how I can go about fixing this. She might not be open to it, but fuck, I have to try. Maybe I should talk to Harper about it. I think out of her three roommates Harper is the one Mazzy is more herself with. When she is around Serafina, I can see that Mazzy is struggling to contain something. I see her eyes roll when Serafina comes into the station all bouncy, suggesting another night out or shopping trip.

I overheard Serafina talking with Clay one day. She was asking if she did something to piss off Mazzy because she feels Mazzy has been avoiding her. I thought it could have been because of the mate bond and having her friend's scent on me and my scent on her friend, but now I'm thinking it's more likely Mazzy only tolerates Serafina out of respect for Archer.

A loud thud pulls me from my thoughts. What the fuck was that? I'm in my room, and the twins are supposed to be cooking dinner. But from that loud thud, I'm guessing it's not going as planned. Rolling my eyes, I decide to forgo the nap, not like my mind is letting me sleep anyway. I should go see what my two idiot younger brothers have managed to fuck up now.

Walking out of my bedroom, I'm not surprised to see the kitchen area empty. Scanning the rest of the apartment, I find my idiot brothers in the middle of a wrestling match on the living room floor.

Can they not complete one simple task without fighting?

"HEY," I yell trying to get their attention, and it does…for two seconds. Jayce pauses his assault on Zyon and casts his eyes up at me, and in that moment, Zyon throat punches Jayce. It was not hard enough to cause permanent damage but hard enough to make it difficult to breathe for a bit. I chuckle to myself. No matter how mad they make me with this fighting, it's kind of comical.

That was a cheap shot.

"Will you two knock it off? You told me you were handling dinner. I can see that's going well," I say, trying to show I'm not amused by their lack of focus.

I swear these two spend more time fighting than getting along. I don't see blood all over the place, so that's a good sign. The last fight had sharp objects involved and a lot of blood to clean off white carpets.

Shaking my head at my brothers, I turn and head to the kitchen. Let's see how much of dinner they got started before their tussle. Searching the small space, I notice that dinner is not even close to being started, let alone done. The raw steaks are set out on the counter next to the pan on the stovetop. The veggies are sitting on a cutting board on the adjacent countertop with a knife balancing half off the cutting board. Well, I can see where it started.

One task. Could they complete one task?

I wash my hands in the sink and head to the stove. I can hear a ruckus going on to my right, but I don't care to look. I asked them for one thing, and they can't seem to do it—so I will. As I go to grab the steaks Jayce runs into the kitchen with Zyon on his heels.

"I got it, Loen," he says, panting. Guess he's still trying to get over that throat punch. I roll my eyes and shoo him away.

"I got it," I say annoyed.

I wanted a short nap before my night shift tonight. They know I'm taking some time away from the combat seminar. They don't know exactly why, but they do know part of it has to do with Serafina and her obsession with asking me out. The real reason is to give Mazzy some space while I find a way to fix what I fucked up.

I have explained to Serafina over and over the last three weeks that what we had wasn't a serious relationship kind of thing. I also explained it to Chief Whitlock. He wasn't happy about the one-night stand thing, but he also gave me some advice. He insisted I avoid going on any outings with her, not ghost her but keep telling her I'm not interested or be unavailable every time she asks. He knows his daughter falls for men fast and figured that was what was happening, so he has been helping me by switching shifts at the last minute.

I know it sounds horrible, but this girl won't get it through her head that I'm not interested in her. I had a feeling asking my brothers and I to Scarlet Floor was Serafina's way of trying to get a date out of me, and I was right.

When I overheard her crying to the chief one day, I thought it was about me, but when I listened in it was actually about Mazzy. She was crying about Mazzy being unusually cold toward her, rolling her eyes at her far more than she normally does, and being overly snappy.

She isn't the only one Mazzy has been cold and snappy with.

"Dude, what the fuck?" Jayce shouts. I turn my head to see what the commotion is about. I got lost in my thoughts while cooking and completely tuned out my brothers and their current argument.

"Zyon, seriously, I called dibs, you backstabber," Jayce yells as he runs back at Zyon, throwing his phone on the island. I must have been so focused on the steaks and my thoughts that I didn't hear it go off.

"You two didn't learn anything from the last time?" I ask, shaking my head.

These two, I swear, are so thick-headed sometimes. The twins are only a couple of years younger than me. I'm twenty-seven years old, and they will be twenty-five in a few months. But they still act like teenagers. Maybe I act more grown up because I have to be. I'm the future alpha, and my father is more about being strong and doing the right things. It makes me laugh thinking about it now. It was his idea to use the rumors that I'm this giant dickhead playboy to our advantage and have me act the part even though I'm probably the furthest thing from a dickhead or playboy.

Yeah, sure you are.

Okay, breaking the drunk guy's nose and sleeping with Serafina aside. I am not that much of a dick. I mean what man doesn't have dick moments, but I try hard to listen to my people, help them when they need it, and do whatever I can to fix things for my pack. My father usually takes credit for the good things I do though, so usually the bad things are all that others get to see.

As far as the Playboy rumor, I have only been with two other women, unlike the high twenty-plus women the rumor mill is spreading. Wolves don't have to stay celibate until they meet their mate. Unless they happen to meet their mate at eighteen or nineteen, many have at least one or two sexual partners before meeting their fated mate.

It's not frowned upon, but to have a rumor that I'm a huge fuck boy? I don't understand how playing along with it will do any good in the eyes of the other alphas. I swear my father wants me to fail, to appear incompetent or neglectful of my alpha duties. I don't see how that will benefit him or help our pack at all.

The man is insane. Thank gods, I'm not like him.

A loud smack pulls me from my thoughts again. Wow, I'm distracted tonight. I need to get some sleep, but instead, I'm here running through all the current problems through my mind, hoping to find a solution. Sighing, I turn to the living room. The twins are back at each other. This time, I can tell their wolves are starting to take a little bit of control. This is going to get bloody if I don't stop it now.

"Guys," I say sternly and walk over to them as they tussle on the floor. I grab the back of Zyon's hoodie and the front of Jayce's t-shirt and pull them away from each other. I'm not much taller than them, but I am stronger. Alpha and all.

"If you guys keep this up, we might as well just hand one of us over to Daren." I let go of their clothes and stand between them.

I'm waiting for one of them to try and make a move at the other, but I guess they're not as stupid as I think because they sulk then walk away from each other. Zyon heads to the couch and throws himself face-first onto the couch cushions. Jayce walks himself to the sink and splashes water on his face. Then he stands leaning against the counter.

"Now that we are cooling down, can I get a little context here?" I ask, still standing in the middle of the living room. I have already gathered this was over a girl, but if I can help them get over it, then we can get back to getting dinner done. Maybe I can get a few minutes of shut-eye. Zyon rolls onto his back and places his hands on his chest, lacing his fingers together.

"Z, what's the issue?" I ask.

"I liked this girl, but Jayce being Jayce, after one date with her called dibs. He knows how it's supposed to work. He was supposed to wait, and he didn't," Zyon says with a defeated tone. He sounds like a sad puppy left at home for too long on its own.

That's a cheap trick. Jayce knows better than to mess with Zyon like that. Hell, it was their agreement in the first place. Ever since they were little kids, they had this dibs rule, and they stuck by it. It is a rule never to be broken in their eyes. If one of them calls dibs on something after a fair trade, then the loser can't complain or get in the way. It worked well with toys as kids, snacks, and so on, but I knew it would go out the window when girls got involved. They are so different but have such similar tastes in girls, so I'm not surprised they are fighting over a girl—again. This situation makes me think of one girl in particular who might get them using their brains.

"Z, remember Lacey? The cute little fae girl from high school?" I ask, waiting for him to respond. I know he will remember her. They still talk about her.

"Yeah, what about her?" he asks, sitting up quickly, surprised to hear her name.

"She liked both of you and agreed to go out with both of you, but what happened?" I ask.

"Jayce called dibs, and I went along with our dibs rule." His tone gets soft. "She said she couldn't stay because she wasn't going to have another man make her decision for her," he says, looking at Jayce.

They both shift their gaze to the floor and sigh. Jayce makes his way past me toward the kitchen. Zyon and I stay where we are in the living room.

I thought for sure that Lacey was their mate. They are identical twins. While it's rare for twins to share a mate, it does happen. It was only unlikely because she was a fae. Fae don't have mates or haven't in a long time. They were both so drawn to her even before they turned eighteen, but their little dibs thing went and pushed her away—like Mazzy is trying to do to me.

"That girl should have been your clue to drop that rule right then and there. But no, you just keep repeating the same fight over and over." I'm trying to get my point across. They need to drop this dibs rule and search for different girls. Jayce finally speaks up from the kitchen.

"Steaks will be done soon," he says with a cold tone.

Oh, fuck, you forgot about the steaks on the stove.

"Loen, I'm sorry we woke you up," Jayce says.

There's more to this story, but I'm sure in time, they will open up and work together. Honestly, Lacey was the best thing to happen to the twins, but when she and her family moved, it broke their hearts. She was a sweet little fae with pink hair, green eyes, and freckles across her nose. When I say little, I mean *little*. At seventeen, she only stood four foot eight. She was a tiny thing, most fae are tall, like six foot tall, but for some reason, she was unusually small.

Focus, Loen. Gods, you need sleep.

"Screw dinner. I'll get a snack on the way to work. I need to sleep. I can't stay focused, and that's not a good combination with a gun on my hip," I say and walk to my bedroom door. "Can you two hold off on beating each other until after my shift ends in the morning? I'll help you all talk it out, I promise," I say to them both.

"Yes, sir," they both say as Jayce plates the steaks, and Zyon heads to the kitchen area to help him.

Please, let them get along for a few hours at least.

Heading into my room, I close the door. Standing at my doorway, I know I should go to bed, but their little tussle and bringing up Lacey makes me think about Mazzy. She's pushing me away like Lacey felt the boys were doing. I have an idea of how to give her space but also get her closer to me. I grab my phone and send a text off to Clay.

Me:
Clay, Hey man.
How's the hotel situation going?

Clay:
Hey.
I want to sleep with my wife.

Me:
I don't understand why the chief put the three of you in one room. You're a married couple and I'm sure Mazelynn wants her own space too.

That thought crossed my mind as I walked into my bedroom. She needs her own space. I can give her space while also giving her own space.

Makes sense right?

We are renting a four-bedroom apartment. We use the fourth room as a workout and storage room. It has a Murphy bed and a dresser in it, so she wouldn't need to bring anything but clothes.

Clay:

well duh

Me:

Mazzy back from work yet?

Clay:

Yeah why?

Me:

Do you know if she still has me blocked?

Clay:

What do you think?

Me:

Just check you dick.

Clay:

Hold on

Me:

If I am blocked unblock my number so I can message her.

Clay:

What do you have planned?

She finds out I am screwed.

I would much rather NOT get kicked in the balls by her again for helping you. It fucking hurts dude!

Me:
Just do it.

I'm trying to help you get laid, man

Clay:

...

I unblocked you

If she finds out I did that I'll kick your ass!

Also, you're in her phone as Major Dickhead!

Me:
I got your back.

That's ok she's in my phone as

Cold hearted bitch!

She's not actually in my phone under that name. She's in there as Mazzy. It was May, but I changed it when she reminded me again not to call her that. I have a feeling she is going to say no, but I'm hoping I can persuade her. I start typing a text to Mazzy and hope she doesn't block my number again.

Me:
Mazelynn, it's Loen,
Please don't block my number.

Mazzy:

Loen

How the fuck, I blocked you.

Me:

I have my ways.

> **Mazzy:**
>
> I'm going to kill Clay

Me:

Why do you assume it was Clay?

maybe I'm just that good of a cop

> **Mazzy:**
>
> Ha ha ha sure you are.

Me:

Rude

> **Mazzy:**
>
> What do you want, Loen?
>
> You have three more texts before I block your number again.

Me:

Fine, fine don't get your braid in a knot.

I know your housing situation is technically my fault.

> **Mazzy:**
>
> No shit! Two more

Me:

Seriously, come on.

> **Mazzy:**
>
> One

Me:

Fine. We have a spare room here we don't use. The newlyweds probably want some hanky panky time. Plus, I doubt you have been sleeping the last few nights.

Waiting for a response, I'm hoping she will agree, not only because I want to help her, but also, because I want her close so I can make sure she is safe.

I need to go to bed. It's been a few minutes, and I'm worried she blocked my number again. I'll have to pull out what I have up my sleeve.

Here goes nothing.

Me:

I saw you in the gym having a night terror a few weeks ago. I was going to wake you up, but you seemed to calm down, so I left you alone. From what I did see that's probably every night thing. isn't it?

Mazzy:

{Typing...}

She's either going to block me or kill me. I don't know which one. I lay in bed hoping for a response before I fall asleep. I don't have long before I need to get up for my shift. As I go to shut my eyes, I hear my phone chime.

Mazzy:

I hate you but fine. There will be rules though.

I'm headed to the gym to work out around 7 we can chat when

you get in for your shift.

Thank the gods, she said okay.

Mazzy:

Oh and Loen, don't tell anyone about the night terrors.

….please.

Holy shit she said "please" to me.

She hasn't said a polite word to me since the first day. That's a

step in the right direction for sure. I can let myself fall asleep now. I

relax, knowing she will be where I can keep an eye on her.

Chapter 12: What Did I Agree To?

Mazzy

After throwing my phone down on the couch, I plop myself onto it.

Harper and Clay went out for dinner, and Serafina is in her giant ass

bathtub in her hotel suite taking a bubble bath. I am alone in the room

and now it makes sense why Clay was in such a rush to get them out of

the room for their dinner date. He must have unblocked Loen when I

was in the bathroom.

Note to self, kick his ass and ask him how the hell he got into my phone without my passcode. My heart raced the moment the text came in saying he saw one of my night terrors. I can only assume that he didn't see the stars glowing though. If he did, he would have told Archer or worse the council. I doubt he would keep a secret like that for me.

Shit, shit, shit. What did you agree to?

I have been trying to avoid being near him, but I stupidly agreed to stay in his spare room. I shouldn't have said yes, but he had a good point. I haven't slept more than twenty minutes at a time in the last five days since being in the hotel room with Harper and Clay. I set alarms in my phone and hold it in my hand, so the vibration wakes me up to try to avoid having night terrors. At least if I stay in the spare bedroom, I'll be in my own room behind a closed and locked door. Lowers the risk of someone seeing my markings if I lose control during a night terror.

I hate admitting I have shit to heal from mentally, but I do. My childhood was rocky, and while I had someone loving who raised me, she lost everything, including her life, to keep me safe. I can't even face my sister anymore. She isn't my biological sister, but we were raised by the same wonderful women. I love both of them so much and miss them dearly. My sister and I were fifteen when our mother died. Even though my sister wouldn't say it out loud, I know deep down, she blames me for our mother's death.

It wasn't your fault.

It is my fault, all my fault. No matter how many times my sister tells me she doesn't blame me I know it's why we grew apart. When she turned eighteen, she moved away to do something important. I don't blame her for being mad at me, but I miss her. If she was here, she would be pushing me to be with my mate until we accepted each other—more like I accepted him. I'm sure Loen is accepting of me.

Yeah, for now.

Fuck you, brain. Can I please have two seconds without comments from the peanut gallery? No, I didn't think so. Sighing, I lay on the couch thinking. I don't think Loen will accept me when he realizes I'm a Nova. He will turn me in to protect himself and his pack.

If he did see the markings and tries to hide or protect me, he would be putting his life and his pack in way more danger.

I'm not worth that risk.

It's just the stupid mate bond. Without it, I doubt we would be interested in each other. Yeah, he is absolutely attractive as fuck, but if the rumors about him are true, who knows how long he would actually stick around. The girls he's into are tall skinny models, like Serafina, not short girls with a little bit of extra cushioning. I mean, yeah, my chest would get his attention. But my big hips and thicker thighs? Probably not.

You could lose weight…

Fuck that. It's just the stupid mate bond making him attracted to me. It makes falling for your mate quicker. It's a lust-to-love kind of thing. I won't lie though. When I catch him staring at me, it makes my heart skip a beat. His gaze is always soft when he looks at me. I don't think he knows I have caught him staring, but I have.

Well, until he started switching to night shift after the nightclub incident. I kind of miss having him around when it's sparring time. I know when I fight, he thinks it's hot. He gets all antsy and tense. I swear sometimes I heard his heart rate pick up. I know he is struggling to hold back his wolf when he starts to shift his stance, so his hands are covering a certain part of himself. I have refused to spar with him, but now he isn't around for me to spar with even if I wanted.

You want to.

Fuck off, will you? This is hard enough without my brain fighting me every step of the way. It's not love. It's a fate bond, and fate has a twisted sense of humor. She's getting her rocks off watching my life crash and burn. I'll bet money on it.

I already put more magic into the bond-blocking spell, but I don't have enough energy or magic to block it entirely. Hell, I don't know why but I have been feeling weaker than normal. I figure it's a lack of sleep issue or stress. Magic is attached to the user's emotions and physical well-being, so if someone is feeling stressed or sick, their connection to their magic can be a little wonky.

I guess it's time to start packing up. I stand from the couch and grab my backpack. I don't have a lot of things in it, just a few changes of clothes. I'm hoping Loen will be okay with running me to my apartment to get a few things. I'll have to clear it by Archer first, but as long as the cop who is supposed to be keeping an eye on the place is there, I don't see why it would be an issue.

I pack up my backpack with my stuff, grab my helmet, and head out the door. I'm leaving earlier than I want to, but it leaves me with a little bit longer workout. Two hours. I have two hours until Loen is due in. That's two hours to stop the panic in my chest.

Chapter 13: Crash

Mazzy

Leaning against Loen's desk, I'm patiently—okay not so patiently—

waiting for Loen to get here. He was due about fifteen minutes ago,

and it doesn't look good that he's late. My gut is in knots. Something

feels off, and that makes me think something is wrong. I reach into my

back pocket and pull out my phone, unlocking it. I'm hoping maybe I

missed a text from him saying he's running late but nothing. I bite the inside of my cheek, contemplating whether I should message him or wait longer.

It's far too quiet for me here in the offices, so I head outside. Sitting on the steps of the station, I finally decide to message him.

Me:
Did you crash?
I knew you sucked at riding that bike.

Loen:

....

What kind of response is that? I go to text back, but another message from him comes through. This time it's a video message. Why would he send me a video message? Opening the message, I watch the video.

Oh shit.

I nearly drop my phone when I stand and rush up the steps to Archer's office where I left my helmet. The call must have just come through the station because the once too-quiet station is now busy as officers start to rush around heading out the door. I put my phone in my back pocket, grab my helmet off his desk, and rush back out the door to my bike. I left my bags by his desk, but they will be fine there. I rush to my bike and start it up, throwing my helmet on. I hear a bunch of sirens drawing closer.

The loud sirens wail loudly as an ambulance speeds by the station followed by a cop cars. I follow a few of the squad cars out of the parking lot all heading in that same direction. Eventually catching up to the ambulance, we follow close behind.

As the ambulance starts to slow down, I back off the and find a place to park my bike. Another ambulance, a few police cars, and two fire trucks show up as I park on the opposite side of the road to keep my bike out of the way. There's a black sports bike with blue decals on its side and a black helmet on the ground next to it. I can't tell from here if the bike is damaged at all, but I know that's Loen's bike. My stomach twists as I cross the street to the ambulances and officers at the scene.

"Here to help," I say to the female officer, Fran. She's a sweet but tough lady. She is taking control of the scene while her partner, Clif, is on his radio relaying information. I toss him a quick head nod, and he nods back.

"Mazelynn, the EMTs are getting their stuff, then heading down to the crash," she says and points down the small embankment.

My heart is in my throat, and my anxiety is at it an all-time high. That's normal for a scene like this, but knowing Loen was down there makes me feel like I'm going to throw up. I know he is alive. He messaged me, but I can't help the feeling in my gut that this event is going to change things.

"Fran, I'm headed down now to get more eyes on the conditions of the people inside. Sent the EMTs and any extra hands down as soon as possible," I say as I start running down the embankment. As I pass the EMTs, they nod at me. I know they will be just a few feet behind me. I have to prepare myself for what I might see there.

Once I'm closer to the crash, I start to see how bad the accident is. All I can smell is blood and freshly dug-up dirt. Taking a deep breath, I reach the crash at the bottom of the embankment. My breath hitches as I look at the reck. The shredded yellow metal of the bus sends a chill down my spine.

A school bus.

The bus is upside down, pinned between a hill and a stone wall. Just looking at the bus, I can tell the bus rolled a few times. It left a trail of metal and other debris on its descent down the steep hill. Close by, there are a handful of backpacks that were thrown as the bus rolled and a ripped-up sign. Even with the sign torn from the bus as it flipped, I could make it out: *Whitlock School District.* The rest of the sign is missing.

Gods, a bus full of kids.

"Loen," I yell, trying to find a safe way to crawl into this bus. The bus is pinned and crushed like a hotdog in a hot dog bun. The bus is the hot dog, and the embankment is on one side and a solid stone wall on the other are the bun. The side windows are not an option. I don't think I can fit through any of them. I came down in front of the bus. If I climb over it might be able to get to the back where the emergency door is if it isn't jammed shut.

"May, be careful but get your ass in here," Loen yells from the inside of the bus.

"Hey, watch your mouth," I say. He gets a pass for calling me May for the moment. Honestly, hearing him say it calmed my racing heart a little. Fuck this stupid mate bond is getting harder to ignore.

Focus, Mazzy.

I guess there's only one option. Through the busted-out windshield, it is. The twisted metal of the front end of the bus is going to make it hard to get in or out. I try to carefully climb through it while avoiding getting cut. Once on the bus, I stand up and take a look around. I'm both relieved and heartbroken at the same time. It's older kids. The first few I see are wide-eyed and blankly staring at me. They have blood and cuts, but the fact that they are awake is a good sign. The blank look tells me they are scared and in shock. Going over to check on the kids, I have yet to put eyes on Loen from the video he sent. He's bleeding too and that has my heart racing.

He's a wolf, you idiot. He heals. He's up and moving around. He's fine.

Finally my eyes land on Loen, he's at the back of the bus helping a young male. My instinct is telling me to go to him, but I know that's only the mate bond talking. I need to focus on helping the kids on this bus. Loen is fine.

"Head count," I yell. Needing confirmation on how many kids we are talking about here.

"Twelve," he says. His focus is right where it should be—on the kids.

"We need more hands," I say.

Assessing the conditions of a handful of kids on the bus as I look around. Even the ones with minor injuries that I can see aren't going to be able to climb out on their own. The bus landed just right or just wrong depending on how you think about it. Getting the kids out of here is going to take a team effort. Thank gods, the wall was there. If it wasn't this bus would have continued down the hill another twenty feet into the river.

This is going to be a long night.

Climbing back to the busted-out windshield, I get visual of the EMTs as they rush down the hill with their gear. We still me need more, so I yell to the EMTs that are nearly here.

"We need way more than just you two. Twelve kids total. No idea where the driver is," I shout, peering out the best I can. They start to pass their bags through the opening to me, and I set them down on the bus.

"The back emergency exit is mangled. We need to cut a hole to get these kids out," Loen shouts from the back of the bus. One EMT stops trying to climb into the bus to radio Fran, telling her we need more help and the Jaws of Life to try to get an opening big enough to safely get the kids out of there.

"Be careful on your way through. Glass and metal are everywhere, and it's a tight fit," I say as I climb back onto the bus with them behind me.

We got this.

Chapter 14: One Rule

Mazzy

That crash was an absolute nightmare. The position of the bus made it so difficult to get the kids out that the firefighters had to use the Jaws of Life to cut exit points. Those of us on the bus did everything we could to help and calm the kids inside the bus while they cut. A few of the other officers searched around and eventually found the bus driver alive. He got lucky.

"Thank you all for joining me this late. It has been a rough evening." Chief Archer's normally loud voice is hushed and scratchy.

"Any word on the kids?" Cliff asks.

"Are they okay?" Fran blurts out.

"What about the driver?" Jordan asks. The chief slams his hands down on the black tabletop, making the table rattle.

"If you all would shut up, we will go over all of that," he snaps, clearly over the day and ready to go home. "As you know, we have several children in the hospital getting treatment for a variety of injuries from the crash. As of a few moments ago, those at the hospital seems to be in a stable condition."

You can see it in his eyes that this situation has upset him. It upset all of us. Even with the magic of our fae officers and EMTS, we couldn't change what happened. We did everything we could.

"Chief, the driver?" Loen asks.

Sitting at the large table across from me, I have been trying hard not to stare at him while we waited for the chief to come into the briefing room. He refused to be seen by medical, insisting the cut on his head was the only injury and that it was healed thanks to his enhanced healing abilities. He is a liar. The way he walks with a limp and the slight mate bond tell me his leg is injured. But the stubborn thick-skulled alpha is too proud to get help I guess.

"The driver is stable as well. He has minimal injuries. He got lucky," Chief says, pausing for a moment then sighs. "This crash was originally thought to be an accident, but it is now under investigation, as a suspected DUI."

Gasps sound through the large room from everyone. The pained, saddened look that Chief Archer has on his face makes more sense now. We were all under the impression the driver fell asleep, or the bus blew a tire, and he overcorrected but not that he was drunk. I didn't smell any alcohol at the scene, and I was near the driver a few times after he was found.

"Sir, the bus driver was drunk?" I ask.

"Yes," chief says sadness in his tone.

"Fucking hell, are you serious? That fucker drove a bus of twelve teenagers drunk?" Jordan snaps.

Jordan is a new father. He welcomed twin girls a few weeks ago. You can tell that this information has triggered him and everyone else. The room is now full of people chatting among themselves. A lot of swearing but most are venting angrily over the information we just got. My heart feels so much pain for the children and their families. These poor kids were just trying to have a fun night celebrating a win during a camp tournament.

"How is that fair? How is it a drunk gets ejected from a flipping bus and walks away with a few broken bones and bruises?" Cliff asks. His voice booms over the background chatter.

"Okay, everyone. Please, I know that this is upsetting news, but those are the facts at the moment. We will be investigating this driver and doing everything we can to help the children and families affected," Chief says loudly. His deep voice cracks a little when he mentions the children.

"Three children lost their lives tonight, and he got to just walk away," I say then something hits me. If we just got the information, the families might not even know yet. "Chief, do those families know about the possible DUI?" I ask. Loen's eyes dart quickly to mine then back to the chief.

"Not yet. I am going to give them the night and visit with each family to discuss the investigation," Chief explains.

Nodding, we all agree with the chief. The chief continues his debriefing after a few moments of silence.

***

It's the middle of the night, and we just got released from that debriefing. I'm covered in dirt, sweat, and dried blood, definitely in need of another shower. I can't stop thinking about those kids—the three that should be here but are no longer alive. Something felt weird to me. I knew the one Loen was caring for died before he did. I felt it. I had to stop him from continuing CPR. He was so determined to save him, but at that point, he didn't want to see that the kids was gone. The same with the other two kids. It was like I felt their souls leave. I had to do everything I could to keep myself from crying or losing control of my magic.

That's the first time that has ever happened to me. I have watched people die before, held their hands, but I've never felt anything like what I did tonight. Instead of heading directly to the showers, I decide to go outside for some air first. I can't wrap my head around everything without some air.

As I walk out the doors, I look up. The moon is out, and she is stunning. The moon always brings me a sense of peace and strength when I'm feeling overwhelmed or weak. I know that sounds silly, but it's true. It's just as quiet out here as it is inside. The entire station is creepy with how dead silent it is. The only sounds are those of fingers on keyboards, typing away. I head down the steps and sit on the bottom one with my knees to my chest. I rest my arms on my knees and just collapse into myself.

It's okay to cry, Mazzy.

I bring my eyes to the sky again, getting a sense of peace for a few seconds before I get a sense of dread and pain. Something isn't right. The moon has never made me feel this way before. The stars and the night sky are usually my happy place, but right now, my gut is saying something is wrong. Focusing back on the moon, I take a deep breath.

"Hello, Moon," I whisper before I crash my head back into my hands.

I don't know how long I it there before I hear steps from behind me. Not picking my head up from my hands, I just sit still.

"Did you just say hello to the moon?" a voice from behind me asks.

I pick up my head and turn my upper body to see who it is. The voice should have sounded familiar, but it was scratchier than normal. He is exhausted and still has a full night shift ahead of him.

"Loen, not now. I just needed some air," I say and turn back away from him. Instead of saying something sarcastic or teasing, he doesn't say a word. He just walks down the steps and sits next to me.

Go away, Loen. Please.

"It's okay. I talk to the moon, too. The moon goddess is in there waiting to listen to us," he says.

Moon goddess, huh?

I never pictured him believing the "myths" of the moon goddess or the Novas. I wonder why he thinks she is up there, waiting to listen to us?

"Shut up," I say with a slight laugh. I'm surprised that my eyes aren't drawn to the moon when I glance back up to the sky. I'm drawn to an oddly dark part of the sky. I tilt my head, trying to focus on it more.

"Huh," I say. Dang it. I didn't mean to say that out loud.

"What's up?" Loen asks and waits for a response.

"What? Oh, umm, nothing," I say, pausing so I can think of what lie to tell him. "I just got lost in thought that's all." Leaning forward, he just sits next to me like he wants to say something but isn't sure how to say it. "Are you okay?" I ask. He gives me a confused expression but then smirks a little.

"Aww, you were worried about me," he says, almost cocky sounding with a fake grin plastered to his tired but handsome face.

"Would you believe me if I said no?" I joke.

"Not one bit." He laughs. This is the first time we have had a back-and-forth conversation where neither of us was being an ass hat to the other. Go figure, we can only have a civil interaction after a tragedy.

"Fine," I say rolling my eyes at him. "I was, so sue me."

"Mazzy," Loen says, but the moment I turn to him, he stops talking. This back-and-forth is surprisingly nice. In this moment, I start to see why he is meant for me. I'm about to hate myself, even more then I already do.

"Loen, the rule I mentioned. If I stay at your place, I need one thing," I say, making sure to I keep eye contact with him.

Man, those eyes are calling to me. Fuck my life, I don't want to do this, but I have to.

"Name it," he says without hesitation. The way he says that sounds like he would give me the moon or stars on a silver plate if I asked—even if it would burn him.

I'm really, really going to hate myself.

"I need you to…" I pause and take a breath. "I need you to keep your distance from me. Whatever you think you feel, I don't. I don't want you to get your hopes up. I'm not and will never be your mate," I say.

The moment I finish the sentence, pain shoots through me. The look on his face is one of pain and a little bit of anger. The sadness from the night gone replaced with sadness I caused him.

"I'm sorry," I whisper.

So, so sorry.

My chest feels like it's on fire and being stabbed repeatedly by a sharp silver blade. My heart feels as if it's on the verge of stopping. Instead of blocking the bond more with magic, I took it down. I deserve to feel the pain and take some of his pain away. Another spell I used on him that he won't ever know about. I was not able to remove all of his pain, or he would have known something was up, but I lessened the blow.

I rejected the bond that ties us together, and now I have to pretend I feel nothing, not an ounce of searing pain and heartbreak. I have to be cold like it didn't matter one bit when it actually feels like I am killing a part of my soul.

"I can do that," he says flatly as he stands and doesn't even turn to my direction. I gasp and turn away from him as he turns the other way and makes his way back up the steps into the station. I didn't think he would agree like that. I thought he would fight me on it, but he didn't.

"I'm sorry," I whisper again, knowing by this point he doesn't hear me.

Don't let him go.

I have to. I had to break the bond. The feelings I have now will fade, hopefully. The bond is the only reason they are there anyway. It was only the mate bond that pushed us to feel anything for each other. The god or goddess of fate made the wrong match. He will get another chance.

I take one last gaze at the moon and head back inside. It's time for a shower, and then I'm crashing on the sparring mats until Loen is done with his shift. Let's hope this doesn't make him change his mind about letting me stay in the spare room. I'll understand if it does though.

You need him.

Chapter 15: Yup, Bad Idea

Mazzy

Buzz, buzz, buzz.

My phone buzzing in my hand wakes me up for the millionth time. I didn't trust myself to sleep without it just in case I had a night terror. Every twenty minutes, I woke up, scanned the room, and went back to sleep. Sitting up, I flip it over and press the stop button.

"Eight a.m. Time to get up," I mumble.

Loen's shift ends at eight, so I need to find him to talk about the room situation. If he even wants to let me use it still. As I stand and look around the gym, I am shocked to see Loen sitting against the mirror next to the punching bags. His head is hung low, and his breathing is slow and steady. Is he sleeping? That looks uncomfortable. Walking over quietly, I squat down next to him and reach for his arm. I tap on Loen's forearm and wait for him to move, but he doesn't.

"Loen," I say in a hushed tone slightly above a whisper. I don't want to startle him too much. Not the best idea to startle a full-grown alpha shifter unless you want broken bones or death. Still nothing, so I give him a hard tap on the arm, not even a twitch.

He sleeps like a rock, a big dumb handsome rock.

Sitting slightly to the left of Loen are soft punching blocks, ones typically used in martial arts for practicing kicks. A smirk dances across my face as a mischievous idea crosses my mind. This is payback for the kiss in the alley way and the times he called me May without permission.

Grabbing one of the soft punching blocks, I hold it firmly in my right hand. This won't hurt him. It is slightly harder than a memory foam pillow. This is a bad idea, but hey, it might be funny. I need a laugh right now anyway. I take a step back just far enough so I can get a decent swing.

"LOEN, HEADS UP," I yell and throw the block toward his head. It hits his face then bounces off, falling to the ground next to him. He didn't even move. Is he dead? Stepping closer to him, I go to touch his arm. There's a low chuckle, followed by a strong hand on my right thigh, and then a thud as I hit the mat. Loen is still chuckling on top of me, pinning me to the sparing mat.

"What the fuck?" I shout, trying to wiggle from his hold.

His body is straddling mine. I have just enough room to wiggle a little but not enough to flip him off me. I do have one option. I could try to knee him in the balls. I decide against that for the moment. With him so close to me, I am slightly surprised and relieved that I don't feel anything remotely close to a mate pull to him.

Thank gods.

"You know, hitting someone with a foam block isn't a nice way to wake someone up, Princess," he says in a low tone. The way he says "princess" has me feeling things in places I shouldn't be feeling things, especially with the broken bond.

What the fuck, lady parts? Get with the program here. We aren't mates anymore.

"Get off me, Loen," I say as he starts laughing at me again. "If you don't move, you'll be icing your junk for a week," I say with a stern tone. The look on his face looks more like amusement than fear I'll knee him in the balls.

"Why are you thinking about my dick, Princess?" Loen teases me with a hot as fuck smirk on his face as my eyes go wide. My heart skips a beat.

What the actual fuck?

"I warned you," I say harshly. The moment my knee conjects between his legs, he lets out a pained groan as he rolls off me and grabs himself.

"Fuck, fuck, fuck," he says nearly rolling around on the floor holding himself. I jump up and turn to him rolling my eyes.

"I warned you, didn't it?" I say, making sure to coat it as much sass as I can. "If you want to act like a brat, I'll act like one too."

"Fucking hell, Mazzy. I was about to let you up," he says still curled on the floor.

Yeah, sure you were.

"Oh, come on! It wasn't that good of a hit," I say. This is already more bearable than the last twenty-two days. A silver lining, I guess.

"Did you just get off shift?" I ask. Ignoring him still laying on the floor, I walk over to my duffle on the mat next to where I slept.

"Nope," he says slowly starting to stand up. "Been off shift for about an hour. I wanted to let you sleep."

"You have been waiting there for an hour watching me sleep? That's not the list bit creepy," I say, knowing damn well I was up every twenty minutes looking around, and he wasn't there my last check.

"No, I have only been in here for like twenty minutes, give or take. The last time your phone alarm went off and you dozed back off," he says standing and retrieving his own stuff from near the mirror. "The chief wanted to talk about the bounty hunter situation. I guess he's not too thrilled about paying for the hotel accommodations."

"Serafina doesn't have cheap taste. That's for sure," I say as we start to walk out of the gym. "Speaking of accommodations, what are we doing about me staying in your spare room? Does the offer still stand, or did I royally fuck that up?" I ask and wait for his response.

"Offer still stands, Mazzy. Just no more kneeing me in the balls, okay?" he grumbles adjusting himself then shoving me with his broad shoulders. "Oh, also we have our own rule. No walking around the apartment in just a t-shirt," he says, giving me a wink then walking ahead of me.

"I wouldn't do that. I have more modesty then that," I say with a gasp as I try to catch up to his long strides.

"Just saying we like to keep the apartment hot, so don't be surprised if we are walking around in our boxers," he deadpans, and I freeze in place.

He can't be serious. While the twins look similar to Loen in build, they have different eyes and faces. The twin are still attractive but are more boy band model cute. All three are built like gods though. Loen in just boxers walking around with all those fabulous muscle on display.

Hell yes, please.

Just because I broke the bond doesn't mean I'm too good to admit he is attractive, right? I mean a rock would find him attractive, so fuck it. Not like there's anything more to it now. No emotions attached to him. No fated mate bond pulling us together. I can look without worry that I have to keep a bond from forming.

Right?

"The twins have the car. They are on their way in for their shift. We'll throw your bags in the car and drive it to my place. We can return the car later and get our bikes. Sound good to you, Princess?" he says and that pulls me from my thoughts.

"Stop calling me that," I snap at him. It's not that I hate it. It's that I think I like it, and he needs to stop.

"Calling you what?" he asks, pretending he doesn't know. That smirk on his face is hot as hell and mischievous at the same time. He has a dimple on the right cheek when he smirks.

Cute.

"Nothing," I say.

"If you say so, Princess," he says, making sure to say "princess" with a deep husky voice.

This was a bad idea!

Chapter 16: Sassy and I Like It

Loen

She wanted to get a few things that she couldn't grab before they got kicked out of the apartment by the chief. She insisted on going inside alone. I don't like that idea just in case the bounty hunters are still there, but with officers watching the place it was probably safe enough. So, I here I sit, waiting in the car.

Starting to get impatient, I start to leave the car when I notice her walking back with a huge duffle bag and another large backpack.

How much stuff does one girl need?

"Do you need a hand?" I ask out the car window.

"Nope," she says with a pop of the *P* at the end. *Brat.*

"Fine, have it your way," I say, leaning back and waiting for her to get in the car. Out of the corner of my eye, I can tell she's being extra careful with the extra-large duffle bag.

"So, what's in the giant bag? A body? Should I worried about you murdering me in my sleep?" I ask, making sure to throw a joke in there. The last few weeks have been far too miserable to carry on this alpha hole attitude.

"Ha, ha, very funny," she mocks back. "It's not a body and as for the other part. Only time will tell. Let's get going," she says as she slams the back door before jumping into the seat beside me.

I felt the bond break last night, and I had to walk away from her. I knew by morning the pain and pull to her would be less noticeable or gone altogether. I wasn't expecting her to say she wanted me to keep my distance from her. She didn't reject me in the typical way by saying *"I reject you as my mate,"* but her *"I'm not and will never be your mate."* That did the trick. That pain sucked ass, and I had to try hard not to show her it hurt me.

She didn't even flinch though. Not even a slight wince of pain. I tried to search her eyes to see if she felt something when it broke, but my guess is she used her magic to dull her pain. I felt like I got kicked in the chest by a horse for a few hours. It wasn't as bad as others have described it though.

"Loen," she says. I turn to look at her she has an inpatient look on her face like she has been waiting ages for me to start driving. I must have zoned out for a minute.

"Ready?" I ask pretending I wasn't just lost in my own thoughts.

"You okay?" she asks, staring at me with those amazing eyes of hers. "You can change your mind. I can go back to sleeping in the gym or bunks at the station. Hell, I'll sleep on the floor in the lobby if I have to."

I wasn't expecting her to ask that. I was expecting a sassy "yup" or something along those lines. I can't help but stare at her. She sounds like she wants me to change my mind.

"Any day now, old man," she teases. Apparently I was taking too long to answer.

"Hey, I'm only two years older than you," I say shaking my head. "I'm not changing my mind. You need somewhere to stay where you feel safe."

"Yup, old," she says and then gets out her phone and starts messing around with it. Pushing on the gas, the engine revs but the car stays still. She lets out a soft giggle before opening that sassy mouth of hers.

"Still in park." She laughs.

Her laugh. Fuck, that sounds heavenly.

I don't care how embarrassing that was. Her laugh is amazing. Why has it taken me twenty-two days to finally hear this girl laugh? Shifting into drive, we start the journey to my apartment.

"Thank you," she whispers.

***

Every now and then, she'll laugh at whatever she's gawking at on her phone, but that's it. She's hiding more than just her abilities from everyone. Does she truly feel she can be herself or show the world who she is? It honestly angers me that she feels she has to be a different person. I want to know the girl she's hiding from everyone. The girl I saw talking to the moon.

"What is your issue?" she asks. I realize I have been looking at her a lot. "Do I have something on my face or are you trying to kill us by keeping your eye on me instead of the road?" she asks with a stunning smile. Her smile is beautiful, genuine. She seems far more relaxed around me now. Maybe the bond breaking is a good thing. Maybe we aren't meant to be mates but friends.

Before I get a chance to say anything, my phone starts to ring through my car's speakers. I love the hands-free technology. Glancing briefly at the dash screen, a name I would rather not see shows on the screen. Fuck, it's Eliza, one of my ex-girlfriends. Pressing the accept button on the steering wheel, I give Mazzy a quiet motion with my hands.

"Hey, E, you're on speakerphone. I have…a coworker in the car with me. What's up?" I ask, peaking at Mazelynn to see if she reacted in any way.

Nope, nothing.

"Hey there, Loen and…Coworker" she says with her fake giggle. I want to cringe. Her laugh is like nails on a chalkboard. "Hey Loen, I heard from a little birdy you are in Chief Whitlock's department for a little while."

"You heard correctly," I say. Mazzy has not even looked up from her phone.

"What are you up to this weekend? I'll be in the area," Eliza says. Out of the corner of my eye, Mazzy's eyes go slightly wide for a second, and she clenches her jaw.

Oh, that got her attention.

"This weekend, I think I'm on duty. Hold on," I say, pushing the mute button. "Is there a problem, Princess?" I ask in a slightly sarcastic, cocky tone.

"No, no problem, but if you blow off combat training for a booty call, Chief Whitlock will hang you by your dick from the rafters of the gym," she says and then presses the button on the screen to unmute the call before I even have a chance to respond.

What was that jealousy?

"E, I have work this weekend. What about next weekend?" I ask.

"Darn, come on, Lo. I really want to see you, and I can't wait until next weekend. I don't want to miss spending time with you." Her voice is high pitched and whiny. As I go to open my mouth to respond, I hear Mazzy clear her throat.

"He will be off this weekend," Mazzy says loudly and smirks at me with a devilish look in her blue turquoise eyes. That look tells me I should fear the next words out of her mouth. I don't have the response she wanted though because that look was sexy.

"Who's that?" Eliza snaps.

"Hi yeah, I'm the coworker. Nice to meet you. E, is it?" she says with a snarky tone, pausing for dramatic effect. "He will be free this weekend. I'll make sure of it. Just for you darlin'." The look she has on her face is one I'm starting to be concerned about. Who knew the Ice Queen has a mischievous side? She is suddenly so funny and extra sassy. I like it.

"Aww, bless your heart," Eliza says, and the moment the words leave her mouth, I want to stop the car and watch the show. Eliza is from the South where "bless your heart" isn't meant as a good thing, and I can tell this wasn't. Eliza is jealous, and something tells me Mazzy knows that and is about to set Eliza on fire.

"No problem, girly pop," Mazzy says, and I see the corner of her mouth curl up a little before she opens her mouth to speak again. "You obviously need to get fucked, and that should be his top priority. Plus, sometimes the only way to shut up a needy kitty is to shove something into its mouth," she says without even a hint of a smile on her face. She just drops it like it's nothing.

I am, however, trying very, very, VERY hard not to burst out laughing. That was definitely not something I expected to come out of her. I'm having to literally bite my tongue, so I don't laugh. A loud high-pitched gasp echoes through the car speakers.

"Well, I never. That's just rude. Loen, are you going to let her talk to me like that?" Eliza whines again.

"E, she's just teasing," I manage to say without laughing. I toss a cool it glance to Mazzy who just winks at me.

Oh fuck.

"Yeah, I'm just teasing, E. Don't get your panties in a twist," Mazzy snaps back. This girl is a sassy one, and I'm fucking here for it. I wish I would have seen this side of her before now. Everyone should see this side of her.

"Yeah, sure you are. Is she your current fu—" Eliza starts.

"Finish that sentence, Eliza, and I promise you won't like the outcome," I interrupt her in a deep alpha tone that causes Eliza to shut up instantly.

Eliza is from my pack, she knows that tone means to back the fuck off. It was Mazzy's reaction that caught my attention. Even out of the corner of my eye I noticed it. Her eyes widened as she tries to resist the urge to bow her head and move away from me. I know now that Mazzy is a Nova, the stars on her skin gave that away, but not once have I sensed a wolf in her not even when her star markings were glowing bright during her night terror.

I thought about it a lot last night. The only way she wouldn't have felt the pain from the mate bond breaking was if she didn't have one. However, what I saw just now, was a hint of a wolf reacting to an alpha.

She has a wolf?

"Sorry, Alpha. I didn't mean anything by it." Eliza tries to backpedal. Noticing that Eliza gets a reaction out of Mazzy, I think I want to test something. This might be a bad idca but fuck it.

"Well, E, it looks like I'm free this weekend after all," I say. "What do you have in mind?"

"Goodie, there's a new bar close to the station that does the singing thing I hate, but I heard they have decently priced drinks and a live singer on Saturdays," Eliza says with excitement. Mazelynn's eyes go even bigger.

Interesting.

"That sounds amazing. Let's plan for seven on Saturday?" I say with fake excitement.

"You mean tomorrow, you goofball. It's Friday."

"I worked a few night shifts this week, so excuse me if I'm thrown off a day or so," I say.

Mazzy starts fiddling with her fingers in her lap. I hadn't noticed she put her phone down. Rolling up to a stop light, I turn to Mazzy and tilt my head. I know she sees me looking at her because it takes her only a second to flip me off with a sassy but somewhat fake smile.

Oh, this fucking girl is a hidden wildcard. Hell, yes!

"It's okay, Loen. I'll meet you at the bar tomorrow at seven. I can't wait to see you. I have missed you *so* much," Eliza says in her *hoping to get laid* tone.

She only ever calls me when she is in between boyfriends and wants to fuck. Fate hasn't given her a mate yet, and if she keeps up her pattern, she probably won't accept one anyway. She likes sex too much. I usually ghost her or tell her I'm busy, but something about her riling Mazzy up has me agreeing to go out with her. Maybe this is me wanting to get back at Mazzy for breaking the bond a little, or maybe I'm hoping this will make her jealous. Before I get a chance to say anything, Mazzy hits the end button on the screen with her palm as she slams her hand on the screen.

"Oops, sorry, Lo. There was a bug on the screen," she says. "Oh, and the light is green."

Only after she says that do the sounds of honking car horns reach my ears. Waving my hand high enough to apologize to the car behind me, I accelerate. Why on earth does she hide this girl from others? Fuck, she's funny and sassy. She shows the world this cold-hearted Ice Queen, but she's not that at all. My phone rings again, but before I can answer, Mazzy does.

Shit.

"Sorry, Darlin', I lost my balance trying to get back in my seat and accidentally hung up on you, my bad," Mazzy says with major fucking sass.

"What the fuck, Loen?"

"Chill, girl. There was a bug on the screen. I tried to squash it. I guess I missed 'cause it called…I mean…came back." Mazzy smirks and then picks her phone up again. Giving me a waving motion, she turns her body somewhat away. I guess that means she's done fucking with Eliza.

Too bad. That was entertaining.

"Eliza, my coworker here is being extra today. I'll have to let you go so I can deal with her. Since I'm her boss, I guess that means I'll have to dish out some kind of punishment. I'll see you tomorrow," I tell Eliza, but it isn't her response I'm waiting for. It's Mazzy's. She just drops her phone and looks at me.

"Okay, if you must, but if you plan to fu—"

"Bye, E," I say and hang up the phone.

"She sounds like a peach," Mazelynn grumbles.

"She's a lovely woman and pretty. She was the first girl I slept with, so she has a special place in my heart," I say.

I mean, it's not all a lie. Eliza is a pretty woman, but she doesn't hold a candle to Mazzy. Even though she was the first woman

I slept with, that girl takes up zero space in my heart—not even a centimeter.

A few more turns before the apartment, I glance over at Mazzy again. She tucks her knees up to her chest, turns her face away from me, and rests her head on her knees. A complete shutdown to what she just was. How the hell did she just go from sassy as fuck to trying to become invisible that quickly? I wanted to see a reaction but not that kind of reaction.

What did I say?

"Mazzy, I didn't mean to upset you," I say as we pull into the apartment building parking lot. She says nothing, just keeps looking out the window and hugging her knees to her chest. Her phone pings a few times, but she doesn't reach for it. Once parked, I reach for it on the floor in front of her and try to hand it to her.

"Hey, I was playing around, Sorry if I took it too far."

She releases her knees, and without a word or even a glance in my direction, she grabs the phone from my hand and opens the car door, stepping out. I get out of the car and head around to her side. She has already started getting the bags out of the car. Rushing over, I grab the large black duffle bag. Surprised by the weight, I nearly dropped it.

"The fuck is in here. I'm starting to think it really is a dead body?" I joke, trying to break the awkward silence.

"Don't drop that," she says, grabbing the other stuff and closing the back door of the car.

"Listen, if you want to come with us—" I say, but this time, she interrupts me.

"I'm going to stop you right there," she snaps glaring at me. "I'm not being your third wheel. I'm busy Saturday. That's why I needed the giant bag."

"Okay, okay, no need to get snappy. Let's get your stuff to my apartment and get you settled for a bit before swapping with my brothers for the bikes," I say as I point her in the direction of the front doors.

"You didn't say anything wrong. I just remembered something. That's all," she says quietly.

I don't believe that for one moment.

Chapter 17: Who Is He?

Loen

Mazzy left about an hour ago to go do whatever she had planned for

tonight. I'm guessing something that has to do with beating someone

up with heavy equipment. That duffle bag was not light, but even

though she said she needed it, she only took a smaller one with her

when she left. Still, I'm curious what she's up to. I have been trying to

pick out something to wear to this bar, and I decide to just keep it casual—a black V-neck t-shirt, black jeans with a black belt, and my

leather jacket. As I'm heading for the island, my phone goes off with a

text. I wasn't expecting the text to be from Mazzy.

Mazzy:

I hate asking this, but I forgot something in my duffle bag and don't have time to come back and get it.

Me:

What is it?

I'll grab it for you and drop it off at the way to the bar I'm heading out now.

Mazzy:

in the big black duffle, you said was too heavy for me to carry, there is a keyboard.

If you look under the keyboard there should be a power strip with like a billion outlets on it.

I need that.

In the room we set her up in last night, it only takes me a few

seconds to find the big black duffle bag. On the floor near the closet,

it's unzipped and has a corner folded up. The corner of an electric

piano is peeking out from the folded-up top. I dig through the bag and

find the power strip she is searching for. I close the duffle up and zip it

for her. It's a nice keyboard. I don't want it ruined.

Me:

Got the cord thingy you need, where am I bringing it?

Mazzy:

The bar

Me:

What bar, the same bar as my date?

That bar?

Mazzy:

Yup that one

Now get here I need that cord.

Me:

You know you are sexy when you're bossy.

Oh, gods I did not just send that text.

Without even thinking, I just typed and hit send. I can see her typing bubble which means she is typing, and I'm now wondering if I should just pretend my brother stole my phone and send that or play stupid.

Still typing... Fuck me.

Mazzy:

oooooo

Your date is here fuck boy!

You better hurry up!!!

Me:

I'm on my way.

As I'm walking out of the apartment and heading to my bike, I get another text notification. Looking at the time on my watch, it's only 6:45. Eliza better not be texting me asking where I am. She showed up early. That's on her. Checking my phone, I'm surprised that it's not Eliza but Mazzy again.

Mazzy:

You should see the dress your date has on.

wow

It's a little black strappy dress barely holding her in

it's a little see through too

Oh shit

Someone has plans for tonight, she has no panties on!

Better hurry!

Well, that's not what I expected. All day today, she avoided talking to me or the twins. She hid in her new room for most of it and only came out to eat when we told her we ordered her something for lunch from a local Chinese joint. She said thank you and that was the most she spoke to me until she texted, needing me to get that cord out of the bag.

Me:

Are you drunk?

Mazelynn:

N

O

P

EE

oops, too many E's

Wow, she's drunk texting. How many shots did she do to get that buzzed that quick? Making sure I have the cord Mazzy needed, I head to the bar. I want to see what Mazzy needs that cord for. Maybe she plays piano there or helps with the live music. That would be cool, but more importantly, I want to make sure she is okay. This is definitely way out of character for her from what I have gathered from Clay and Harper.

Pulling into the bar parking lot on my bike, I notice there are a lot of people here. I know Mazzy definitely isn't for crowds. I learned that quickly. That somewhat explains the drunk texts. I find a spot and head to the door, shocked when I see Mazzy waiting by the door with a somewhat panicked look on her face—her sweet, soft, beautiful, drunk face.

Stop that, Loen. You are here to see Eliza.

"Loen, thanks so much," Mazzy says as she stumbles over her own feet to get to me. Her cheeks are slightly pink, I would have thought it was her make up but she barely has any on—just some dark eyeliner and reddish lipstick. The pink in her cheeks is either because she was blushing or from being drunk.

"Hold up," I say as I catch her before she falls. "How much have you had to drink, May?" I ask her, accidentally using a nickname I know she won't be okay with.

Please don't notice. Please don't notice.

"I got it, Loen. Thanks again." She giggles, catching me off guard. She goes to walk away.

"May, the cord?" I ask. Using the nickname again, I am pushing my luck here. She spins back around with a soft smile on her face.

"Oh, thanks. Also, I lost count," she says, snatches the cord from my hand, and tries to run back inside.

Only as she's running away, I realize it isn't just that booze that tripped her up, but the heels she's wearing—high black stiletto heels. How did I not notice she has on a short black strappy dress? It fits her shockingly well. It hugs all the curves. I had a feeling she was hiding under her tight sports bras and baggy workout clothes.

I tilt my head to the side and watch her as she moves out of sight. Oh fuck. She looks amazing in that dress. I need to get another look. Completely forgetting that I'm there to meet Eliza, I head inside, looking for Mazzy. She's wobbly on those heels, so she can't have gone too far. I scan the room with no sight of her at all. Where the heck did she go that fast? I wasn't that far behind her. Turning to the bar, I feel hands sneak up my ribs to my pecs. I place my hands on top of them and know who it is the moment my hand touches hers.

"Hello, Eliza," I say and turn my head to look over my shoulder at her.

"Hey there handsome," she flirts. Umm, hold up. Mazzy said in her text that my date was here in a black dress. Eliza's dress isn't black. It's burgundy and isn't nearly as skimpy as Mazzy's dress. Did she text me what she was wearing? I shouldn't have thought that. I turn to the bar and adjust myself because the thought of Mazzy not wearing anything under that black dress gives me a raging hard-on. No mate bond needed. I want her.

"Hey, you good?" Eliza asks as she leans into my back.

"I'm fine. Let's find a seat and get some drinks," I say as I adjust and then escort Eliza to a table on the right of the stage.

It's a red high-top table with four seats and a good view of a large stage. I guess it's live singers tonight like an open mic night kind of thing. Makes sense as to why so many people are here now.

I leave Eliza at the table and head to the bar for our drinks. The bartender is great at his job, serving those at the bar, so the lines aren't long. I sit at the table, scanning the crowd with my drink in my hand. I have yet to take a sip of it. We have only been sitting for about fifteen to maybe twenty minutes when the club music stops, and a DJ announces the singer for tonight. I was under the impression it was multiple singers, but it's just one. Let's hope they're good.

"Back by popular demand, I am pleased to welcome back to the stage… the amazing Mazelynn," the announcer says.

Mazelynn.

I almost drop the drink in my hand and start scanning the stage for her. I must not have been subtle about it because Eliza places her hand on mine and gives it a tight squeeze. Turning to her for a second, she looks super annoyed.

"Who are you looking for?" she asks.

"Oh, the singer. I know her," I say, not taking my eyes off the stage.

"Really? Is she the coworker from yesterday?" she asks with a lot of jealousy in her tone.

I choose not to answer her. The music starts playing. It's kind of upbeat but also a little soft. I have heard this song before. It sounds like she's going to sing a cover of a song, but I can't remember the name. I hear a soft, sweet voice before she steps out onto the stage. The moment she does, the crowd is in awe, and so am I.

Her voice is amazing, and she's up there moving around like she hasn't had too much to drink. I can't take my eyes off her. I don't want to take my eyes off her. Something mid-song made her do a double take at the bar, which caught my attention. I look at the bar, but not knowing what to look for, I turn back to watch her.

When the final verse that she sang in such a sweet, perfect pitch, Mazzy stops in the center of the stage. The lights dim a little, and she bows her head down, flicking the mic off. Her shoulder heaves a little, and I swear I see tears streaming down her face. Without looking up, she turns around and leaves the stage rather quickly.

Go to her.

Yep, I'm going after her. Something is off, and I can't just sit here. I start to stand, but Eliza grabs my arm and tugs me back down.

"Hey, where are you going?" she asks. The look on her face is a mix of anger and jealousy.

"Something seems off. I just want to check on her," I say and pull my wrist from her grasp. "I'll be right back."

Standing, I head for the hall I'm hoping leads to the back of the stage. The DJ comes on and announces that there will be a pause in singing because they are having technical difficulties with some of the vocal equipment. That's a cover. Something is up with Mazzy.

I guessed right. This hall leads to the back of the stage. I walk through the door and ask the first person I see where Mazzy is. The stagehand looks confused and a bit defensive.

"She's not here," the stagehand says with a somewhat guarded tone.

"What? She just got off the stage. Where did she go?" I demand.

"Listen, I don't know who you are, but you're the reason she just took off so leave before we call the cops on you," he says in a protective way and is no longer looking like a tiny stagchand.

"My name is Loen. I'm a coworker and not the reason she took off. I'll show you my ID if you want proof of who I am." The man relaxes a little when I show him my ID. He eyes the ID and looks at me, not sure if he should let me through or call security on me. "She knew I was here. Whatever she saw at the bar freaked her out. I need to ask her what's wrong."

"All she said before she left was that she can't be near Tristen. When one of the bouncers went to grab her arm to stop her from leaving, she slapped him hard across the face. He was more shocked than anything. That's not like the Mazelynn. We see here on Saturdays," the stagehand says. "I'm worried about her."

"Then tell me where she went," I demand, and he nods his head.

"She went out the back door, just over there. I doubt she's gotten far," he says, pointing over his shoulder to a door that likely leads to the alley behind the bar.

I don't hesitate to go right through that door. Stepping out into the back alley, I look around and see no sign of her. Closing the door behind me, I start walking down the alley.

"May?" I call out and walk down the alley. "May? May, where are you?" I call out again and again.

I have a bad feeling in my gut. How did she just disappear? Stopping for a second, I take a deep breath, and as I'm releasing it, I look to the sky. The lights of the alley must be too bright or something because I don't see the stars. The sky above me is solid black. That's odd.

Walking to the end of the alley and back to the main road, I look up again. A patch of stars seems to be missing from the sky, like a large patch. Hanging my head, I start to think about where Mazzy could have gone. Her bike isn't here. She had her roommate Harper bring her here in her SUV. My phone goes off in my pocket, and for a second, I choose to ignore it but decided to check it just in case.

Eliza:
Where did you go?

Great, I don't want to deal with her right now. As I start to text Eliza back, another message comes in. I thought about not checking the phone, but I glance at it quickly. Her name across my screen eases my rising panic.

Mazzy:
Take me home, please!

Me:
Where are you Princess?

Mazzy:
By your bike.

It took me no time to turn on my heels and get my ass back to my bike. Was she there the entire time? I look near my bike but don't see her. I can see my bike, and I cannot see May anywhere near it. I walk to it, and that's when I finally see her. She's curled up on the ground on the other side of my bike hidden from view. Going around my bike, I squat down next to her and go to reach for her, but I remember how she reacted to the bouncer inside.

"May?" I ask softly, not wanting to startle her. "May, are you okay? Let's get you off the ground. Can I pick you up?" I ask her and wait for her to respond, still not touching her.

"Please," she barely squeaks out.

This is nothing like the cold-hearted Ice Queen I have seen the last three and a half weeks or that sassy brat she showed yesterday. This is someone terrified and hurting. Knowing that's not a yes in her book, I wait. I look up for a moment and notice a man has come out of the bar looking around like he's searching for someone. Is he the man that she ran from?

"May, I don't know what's going on, but I'm picking you up and putting you on my bike," I say, grabbing my helmet and placing it on her head. Making sure it's on her well, I scoop her up. I set her on the bike and get on in front of her. She wraps her arms around my waist the moment I'm seated in front of her and leans her body against my back. Starting the bike and getting us the fuck out of here, I notice the man has spotted us. His face contorts with an evil smirk.

Not caring to focus on his face, I'm more worried that if I do, I'll stop the bike and beat that smirk off his smug face. So, I focus on May, who's holding onto me so tight like she's afraid I'll let her go. *Not happening, Princess*, I think as we speed down the road away from the bar.

As we drive, I think about that man. He must be Tristen, the man who caused the normally brave-faced woman I knew to crumble in seconds. The look on his face told me he knew his effect on Mazzy and got sick enjoyment out of seeing her hurt like that. What had he done to cause her to react that way? Then it clicks. He's hurt her somehow. He hurt Mazzy.

My Mazzy.

I need to find out what he did to her.

Chapter 18: Something I Can't Have

Mazzy

The moment I wrap my arms around him, I lean my body against his

back and a sense of comfort flows through me. I close my eyes and

just hold onto him as we take off. He is risking his life riding without

his helmet, but it was sweet of him to put it on me to keep me safe.

The first and only person that I wanted, no needed, when I saw Tristen was Loen. I needed him in that moment, but with no mate bond between us anymore, I shouldn't have needed him that much.

Told you so. You need him.

I sobered up when I saw Tristen's face at the bar, so obviously, it isn't booze talking. Once the bond breaks, mates usually don't fall for each other. Hell, they usually hate each other so much that they either want to kill each other or be nowhere near one another. The wind whips at my skin as we ride the bike, making me shiver.

Stupid black dress.

I regretted this damn dress the moment I took my coat off. The stagehands couldn't take their eyes off my chest, and the amount of drunk guys throwing pick up lines at me was making me want to throat punch someone. This dress held nothing to the imagination and hardly held in my C-sized chest. Now on this bike, it's an even bigger regret because I am freezing. I don't know what made me wear this dress.

Yes, you do.

Okay, *fine*, I did. I wanted to see Loen's reaction. I was slightly upset he seemed so eager to go on that date with his ex, Eliza. I usually wear a tight sports bra. I don't like showing off my curves that much, but this dress, for sure, showed off every curve I have. I thought Loen's eyes were going to pop out of his head when he saw me in the dress. It made me giggle at his reaction.

So, so cold.

"Hey." He takes one hand off the handlebars for a second and taps my hands on his waist then places his hand back on the handlebars. "Almost home, okay?"

Tapping my hand on his abs, I let him know I hear him. He nods his head. Adjusting my grip on his waist as we roll up to a stop light. Instead of keeping both hands on the handlebars, he takes one hand off, places it on my upper thigh, and rubs his thumb back and forth attempting to soothe me.

A few more stop lights later, we are finally at his apartment complex. Loen doesn't say a word as he stops the bike, gets off, and then takes his helmet off my head. Opening my mouth, I go to say something, but I freeze up. He is being so gentle with me. For a large alpha shifter, he has such a gentle touch. I start to get off the bike, but he stops me by scooping me up into his strong arms.

"I can walk," I say softly.

"I know," is all he says, but he doesn't put me down—just keeps walking.

Screw it.

Instead of fighting this, I just lean into him and hide my face in his chest as he carries me to the elevator. I know I will have to explain things to him, but I'm hoping it won't be the moment we get into the apartment. *Please give me time*, is the only thing running through my head as we ride the elevator to our floor. When the elevator doors open on our floor, he carries me down the hall until we reach the apartment door.

"I'm putting you down for a second. Don't move," he says as he sets me on my feet, making sure I am steady before letting me go to get his keys out of his leather jacket.

I hate these heels. They are killing my feet, and my legs feel weaker than I want to admit. How can seeing one man's face cause my entire body to betray me? I know it's a trauma response. But it's been five years now. I should be able to hold myself together better than this. I stand next to him with my head down, just staring at my feet.

When he opens the door, I go to take a step in, but he scoops me up again.

"I said don't move," he says in a low gravelly tone as he walks us into the apartment, kicking the door shut with his foot after we clear the doorway. I'm expecting him to put me down in the living room or on the island stool, but he doesn't. He carries me to my bedroom and sets me on the edge of the small Murphy bed. I guess it's a good thing I was lazy before I left and didn't put it back up.

I sit on the edge of the bed with my legs over the side, hanging my head. I just sit there quietly waiting for him to ask or leave the room, but he doesn't do either. Instead, he gets down on his knees and slides his hand down my right calf until he reaches the strap of my heel at my ankle.

"I can do—" I start to say, but he interrupts me with a simple glance up at me. I stop talking and just sit there waiting. He undoes the strap on my right ankle and takes the heel off tossing it to the side then moves to the left shoe.

This man seriously isn't who he shows everyone else.

Loen stands up, grabbing the black heels and places them in my closet nicely.. His face is gentle, but his eyes tell me he has a lot of questions.

"Loen, I can—" I start to say, but he tosses me a look that shuts me up quickly. This isn't the woman he has seen. I'm still just unsure of what to say, so I just look at him. He's so tall. I wish he would squat back down. Looking up at him from this position has me thinking of some not-so-wholesome things.

Get your mind out of the gutter, Mazzy.

"You do not have to answer with words just a nod, okay?" he says. I nod my head, letting him know I understand.

"I'm going to start the shower for you," Loen says. I nod. "That isn't the question I need a response to, Princess."

Fuck, he has to stop calling me that. The way he says it in his gravely deep voice heats my core and makes my body tingle. He gently grabs my chin and tilts my face to his.

"Do you want me to stay close to you?" he asks with a little hesitation like he's afraid I'll say no. I nod. That must have reassured him. He's now smirking a little. I like his little smirk.

"Anything for you, Princess," he says as he yet again scoops me up and carries me to the bathroom.

After setting me on the counter so he can start the shower, he doesn't seem mad at me. But he does seem like something is bothering him. I can't help but feel like it's me. I'm bothering him. I'm so frozen and can't even take care of myself. I haven't seen Tristen in almost five years, and when I do, I turn into a big baby who can't take care of herself. I look down at my hands on my lap and start playing with my hands nervously.

You're pathetic.

I drop my head lower and close my eyes. As if he hears my inner voice berating itself, Loen turns from the bathtub and walks over to me. He gently grabs my chin and tilts my face up so I'm looking at him. I can't make eye contact with him right now, so I shut my eyes. My eyes will give everything away. I can't show him how pathetic I feel. I broke the mate bond by asking him to keep his distance from me. That's a rejection of the bond, and it broke, leaving both of us feeling pain and sadness. I broke what was made for us, but here he is taking care of me.

"You're not pathetic," he says, and my eyes fly open, catching his right away. He drops my chin and leaves the room without saying anything else. I sit on the counter and stare at the floor for a few minutes. When he doesn't come back in, I lean forward a little just enough to see through the cracked bathroom door.

There he is sitting on the floor with his back against the bathroom door frame. He's staying close but also giving me privacy. I hop off the counter and undress, hoping in the shower.

The water is so warm. It feels good on my skin. I turn to look for shampoo and soap, and that's when I see my shower stuff sitting neatly on the shower shelf. I feel a lump in my throat and tears burn my eyes, trying to break free.

Don't cry. You are stronger than this, Mazzy.

I'm not sure I have enough energy to hold back the tears. I have been holding back my emotions for far too long, and I feel like the cap holding them in is about to break. I am twenty-five years old, and my life has been full of loss and pain. I can't even talk to my best friends or anyone about half of it. No more holding it back. At least not right now. I let the tears fall and sink to the floor of the shower.

I don't know how long I'm on the floor of the shower letting myself cry. It takes me a little bit to find the energy to stand and finish my shower. After I finish washing my body and hair, I braid my hair before peeking my head out from behind the curtain. I know Loen said he's staying close, but I've been in there for a while. I didn't think to ask for a towel.

I scan the room, and when I look at the counter, I see it. A big fluffy navy blue towel is folded nicely, and next to it, is a big t-shirt and a pair of plaid pajama pants. Those aren't mine. They look like they are Loen's. I try to peek to see if he is still sitting on the floor outside the door before opening the curtain.

"I'm still here, Princess," he says.

"Thank you," I manage to squeak out somewhat shocked he is still on the floor.

I dry off and put his t-shirt on. The pants on are way too big. I try to cinch them with the tie in the waistband as much as I can. I'm a little worried about them falling off while I walk, but luckily, this is one of Loen's t-shirt so it goes to my knees easily. If the pants start to fall off, at least I have time to catch them before flashing anyone.

Taking a deep breath, I open the bathroom door the rest of the way, expecting Loan to be on the floor still, but he is standing, leaning against the wall and waiting for me. He tilts his head, giving me a questioning glance like he wants to ask if I'm okay but knows if he does, I'll probably break down again.

I respond by nodding my head and then look at my bedroom door. He steps back and allows me to pass him. Instead of following me to my room, he remains by the bathroom door. I turn before going into my room and know that the morning means likely talking about all of this. I'll need to prepare myself for that. I smile softly at him and thank him again before going into my room and closing the door.

It doesn't take long for sleep to take me, and I welcome that darkness, hoping for a decent night's sleep. I have a feeling though I'm in for a night of night terrors.

Chapter 19: Ice Queen

Mazzy

Waking up without a loud alarm blaring in my ear or buzzing in my hand is new for me. I don't remember the last time I slept in. Rolling over, I reach for my phone. It's not under my pillow. Looking around, I find it plugged into the charger on the bedside table. He must have plugged my phone in for me. That was nice of him. Sitting up, I grab my phone and text Harper.

Me:

Hey. How was your night with the hubby?

Harper:

Better than yours by far

Me:

Ewww I don't need to know the dirty details.

Harper:

You asked

Me:

Smartass

Harper:

What's wrong?

Me:

What? Nothing's wrong.

Harper:

You don't do this small chit-chat shit unless something's wrong.

SPILL!!!!

Me:

Have time to call me? is clay there?

Harper:

I will make time to talk to you and no.

He went to work out at the station.

Let me pee and then I'll call you!!

Me:

Sounds good, Thanks, Harper

Looking around while I wait for Harper to give me a call, I try to gather my thoughts. I need someone to talk to. I can't keep this all in anymore. I trust Harper, I think. I decide to take it easy today. I grabbed a few of my books off my bookshelf when we stopped by my apartment Friday. I get off the bed long enough to get one out of the backpack. *It's snuggling in bed with a book in the morning.*

As I start to read my book, a small-town romance, my phone chimes with a text notification. Harper said she was going to call me, not text me. Oh, it's from the chief. Oh, boy.

Archer "Chief":
We have a new assistant coming in to help for the next week or two. His name is Tristen Portlan,
he's a cop in Blackheart.

Me:
why?

Breath, Mazzy, just breathe.

Who am I kidding? I can't fucking breathe.

Archer "Chief":
So, we can get information out of him about his bestie the alpha of Blackheart that's why
Is there a problem with that?

No, Sir, No problem, when does he start?

Archer "Chief":
Tomorrow

Fuck my life.

"Seriously gods, are you having a laugh up there watching my life go from one disaster to another?" I ask the empty room. Sighing, I remember to talk myself down. *"You are okay, you are safe, he is not here."* Yeah, that's not working at all. Fuck, I'm panicking. Just as I feel my chest get tight my phone ringing makes me jump. Harper.

"Hey," I say with a shaky voice.

"What's wrong? What happened? Did someone hurt you?" Harper asks, rattling off question after question.

"Are you planning on letting me answer any of those questions or do you have more?" I tease. It's half-assed though. I'm hardly in a teasing mood at the moment.

"Mazzy, I can hear it in your voice. What's wrong?" she asks. I could use a hug, but I'll settle for her voice for now. I'll get a hug from her later.

"Are you in the right headspace to listen to some traumatic stuff?" I ask. I don't want to surprise her, but I can't keep this to myself anymore. Verena won't message me back, and other than her, Harper is the only other one I trust.

"For you, always babe," she says. "I'm on my way. This sounds like a you'll need a hug kind of talk."

"Yeah" is all I say.

Not even fifteen minutes later, Harper is buzzing up to the apartment. She didn't waste any time coming over. That's why I called her. She is always ready to listen to us and hug those who need it. I'm still scared to fill her in on everything. Well, not everything, just the Tristen thing. I can't work with him for the next two weeks. I won't be able to. Letting Harper in the apartment, we head right to my room.

"Holy shit. This place is huge," she says as she looks around the apartment.

"No kidding," I say with a chuckle as we reach my bedroom door.

We head into my bedroom, locking the door behind us. This is going to be a hard conversation as it is. I don't need the risk of one of the Dolton boys walking in. I ask Harper to use her magic to cast an eavesdropping spell, and she does without hesitation. I could have done it myself, but revealing I'm a Nova is not the plan for this conversation.

"Ready?" I ask her as we get comfortable on my bed.

"Fire away, babe," she says.

Here goes nothing.

Chapter 20: What Did He Do?

Loen

The Mazelynn we have seen the last two days at the station is a

complete shut-off, cold person, the true definition of an Ice Queen. I

want to know what is going on with her. I wonder if this is because of

the other night at the bar. I told her I wouldn't tell anyone about her

singing or her little breakdown.

Well, what I didn't know was that the man who caused her to have a massive panic attack and mental breakdown was here, in the station, in the same room as her. It also makes sense why she was so adamant that I deal with the outdoor training all day, which kept me from noticing the jackass was here. When my brothers came out a few hours ago to mention that the way the new guy Tristen looks at Mazzy is creepy, I put two and two together. I ended the outdoor training rather quickly after that.

I didn't enter the gym floor. She gave me a look that told me not to, so I'll respect that. But no way in hell am I going back outside. I'm staying right here at the entrance of the gym, keeping my eyes on this creep. I'm watching this man look at Mazzy like she's a piece of meat, but when she glances his way, it turns evil and menacing. This dude is a real creep. I can see that he makes her uncomfortable and that makes me want to kick his ass.

Leaning my back on the wall, I cross my arms and wait for the training session to be over. It was supposed to be over about ten minutes ago, but they are running behind. I don't mind if I get to watch

Mazzy kick trainees' asses, and it makes for a good laugh. The view isn't too bad either.

Knock that off. How are you acting any differently than Mr. Slim Ball over there?

Taking my eyes off Mazzy, I turn back to Tristen. He is a lanky man—pale with hardly any real muscle on his body and a crooked grin. His black hair is a little on the long side and greasy looking. The dude needs to wash his hair. He has a five o'clock shadow going on, but his growth is patchy as hell. The way he is still looking at her is making me want to go over there and knock his teeth out.

"You want to hit him, don't you?" a voice says from behind me, and I startle a little. I was so focused on Mazzy and the creep that I didn't hear someone come up behind me. Turning a little, I notice it's Bex, one of the female shifter officers.

"Hello, Bex, I wasn't thinking about hitting anyone," I lie and turn my gaze back into the gym.

"Sure, you weren't. The look on your face doesn't give off *'Keep looking at her and I'll fucking kill you'* vibes at all," she says sarcastically. I roll my eyes and turn my head to look at her.

"I don't like the way he is looking at her. It's creepy," I say

"No kidding. He's a creep. Always has been," Bex says and looks to the floor.

"Always has been. Do you know him? "I ask

"Yeah, Mazzy and I went to the academy with him," she admits with a tone that says she wishes that wasn't true.

"Hey, I have a question for you, Bex. Were they a couple in the academy?" I ask. I don't know why I ask it like that.

"Hell, no! She rejected any of his advances so much so that he started calling her the Ice Queen because she was so cold about her refusal to go out with him," Bex says as she watches Mazzy finish up the sparring training for the day.

"He started that name?" I ask with a questioning look.

"Yup, she hates it but is too nice to tell people to stop," she admits, and I can see she's upset about telling me.

"She hates nicknames, yells at me for calling her May, but refuses to tell people to stop calling her Ice Queen?" I ask. Bex nods with a down cast gaze. There has to be more to the story. No one will call her that anymore, ever. I'll make sure of it.

"Loen, what's going on? Did something happen to Mazzy?" Bex asks with a great deal of concern in her voice. Her eyes dart to the sparing mat and focus on Mazzy for a few moments.

"Forget I said anything," I mutter. I told her I wouldn't say a word about it.

"Loen, please, what happened?" Bex begs. Turning her attention back to me. "Please, what happened?"

"Nothing Bex, drop it okay," I say, standing with my arms crossed and focusing a stone-cold glare on Tristen I try to ignore Bex. She moves to stand in front of me, looking me in the eyes before following my gaze right to Tristen.

"No," Bex says in a panic. Turning quickly, she grabs my arm and yanks me trying to pull me out of the gym door.

"Hey, now," I say as I'm yanked out the door. For a tiny shifter female, she is rather strong.

"Shut up and come with me," she says, so I follow her down the hall. We pass the reception desk and head to a vacant office. Once inside, she locks the door and turns to me.

"Care to explain?" I ask.

"I shouldn't because I don't think she knows that I know," she says.

Well, that clears things up a whole lot, thanks Bex.

"You, okay?" I asked her.

"No, not one bit. Tristen is a bad guy, Loen. He has hurt woman. A lot of them," she says, struggling to get the words out. I don't push her. After taking a deep breath and releasing it, she starts again. "Tristen is a serial rapist. He assaulted at least ten girls, if not more, during his time at the academy," she says, tears forming in her eyes.

"Bex, that's a big accusation," I say, trying hard not to lose my shit.

That would explain Mazzy's reaction to seeing him at the bar. The alpha rage inside me wants to leave this room, storm over to that creep, and rip his fucking head off. I have not been here long, but the little time I have been, Bex has given me no indication of being a liar.

Easy now, she isn't your mate anymore...remember.

"Loen, I know it is, and there is more to it," she says, taking a deep breath again like she's about to go on a long tangent. "Tristen Portlan was rumored to use his best friend connections with the alpha of Blackheart to force witches to help him assault women, but no one could prove anything." She pauses choking on her words. Sadness and fear riddles her face. "I already told you he was the one who started the Ice Queen nickname for her. Well, about a week before graduation, he started bragging that he finally banged the Ice Queen." She paused again, looking to the closed door, then to me again. She is clearly uncomfortable talking about this. I don't know if I should ask questions or let her continue. My skin is starting to crawl. I can feel the control over my anger slipping.

If he hurt her, he is a dead man.

"He, um," she says and looks down. "He assaulted her, then bragged about it, making it sound consensual when it wasn't. And not just her," she says as she looks up at me with tears streaming down her face. The look in her eyes looks just like Mazzy's. That monster hurt Bex, too.

"Why wasn't he charged?" I ask, trying to understand this situation, while also trying to remind myself that I can't just go ripping heads off people.

"The other girls including myself and Mazzy couldn't remember anything. Not at first. I got my memory of it back after a few weeks and was too ashamed to come forward with it. I'm guessing Mazzy was the same." She rocks on her feet.

"He used a witch to put a memory spell on you," I say, which makes more sense.

"Along with another spell, one that made our bodies go limp, leaving us unable to move, defend ourselves, or even talk. All we could do was scream in our minds, watch, and feel... The spell was powerful enough to mess up magic and shifting abilities," she chokes out as she hugs herself tightly.

"It felt like it was a dream when I woke up the next day, and then the memory of the dream was gone within minutes of waking up," she says and bursts into tears. Her legs are shaking, so I rush to her and catch her as she collapses. This is the second time I have had to hold a woman this man has hurt. He won't hurt anyone else, and he is done tormenting Mazzy with his presence.

"I got you, Bex," I say as I guide her to the floor safely.

She's not lying. Her reaction is genuine and so was Mazzy's. This fucker got away with sexually assaulting women, and now he's continuing his sick game by being here around Mazzy and Bex.

"He won't get away with this Bex, I promise," I say to her, trying to comfort her. I don't care how much trouble this gets me in. He hurt women, used them for what he wanted, and took things from them against their will. He has forever scared them. Broken mate bond or not, he hurt my mate. I'm going to make him regret even looking at her.

My soul will not rest until he has seen a jail cell or death.

Chapter 21: Loen, Where Are You?

Mazzy

Where the hell has Loen been? I have not seen him at the station or his apartment in nearly three days. His brothers aren't much help. *He's out, I'm sure he's around somewhere,* and *He will be back soon* are all lies, and it's annoying. Even texts to him go unread.

Why do you care?

Well, that's just rude. I care because I, fuck it, I like him, and I'm worried. My phone chimes, and my heart rate speeds up. Is it him?

Getting off my bed, I get my phone out of my duffle bag. I was getting ready to go to work, but panic took over. I text Archer that I'm not coming in today and then toss my phone in my bag. I normally don't call out unless I'm sick or hurt, so I'm sure Archer is going to be worried.

I would normally expect a visit from Serafina at some point if I call out. Archer always sends her to check on me, but because of my lack of anger control when she's around me, I have not spoken to her in a little bit. I screwed up when it came to dealing with the Serafina fucking my mate thing. She didn't know. The anger didn't go away until I broke the bond. Then, I was just filled with guilt.

I doubt I'll be seeing her anytime soon. She even had Archer move her to a different hotel. Fuck. My life is a disaster. My phone chimes. Hoping it's Loen, I check it quickly. It's not him, I wanted it to be him. She has been constantly messaging me since I told her about what happened at the academy years ago. She gets that the man that hurt me had connections and those connections could get him out of trouble in a snap of their fingers. She doesn't know his name. She doesn't know it's the man Archer has assisting me with the combat seminar right now. She doesn't know the darker details. I didn't feel she was in a good space to hear all that.

Me:

Morning Harper, I got some sleep.

Harper:

Good! Hey, lunch today?

Me:

No, I called out sick!

Harper:

HOLY SHIT

Do I need to call 911?

Me:

Ha, Ha, Ha

Very Funny!

Harper:

You know I love you girly

I'll stop by later after my shift.

Me:

Sure thing! Love you!

I love her. She's acting a little bit like a mama bear though. I think she's going to make a great mom. While I have my phone out, I send another text to Loen. I hope this time he responds.

Me:

A text saying you're alive would be nice.

I really hope he answers this time, but I have a feeling he won't. After a few minutes of no response, I decide to send a few more. He could at least let me know he is alive.

Me:

I'm not worried.

I just don't want to explain to the chief that you died doing something stupid.

Yeah, Mazzy, because that's convincing.

I need to stop being so worried about him. He's an adult, and I'm not his girlfriend or anything. But it's making me anxious that he hasn't messaged back or been to work or his apartment. My gut says something is wrong. My phone chimes, and I figure it's Harper getting back to me. The moment I see his name on my phone, I get excited and feel a sense of relief.

Loen:

Alive

Real helpful, jackass.

What a dick. I'm trying not to get too upset. Even if it's one word, he at least told me he was alive. Putting my phone in my pajama pants pocket, I decide I should probably get something to eat. Slipping on a pair of slippers, I leave my bedroom and see Zyon at the island. When I get to the kitchen, Zyon looks at his phone with a giant grin. Someone's happy this morning.

"Morning, Zyon," I say as I walk past him into the kitchen area.

"Morning," he says.

"Wow, a man of few words, huh? Must run in the family," I say sarcastically. I hate that these men have been so secretive.

"What?" he asks, peeking up at me from his phone.

"Loen finally responded to my text today. One word, *Alive*. He was being super helpful, you know," I say as I search the cabinets for something to cook.

"Oh," Zyon says and gets back to giving his phone goo-goo eyes. It must be a girl he's talking to.

Loen and I have spent the last twenty-ish days being cold to each other, avoiding each other, and, in my case, fighting the mate pull to him. The night at the bar showed me he isn't what he portrays to everyone else. It's seems more like an act he's putting on to hide the truth, but what is the truth? And why is he pulling a disappearing act?

Oooo, pancakes!

I find a box of pancake mix in the cabinet, and my stomach practically screams at me, *YES!* I might not be the best cook, but I can make decent pancakes. Once I have things gathered up, I set it down on the island across from Zyon.

"Hey, Z, want some?" I ask Zyon and show him the box as he looks up at me.

"Oh, hell yeah!" he responds. "I'll help, hold on," he says, jumping up from the stool and getting fruit out of the fridge.

"Is Jayce home? Should we make him some pancakes?" I ask.

"Nope, he isn't home. Plus, I'm starving, so I might just eat them all," he says with a joking smile.

I guess it's just me and Zyon this morning. Zyon is a nice guy. He has a kind soul even though he plays off being a badass. I waste no time getting the pancakes started. I can't wait to eat these.

After I have finished enough for the two of us, I turn the stove off and head to the island with a plate full. Zyon has already started on the few I finished first for him, and he's about halfway through them. There is enough syrup on those to make even those with the biggest sweet tooth cringe.

"Zyon, do you think you have enough syrup on those?" I ask with a smile.

"Nope," he says with a laugh and then points to pancakes. "These are fantastic."

"Thanks," I say with a smile.

I want to ask him a question, but I'm not sure he will answer it. I know Loen has been talking to his brothers. Anytime I catch them texting him, they hide their phone. They know something I don't. That irritates me like no other, but it's not their fault, I guess.

"Is Loen mad at me?" I ask. My voice comes out a little more insecure than I intended it to.

"No, he isn't mad at you, Mazelynn," Zyon reassures me. He grabs his phone and starts flipping through it and a loud chime has him smiling again. I don't think he noticed that I saw that smile, but whoever he is talking to has this goofball smiling like a kid in a candy store.

"What's that smile for?" I ask him, and he drops the phone on the island face down.

"It's nothing. Do you want something to drink?" he asks, an obvious attempt to distract me from my original question.

"Nope," I say then pause, place my elbow on the table, and rest my chin on the palm of my hand, giving him a knowing look. "Sooo, who's the girl?" I ask. His face turns red, and he turns away from me. "Your face gives you away, Z. You don't have a poker face like Jayce or Loen." I'm just teasing him. He's a sweet guy. A little childish at times, but what man isn't? I smirk at him and continue eating. "No need to be embarrassed. Is it someone I know?"

"Umm, no. I mean, I don't think so," he responds as another chime comes in, and he picks the phone up. That's cute. He has a crush, but something tells me this girl is more than a crush if she's getting that kind of smile out of him. But the smile quickly leaves his face when he opens the message. That can't be a good thing.

"Is everything okay, Zyon?" I ask.

"It was Loen. He, umm, says…" He pauses and looks at me with a blank expression.

"Says what, Zyon?"

"He says he wants me to keep you company today. Doesn't want you alone at all," he explains with a heavy sigh.

He places his phone down on the island and slides it away from himself. He looks disappointed. Sure, Loen messages his brother a full sentence, and I get one word. Asshat. His energy did a complete flip to what it just was.

I don't need a babysitter.

"Ugh, there goes my plans," he says as he picks up his phone and goes to text someone.

"Hey now, no fucking way. I don't need a babysitter," I say push my half-eaten plate of pancakes away from me. I turn to him and wait for him to say something.

"But Loen is my alph…my brother. If he wants me to keep you company, that's what I'll do," he says. He genuinely does have a shit poker face. He's trying to play off like he didn't just slip up. I'm sure he's hoping I didn't pick up on that slipup. I definitely did.

"He's your alpha." I say. His bug-eyed expression and lack of eye contact tell me I am correct.

"I was supposed to have a date with a girl I knew from high school, Lacey. She's a fae visiting the area for a day or so," he says, hoping I'll drop the alpha thing.

I'll give him credit. That's interesting to me, but I'm more interested in the alpha thing. As far as the world is concerned, their father Colak Dolton is still alpha, not Loen.

"Nice try, Zyon. What do you mean he is your alpha?" I make sure my tone is stern, so he knows I'm not backing down on this.

"I can't, Mazelynn," he says and looks down. I know that look. He was ordered by his alpha not to say a word. He wants to but can't.

"Alpha's orders, huh? Okay, fine. So, this Lacey, is she pretty?" I say. I'll let it go for now, but this has me thinking about the situation with the bounty hunters.

"Oh, gods, Mazzy, she's the most beautiful girl." He stops himself, and his eyes go wide. He must have realized he just used a nickname for me.

On the first day of the combat seminar, I informed everyone that they were not allowed to call me by any name but Mazelynn. Nicknames are earned, and they all have done well with it. Until now. I'm not mad at him. Actually, I don't mind it. Zyon has grown on me. Out of the twins, Zyon is the most kind but puts on a front. Jayce is a little more stone-cold and hot-headed like Loen.

"You're good. You can call me Mazzy. Just not May, okay?" I say. He nods in agreement.

We start chatting about this girl, Lacey. It's clear he is absolutely in love with this little fae. Apparently, she is actually little, like four foot ten max, very short for a fae. But from Zyon's descriptions of her, she sounds adorable. A tiny girl with pink hair, fair skin, and bright emerald, green eyes. Zyon says she has the most adorable freckles and smile. I can tell this girl has won his heart just by the way he talks about her, but he explained what happened in high school and how she got so hurt by the twins trying to make her pick one of them that she left.

If she is as small as he says, my mind can't picture how either of them could be with her without breaking her. Like size wise, the math ain't mathing or whatever that saying is. I love how much Zyon lets his emotions out when talking about her. It's sweet, and part of me wants to tell him to never let anything tamp that down and not let his light be dimmed by anything. I would know.

Ice Queen.

It's always ringing around in my mind any time others look at me with a judgmental expression or make comments about how cold I am. I hate thinking about that nickname. I used to wear my emotions on my sleeve when I was young but had to start hiding them, so they weren't used against me. If people knew the real reason for that name, I'm sure they would not call me that. Hell, if they knew the person who started calling me that and what he did, they would forever hate themselves for calling me the Ice Queen to my face.

"Mazzy, what should I do?" Zyon says, and his voice pulls me from my thoughts and back to our conversation.

"Go on your date. It will be fine, promise," I say with a smile and nod my head to his phone. "Seriously, go. You like this girl. Maybe the reason you like her so much is because she's your mate," I say, knowing that's probably not the case. Fae and shifters aren't fated mates pairings, but with how he lights up talking about her, mate or not, he can't hide he wants to see her.

"Loen will kill me. He gave me an order," he says and then stops himself, realizing he slipped up again.

"Zyon, go on your date. Loen can take it up with me. I don't plan on going anywhere today anyway," I say and stand. He gets up and steps in front of me.

"He says he is worried especially with Tri—" he admits.

"I don't need a fucking babysitter," I shout at him "What the fuck did he tell you about Tristen? What does he know about him?" I demand, and he takes a step back.

I know that Loen suspects something happened between Tristen and I. I didn't think he figured it out, but now I'm starting to wonder if Loen avoiding me is because he found out what Tristen did to me. Is he taking that out on me? It's not like it was my fault. Like I chose it. He told me he wouldn't say anything, but he told his brothers about my breakdown? I can't stop my mind from spiraling. I can feel a slight tug at the magic, and without letting Zyon answer any of my questions, I rush to my room and slam the door behind me.

The moment I enter the room and lock the door, my skin lights up with the Nova markings, and I slide my back down the door 'til I'm sitting on the floor.

Seconds to spare, Mazzy. That was too close.

This is why I didn't want to find my mate. Why I broke the bond with Loen. Why I didn't want anyone to know about what Tristen did or anything. I hide myself because when I feel things and get worked up, this happens. I can't control it. Even though I have been feeling weak recently, I can still manage to lose control like this.

"Shit, shit, shit. Pick up the phone, Jayce," Zyon says in a panic as his voice carries through my closed door.

Great, he's calling his brother. I need to get out of here and get some air.

Chapter 22: Z, You Fucked Up

Jayce

"Dude, you did what?" I ask, hoping I heard wrong.

"She knows Loen is the alpha, and she knows he told me to keep her company," Zyon says. Even through the phone, I can tell he's pacing.

Fantastic, fan-freakin-tastic.

"Loen is going to murder you." I say annoyed. I can't believe my idiot twin slipped up and let the Ice Queen know that Loen is actually our current alpha. He was given the same order I was given. No one can know. Not just yet.

"I know, Jayce. It's not like I did it on purpose," Zyon says with a snarl.

I don't know what our big brother is up to, but he needs to get his head out of his ass. Zyon is acting weird, well weirder than normal, and now Loen is off doing who knows what. He's being secretive, and I don't like it. He hasn't been thinking clearly since Saturday. He wouldn't tell the full details about what happened. Just that something happened at the bar that has him watching Mazelynn closer than before.

"The only thing Loen asked you to do was keep an eye on Mazelynn. How the hell could you fuck it up so badly?" I ask.

"I'll fix it somehow," he says before hanging up.

Tossing the phone onto the passenger seat, I turn the music up in my car. I need something to drown out the thoughts in my head. I can't help either of my brothers if they keep hiding shit from me. I should have stayed home, but the moment I saw an SUV following Loen out of the parking lot, I got a bad feeling. So I followed it as it followed him.

The SUV is just a few cars in front of me, heading down a side street. It lost Loen a few blocks back. It slows down every side street. I bet they are looking for Loen. The SUV doesn't look familiar, but given our pack situation, I can assume this has to do with the whole territory situation with the Blackheart Pack. Alpha Daren Collins is the only one after Loen right now unless Daren got the council involved.

Shit.

I hope it isn't the council. If it is, Loen isn't the only one in trouble. Zyon and I will be too. The SUV turns into a hotel on the opposite side of the city. Instead of following it into the parking lot, I drive past and make a mental note of the location. I'll come back later without the car. Texting Loen quickly, I let him know where the SUV stopped and that I plan to head out a little later to check it out. I also tell him that Zyon accidentally revealed the alpha thing to Mazelynn. I don't think this is going to end well for Z. My twin is too trusting and has a shit poker face. I start to head back to the apartment when a text comes through.

Zyon:

She left the apartment, but I followed her.

Me:

what the fuck dude can you not do what we ask?
just once?

Zyon:

Fuck off.

Me:

Loen is going to kill you.
Find her. I'll let Loen know your fucked up.

Shaking my head, I find the chat with Loen. I need to make sure I word this in a way that doesn't end with us having out asses handed to us by our older brother. Loen isn't our father, but he isn't a push over either.

Me:

Loen, the Ice Queen left the apartment.

Loen:

DO NOT CALL HER THAT.

Me:

Sorry, Sir. Mazelynn is on foot headed somewhere but Z says he is following her.

Loen:

For fuck sake you two.

She called out

I just wanted you to keep an eye on her while I figured out more about something.

Me:

Figure what out?

Dude you have been MIA for three days. Show up for a few hours this morning then left again before she could see you.

Then a random message to keep an eye on her.

Did Daren send more bounty hunters?

Loen:

No, this is something else.

Find them and get her back to the apartment.

I'm heading back to a friend.

We need to continue our little chat.

Me:

Who? What chat?

Dude let me help you.

No response. Fucking hell, I hate that he won't let me help

him. I scan the sidewalks as I drive getting closer and closer to the

apartment complex when I finally see Zyon and Mazelynn sitting on a bench outside a small park. Pulling into a parking spot, I put the car in the park and text Loen.

Me:
Found them at the park two blocks from the apartment.

Putting my phone in my pocket, I get out of the car. As I get closer, Zyon looks in my direction and gives me a back-off glare, so I stop in my tracks. He isn't usually serious like that, so I'll give them space for a few minutes. Zyon stands from the bench and holds his hand out to Mazelynn. She swats it away with a playful smile then glares in my direction. Safe to say she isn't happy with me at the moment. I don't even know why. I just got here.

"I guess you are here to take us back to the apartment?" she asks when they reach me. Nodding, I turn back to the car and open the passenger door for her. Zyon gets in the back seat, slamming the door.

This is going to be a long two block ride.

***

"Well," Mazelynn finally asks. She's sitting in the middle of the couch crisscrossed with her arms folded over her chest. Where she has been since we got back into the apartment twenty minutes ago.

"Well, what?" I ask, knowing damn well what she's looking for, but I have orders. And I'm not breaking them. Not like Zyon did.

"Jayce, don't be an asshole," Zyon says with a snappy tone as she pulls out the notebook and pen he got from his room. He is in the armchair to my left. I'm sitting on the floor across from Mazelynn. I kind of wish I picked a different place to sit. The Ice Queen has been giving me glares like no other.

"Dude," I say and leer at him. I can't believe him. Loen is going to lose his shit. Ignoring me, Zyon flips the notebook open and looks at Mazelynn waiting for her to ask a question. This is not going to be good.

"How about I start, and you fill in the blanks," she says, Zyon nods to her. "Okay, a week after the bounty hunters were arrested, I had a day off. I hate days off but turns out staying in the sparring room at night was a good thing. I was able to do research easily," she says.

I'm confused. I thought we were telling her the truth about why we are actually here. Wiggling in my spot, I dart my eyes to Zyon then back to the bossy woman on the couch.

"I can see those wheels turning in that thick skull of yours, Jayce. Don't hurt yourself," she says sarcastically. I don't like that attitude of hers. It's fucking annoying. Like she heard my thoughts, she glares at me with a small smirk.

This chick is crazy.

I guess that checks out because so is Loen. They might be a great pair if they didn't fucking hate each other.

"Anyway, I found the old agreement between your pack and the Blackheart pack and also found the allegations from the council that your father killed a member of the Blackheart pack about five years ago. First question—did he?" she asks and looks at Zyon. He looks down at the notepad and writes the answer down then turns the notebook to face Mazelynn.

No.

"As I thought," she says and pauses for a second. "Daren Collins is framing your pack to gain territory."

That doesn't sound like a question, but she's correct. Zyon and I both nod our heads. I get his plan. We aren't actually saying anything, so we're not actually breaking the order given to us by Loen, our alpha.

Smart way around the rules, Z.

"The council says the man was killed for escorting your sister to her mate's pack, her mate being Alpha Daren. This is not entirely true." She pauses. "Daren Collins is a broken wolf. You know that, right?" she asks.

That information causes both Zyon and I to look at each other in shock. We did not know that. "I'll take those looks as a no... He kidnaped your sister, didn't he?" she asks. Zyon writes on the notebook and flips it around to show Mazelynn.

Yes.

Mazelynn looks down at the floor and then back up at me. I can see concern and empathy in her eyes. There is also something else there like she knows something she isn't telling us. Besides the fact that Alpha Daren Collins is a broken fucking wolf. How could a pack of shifters be ruled by an alpha with no shifting abilities? He's practically human.

How does our human luna know this information and we don't?

Loen didn't have to say it to us, but we know she's his mate. It was clear when he couldn't take his eyes off her and would clench his fists trying to contain himself anytime the other male trainees were sparing with her. He felt the bond, but from what I could see, she didn't. Their bond was bound to break if she didn't feel it. If that's the reason he is avoiding her, I feel kind of sorry for him. I can't imagine feeling the bond and then it breaking because my mate didn't feel it and wanted nothing to do with me.

The only thing that makes me second guess the bond being broken is that he is still being super protective of her. Even though she is supposed to be our luna, I don't trust talking to her about our pack stuff. She's not a shifter. She wouldn't understand. So, this situation is making me uncomfortable.

She doesn't ask more flat-out questions, just wants a nod yes or no to confirm what she's summarizing. She goes over the original agreement between the Blackheart pack and Dolton's pack. We confirm what she found out about it.

Just the basics like the agreement started because our territories were so close together with only a small stream separating them. The Blood River. That's the nickname for the river that runs between our pack and the Blackheart pack. The river saw so much death for so long that the water appeared red from all the blood that was spilled in it or around it.

The original alphas were not friendly with each other but felt the best thing for their pack members was to work on a truce. The agreement said that if an alpha from either pack attacked any member of the other pack, the attacking pack would lose their territory to the other.

"Mazzy, how did you learn about Daren being a broken wolf?" Zyon asks, and I wait for her to snap. He used a nickname she told us never to use but she does nothing but relax her position and look at him with soft expression.

"While most people think I am human, only a select few know a little secret. And by few, I mean Archer and Serafina," she says, pausing for a moment. "Human hearing isn't as good as shifters, or fae, we all know this." She glances to both of us. Zyon and I nod at her both confused on where this is going. "What do you know about the hearing of a broken wolf?" she asks.

Hold the fuck up, what?

"Yeah, broken wolf. So, I don't have the shit hearing everyone thinks I do." She smiles.

I have the feeling she isn't telling the whole story. There's something else she's keeping to herself. We were not aware that she was a broken wolf. We were all under the impression that she was human. But I guess that would explain why she was Loen's mate. She was supposed to have a wolf but doesn't.

I wonder what she's hiding.

"To answer your question about how I know about Daren. Tristen, a guy from the police academy when I was there, has a loudmouth. He is a close human friend to Daren and the alpha's family," she says. The way she said Tristen's name reveals something.

He scares her. Her voice trembled a little saying his name. Just before I get a chance to ask her more about it, the apartment door lock unlocks.

Shit. Loen's home. Let the chaos begin.

Chapter 23: Loen Has Lost It

Mazzy

He's back.

I got the twins talking—well, not really talking, just nodding in agreement. I wanted to see what else I could get out of them. I gave them a little half secret about me to try to show them I trust them, but now that Loen is here, they are going to clam up.

Most if not all of us in the city don't care for the Blackheart pack. If they tell Archer the situation, they will have our support. I decide to stay sitting on the couch as the twins stand and wait for Loen to come in. The moment the door is open. I smell blood and sweat.

What the fuck. He's hurt.

Loen's knuckles are bloody, and he has blood splatter on his face and clothes. I can smell from here it's not his blood thought. Standing up, I look at his face. Oh, those amber eyes look like they are full of fire. He's pissed. The look in his eyes causes the wolf instinct inside me to shy back some. I try to take a step back, forgetting the couch was behind me and end up flopping clumsily back onto the couch with a thud.

Shit.

I don't know what he was doing, but whoever he was hitting probably needs to seek medical treatment. The loud thud of me falling back on the couch causes all three sets of eyes to land on me, but Loen's only linger for a few seconds before shifting to look to his brothers.

Their eyes remain on me longer, but I bet they can feel his eyes burning into the back of their skulls because they quickly turn around to face him and bow their heads. He lets out a deep growl. Without a word or another look in our direction, he walks past the living room and right to the bathroom, slamming that door, too. This time, it felt like the walls shook. He's pissed, like raging alpha pissed.

"Well, that went way better than I expected," Zyon says nervously. Jayce walks up to him and smacks him on the back of the head.

"Shut up," he says in a harsh tone. "We're lucky he didn't come in and start beating your ass."

Jayce's little back-of-the-head slap made me chuckle a little. Even though they fight, you can tell they love each other and will do anything to help their brother. Jayce isn't wrong. Zyon screwed up when he slipped up on his choice of words. It wasn't all his fault. I had my suspicions, and they just confirmed it for me.

Instead of just standing in the middle of the apartment staring at each other, I stand up from the couch again and go to my room. Once inside my room, I grab my phone. This has been an odd day, and

I need some advice. Knowing this will probably get me nowhere, I open a text conversation with my sister.

Me:

Verena, I miss you!

I really could use my sister to talk about something.

I found something and well, I need sisterly advice but understand if you don't want to talk.

I love you, sis.

I'm not super hopeful she will get back to me. She hasn't responded to messages from me in a while, but I could use her thoughts on this mess. And I just miss her so much. I don't like technology sometimes. I can see that she has opened the text. The text that just said delivered now says *read*, but she's not responding. I toss my phone on the charger near my pillow and lay down in bed.

Ugh, please, V.

***

I must have fallen asleep waiting for Verena to text back. When I wake up, I look at my phone and realize it's nearly four in the morning. I fell asleep around seven last night and somehow slept through the night. That hasn't happened in years. I toss the phone back down on the bed and sigh.

I try not to be too upset that there is no text from Verena. I shouldn't have gotten my hopes up that she would message me. I stand up. I'm on autopilot at this point and just go about my morning routine. I take a quick shower, braid my hair, get dressed, and head to the kitchen for something to eat.

I am not hungry. I need to eat, but I'm sitting here poking my breakfast cereal with my spoon. I don't think I have taken more than two bites at this point, and I have lost track of how long I have been here. I glance up at the microwave. It's now six in the morning. I get back to looking at my bowl and just repeatedly poking it with my spoon.

Before I can sink into my thoughts more, the bathroom door flies open, rattling on its hinges. I jump and look toward the bathroom door as a half-naked, soaking wet Loen comes storming out of the bathroom with only a navy blue towel wrapped around his waist. He glances my way, and we make eye contact for a second. I am the one to look away back at my cereal. He is still angry. His door slams off to my right, echoing through the apartment. I have to get ready for work, and so does he.

After cleaning up the breakfast I didn't eat, I get ready for work. I don't know what Loen's issue is. But he obviously needs space, so I'm giving it to him. I'm still mad at him for trying to have his brother babysit me. I'm not weak.

You kind of are, though.

I am slightly weak, I guess. Last night, the moon wasn't in the sky. It should have been but wasn't. The darker the sky gets, the weaker I feel. Since Loen showed up, my magic has been feeling like it's being drained. The Novas in the sky are going dark. Their light is being smothered out. What if that's happening to me? What can I do to stop it?

If my light is going out, then I can't do anything to stop it. Maybe I don't want to. I'll be what I have been pretending to be all these years, and maybe that's a good thing. I flop on my bed and just stare at the ceiling for a while. I should be heading out the door in like twenty minutes. A text goes off on my phone, reminding me I left it on the charger on my bed. Picking it up, it's a text from Loen.

Loen:

Heading out, don't be late

What the hell? Looking at the time, I've somehow lost the twenty minutes. I thought I had to just sit and think. I jump up, grab my gear, and rush out the door. By the time I reach the parking lot, Loen's bike is gone, and I'm not entirely surprised. He is dead set on not being anywhere near me.

I get to work right on time, but I'm shocked Loen's bike isn't here yet. He left before I did. I wait by Lori's desk, chatting with her until he arrives. I want to make sure he is good to handle the trainees today or if he needs to take a day off. When he finally arrives, it's nearly ten after seven. Archer won't be thrilled with how late he is, but as he walks in, I notice he's not dressed in his workout clothes. Instead, he is dressed in casual jeans and a t-shirt. He walks up to Lori's desk not once looking at me. He smiles at her, and then turns and sits on one of the benches.

Has he lost his mind?

Only minutes later, a bunch of large men come into the building—at least thirteen if not more. They are definitely shifters, dressed in all-black suits with guns hidden on their hips. Takes me all of a minute to realize they're the council, and they are here for him. Lori touches my hand before I step away from her desk, causing me to freeze in place.

"Stay here," she whispers.

I turn to look at Loen as he gets his ass arrested. The hot head actually did something so stupid that it got him arrested by the shifter council. I ignore Lori and take a few steps toward Loen and the roughly thirteen large shifters.

"Loen, what did you do?" Lori asks as she picks up the phone and frantically presses the buttons.

She's probably calling the chief to come out here. He won't be able to do anything about this. Lori is a sweet old lady and has grown fond of Loen and his younger brothers. She jokes that if only she were thirty years younger... *Eye roll.* I am only a few steps away from Lori's desk when she calls me back to her and says to stay there. The chief is on his way out to us.

"You are under arrest," one large man in black says as he pulls Loen to his feet from the bench and turns him around. "Hands behind your back," he says as Loen complies but not without commentary.

"No, really? I hadn't guessed," he says in a sarcastic tone.

"Don't be a smart ass. You're in enough trouble alpha, or should I say former alpha," a second man says as he moves in front of Loen.

What does he mean by "former?"

"Fuck off," Loen snaps.

There is a time and place, Loen. Now is not the time. I'm about to say something but the man who called Loen a smart ass pulls back his fist and slams it into Loen's cheek. I cringe at the sound it makes as it echoes through the lobby.

"Hey, you can't just hit him. He wasn't resisting arrest," I shout at the men as I started to walk toward them.

"This man is under arrest for assaulting a member of the Blackheart pack and breaking the treaty agreement," the first man in black says as he tightens the silver cuffs around Loen's wrist. Loen hisses in pain. The man's hands are protected from the silver by thick gloves.

"What?" I ask, looking at Loen, then the man. What member of the Blackheart pack did Loen beat up? I didn't hear any new leads on the other two from Blackheart that have been spying on us. Loen makes eye contact with me as he is yanked backward by the man holding the cuffs with a gloved hand. Those eyes. They feel so comforting, like home. They feel like they can see my soul, the true me, and now, I'm losing that. Why do I feel so drawn to him even when the bond is broken and gone?

"Wait," I say, and I walk fast to catch up as they escort Loen out the doors and down the station steps. "I need to talk to him a second," I say, hoping maybe that will get their attention, and I'm correct. They stop as the men turn toward me. Once I nearly reach the bottom of the steps, I pause.

"Too bad, sweet cheeks. You can chat with him when and if he is released," the man holding Loen's cuffs says. Giving him another yank at the cuffs, Loen tries hard not to react to the pain of the silver on his skin. Fucking dick head knows it hurts and wants to inflict pain.

"Sweet cheeks? I might be a female, but I'm definitely not your sweet cheeks," I holler at the man. Loen gives me a look that tells me to shut up and let it go. I look at him. His eyes are fixed solely on mine. Before breaking eye contact with Loen, I mouth, *Who?* He shakes his head and turns his gaze back to the SUV they are leading him to.

"Loen, you idiot, what did you do?" a deep voice says from behind me, catching my attention. I turn to see a much older version of Loen with dark brown eyes and a stone-cold cocky demeanor. It's Chief Dolton, Loen's father. If the look on his face is any indication of his current mood, he is livid. He storms down the steps to his son and gets nose to nose with him.

"All this over a broken wolf girl?" he says.

My heart rate jumps. Is he talking about me? How does Leon's father know about the broken wolf white lie? Archer promised he wouldn't tell anyone. There are only a few here who think I'm a broken wolf, a shifter-born human with no shifter abilities. It's a white lie, but no one besides my sister knows that. Broken wolves try to hide it.

Archer made a rule that if a broken wolf comes clean, no one outside our department will know. I told him that's what I was to keep my true secret. I have no idea how Chief Dolton found out unless the twins told him, but something tells me it wasn't them.

"Not just any girl, Father," Loen snaps and turns away from us. "Take me away now."

He wants to be arrested. I don't understand. But before I can get a chance to speak again, he is thrown into the SUV with the door swiftly closed behind him. I let out a sigh and glanced over at Loen's father, Colak Dolton. I need to text Jayce or Zyon and see what they know. I make a chat with Jayce, Zyon, and myself.

Me:
What the fuck did your brother do?

Zyon:
????

Jayce:
What's going on?
Mazelynn is he okay?

Me:

No, he is not.

Your brother just got arrested by the council

Do either of you know what the hell is going on?

Jayce:

No ma'am

Me:

Cut the BS Jayce

Zyon:

No, we have no idea. We are telling you the truth.

Me:

I'll believe you for now.

Oh…

Your Father is a peach.

Jayce:

Stay clear of him Mazzy

Zyon:

What Jayce said!

Stay clear

He's a dick who only thinks of himself

Me:

I'll do my best

That last text is a lie. I want to get Colak into a room and have a chat. He knows what Loen got arrested for, and I'm going to find out. Looking at the time, I realize that the trainees are not here yet. They should be.

"Mazzy, we need to talk," Archer shouts from the top of the steps to the station

"Yes, sir" is all I manage to say as I head back up the steps.

So much for a chat alone with Loen's father.

Following Archer and Chief Dolton through the lobby and down the hall to Archer's office, I can't stop thinking about why Loen would beat someone up and willingly let himself get arrested. Once inside the office, I get my answer. Loen beat the shit out of Tristen like in a hospital bed nearly died, in a medically induced coma kind of beating.

The chief called me in to report that Tristen will be going back home to Blackheart Pack as soon as he has recovered enough. The doctors are predicting it will be a few weeks to months. However, he is pressing charges against Loen and that means an investigation. Because Tristen is in a medically induced coma to recover, the alpha of the pack he lives at is the one in charge of pressing charges, and he for sure is. No huge surprise there. Given his alpha is the same one who sent bounty hunters after Loen and the twins.

"Chief, there has to be a reason he did it. He wouldn't beat him up just to beat him up," I say. My voice is showing my concern for Loen and a little bit of fear.

"Well aware, Mazelynn, and unless he decides to open his mouth and defend himself instead of being a sarcastic ass then he is on his own. We can't help him," Archer says, staring at Alpha Dolton, who is standing with his arms crossed in Archer's office.

"That's bullshit," I snap and head to the office door.

"Mazelynn, you stop right now," Archer says in his stern dad voice. I roll my eyes. I stop before I reach the door. I don't care how this looks in front of his old friend. I'm pissed.

"I'm not your daughter. That voice doesn't work on me…Archer," I sass and head out the door.

I'm so pissed that I can't even think straight. Ignoring everyone, I storm down the station hall to the gym expecting to see the trainees waiting but find no one. Not a single trainee in sight.

Where the fuck are they?

Turning around, I go back to the lobby to Lori to ask if any have called sick or something, and as if I summoned them with magic, a few start coming through the doors of the station. The ones dragging their feet are mumbling. A strong scent of alcohol hits my nose and makes my stomach sour.

Drunk trainees. Just what I needed today.

"Showers, now," I yell and don't even wait for them to answer. I'm not in the mood to play games today, and these trainees are about to get a reality check. First reality check, one I got myself a few weeks ago, don't come hungover to training.

I hope they like running and throwing up!

Chapter 24: Get Out of There

Mazzy

My phone ringing wakes me up from a nap I hadn't planned on taking.

I didn't mean to fall asleep. I have spent the last four days pushing the

trainees more and looking into what Loen did. I can't get a straight

answer about it. His father came in here a few times in the last two

days giving me nasty looks. Seriously don't know what his issue is, but someone needs to remove the stick from his ass. What time is it, and who the hell is calling me?

Picking up my phone and looking down at my phone the caller ID says, *Harper*. I answer the phone. She doesn't usually call me.

"Hey, Harper, what's up?" I ask.

"Where are you?" she asks.

"Home, I mean, Loen's apartment," I say.

"Get out of that apartment NOW," she screams into the phone.

What the hell is that about? Context Harper?

"Harper, what's going on?"

"You aren't safe, Mazzy. The council is coming your way right now," she says

"What? Why?" I ask. Are they going to arrest me or his brothers?

"Just get out of the apartment and get your ass to the roller park," she snaps.

"Okay, okay, Miss Bossy Pants," I say as I hang up the phone. I head to the kitchen for my keys and helmet. It's quiet in here. I don't know if I should tell the boys or do what Harper said. A text pings in as I reach my keys.

Harper:
I mean it, Mazzy. Just get out of there now.

Okay, now I'm worried. What in the world is happening right now? I grab my keys swiftly off the island, get my helmet from the coat rack by the door, and head back to my room. I'll go out the fire escape, so they don't hear the door. I wish Harper would give me more context on what is going on, but I'm sure I'll find out soon. Opening the window and looking down at the fire escape, I notice a few black SUVS parked on the street.

Council members and their security?

Working my way down the fire escape, I try to be as quiet as I can. I run back to the parking lot where my bike is, and the twin's car is still there. Odd. They weren't in the apartment. Maybe they were in their rooms. Starting my bike, I head out of the parking lot and toward the park. Harper better be there to explain things to me. I'll be pissed if she doesn't. Reaching the roller park a few minutes later, I notice Harper's SUV parked with the back windows half down but the front windows up.

Oh, shit.

I go up to the SUV and tug the handle it opens, and I see Harper sitting in the driver's seat. I was expecting more than Harper to be in this SUV. The back window half down was our little sign for trouble.

"Get your ass in the car now," she snaps.

I don't waste time and get in the SUV. She looks worried and mad at the same time. I don't know what's happening, but it can't be good. I hope this is pregnancy hormones or something. She is typically chill, but she has a look on her face like she's about to lose it.

After driving around for about two hours, the sun is starting to set, and I'm starting to get annoyed. Harper doesn't say a word. This entire time, she focuses on driving us around, constantly checking the mirrors. We left city limits and have been riding around the towns surrounding the city, the less populated ones. I know something is up, and that makes me nervous.

"Do I get an explanation, Harper, or are we going to continue driving around not speaking?" I finally ask the question I have been waiting for the last two hours.

"Not now," she snaps at me, and that catches me off guard.

"Harper, you call and yell at me to leave the apartment right that second, so I do. We have spent at least two hours in this car. I think I deserve an answer here," I say in a demanding tone.

Sighing, Harper checks her mirrors again before she finally pulls off into a school parking lot. It's nearly 9 p.m., so the parking lot is empty. She stops the car and turns off the headlights before turning herself in my direction.

"Loen came to me asking if I knew about your night terrors and a guy named Tristen. When I told him I didn't know what he was talking about, he told me about something that happened at a bar, some kind of PTSD episode after you saw a man named Tristen," she says.

"Who and what?" I ask softly. I probably should have told her

who it was. That is coming to bite me in the ass now. Harper turns

away from me for a second before turning back to me. I can see she is

trying to hold back tears or anger or maybe both. I should have told

her who it was.

"You didn't tell me it was him," she says as tears start to stream

down her face, but as fast as they came, the tears dry up and what's

left in her eyes is rage. "Why didn't you tell me it was Tristen Portlan?

Why?" she nearly yells. I can't tell if her anger is solely directed at me

for not telling her who it was or angry at who the person is.

"Harper, I didn't— I don't know. Okay? I don't know why I

didn't tell you," I say. It's the truth. I don't know why I kept his name

from her. Maybe telling her his name would have made it more real. I

don't know. All I know is that it was stupid—either stupid to tell her

or stupid not to tell her. Keeping secrets for so long has made me lie to

people I care about.

You're such a hypocrite.

I can't even begin to deny that because I am a hypocrite. I

would be so angry if they lied to me like I have lied to them all these years. Not at them, but that they didn't trust me enough to help them through it.

Fuck.

"Harper, it wasn't that I didn't—"

"Trust us?" she snaps, cutting me off.

"Harper, it's more complicated than that," I say but then stop myself. Is it actually more complicated than that?

"We can address your lack of trust in those you call friends later," she says harshly.

Ouch. That hurt.

"Mazelynn, Loen saw the way Tristen has been watching you during training, and he snapped. I guess Bex pulled him aside and explained it all to him. The moment Bex told him what Tristen did to you and to Bex, he saw red." She pauses. I can see the anger leaving her eyes, and what's left is pity. I hate that look. Don't pity me because I have had trauma. Everyone has at one point or the other, right?

"You know most of the story, Harper. I just didn't give you his name," I say and take a breath.

"No you kept info from me. You didn't tell me how bad it really was," she says, starting to choke up.

"Okay, I'm sorry. Harper, I didn't want to upset you. But if you want to know I will tell you," I say, waiting for her to indicate if she wants to know the details. Harper nods her head. "The rumors that he was assaulting women started a week after we got to the academy. It was hard to prove since the girls said it was a dream but felt real. Turns out, he used magic from witches indebted to his close friend, Daren the alpha of the Blackheart pack, to make it impossible for his victims to get away, defend themselves, or even speak."

"That's awful," she says.

"All I could do was feel every touch, his weight on me, and watch as he assaulted me. Not even my ma—" The tears I tried to keep at bay start falling down my cheek. I started crying at just the right time because I managed to cut myself off from revealing yet another secret part of my life. No one was supposed to find out. I kept it to myself. I had to.

The day he did that was the day I started losing control of the magic I was told never to show anyone. My adoptive mother knew what I was. She knew that as a Nova I would be killed the moment I was found out. Novas are born with glowing stars on their skin. I don't know for sure how other Novas look, but the stars on my skin are usually bright. I have a lot of them like a galaxy of stars all over my body.

Harper and I sit in silence for a while. We're both lost in our thoughts—mine on my past and the secrets I have hidden for so long. After Tristen assaulted me and the night terrors started, I started setting alarms to wake myself up before I accidentally revealed my magic to anyone if I lost control during a night terror. I feel bad I told Harper about the assault but didn't tell her who did it or how he managed to do it.

Oh, my gods.

The night terror at the gym. Loan said he saw one, but did he see the stars? I remember waking up screaming and terrified one night. Luckily, I'd noticed the glow and hid under the blanket. When I finally settled the glow of the stars I searched around the gym, and it didn't appear that anyone had seen it. Did I just not see him? Does Loen know I'm a Nova?

"What did Loen do to Tristen?" I demand as I think back to seeing him come home with blood all over him and busted-up knuckles. If he hurt Tristen, he handed his pack to Alpha Darren of Blackheart on a gold platter. Why did he risk his pack for me? I broke our bond. He should feel nothing toward me but anger.

"Luckily, he didn't kill him even though he probably wanted to. He tried to get him to confess to what he did during the academy, but Tristen wouldn't budge on the 'I didn't do anything' story," she says.

"Harper." I pause. I'm afraid to ask this next part to her. "Take me to where the council is holding Loen," I say but she doesn't move.

"I can't," she says, giving me an apologetic look.

"Please, Harper…. He's my…my mate," I say as I turn away from her, lowering my head and staring at my feet. "If I tell them that they will see it as justified," I say as I look to her again.

I expected to see her sweetheart shaped face with a hint of shock, but there was not an ounce of it. She isn't wide-eyed. Her jaw isn't hanging open in shock. No, this look is more knowing. Her eyes are full of understanding, and she gives me a soft but sad smile.

"You know that already, don't you?" I ask.

"I figured as much. I mean, you snapping at Serafina should have clued me in, but Mazzy, I was hoping you trusted me enough to keep your secret," she says. I give her a puzzled look, and she rolls her eyes at me and sighs. "Loen said he is risking a lot by trusting us, but that he had to try to protect you from the council. He knew you would want to go to the council, which is why you are with me at the moment. He is being transported out of the city, and he wants you unable to stop them," she says, looking around to see if any other cars are around before turning her eyes back to mine. "He told me if you revealed to them that he was your mate, it would put you in danger, and that's not something he was willing to risk."

"He's trying to protect me. After I broke the bond? After I pushed him away?" I ask, starting to ramble a little. Harper places her hand on my leg, causing me to freeze in my descent into panic.

"He didn't want the council hurting you. He wanted to keep you free and alive. He isn't willing to risk the only Nova in our world when he knows what a gift she is," she says, and my breath hitches as my heart feels like it's going to stop beating.

He knew. He has known for weeks. He told her. I don't even know what to say or do so I sit, not moving or saying a word. Frozen in place, the secret I have spent so long trying to hide is known to others, and now they are in danger too. More people I care about are going to die because of me.

I won't let that happen again!

"I'm not telling anyone, Mazzy. I love you more than anything and would *never* hand you over to anyone who would harm you," Harper says, rubbing her hand on my leg.

"But you—"

"But I what? Have a husband, a life, and a baby on the way? So, what? Your life matters to me—to us. Novas were meant to be gifts to our world, but our ancestors were morons. I'll help protect you no matter what the cost, as will Clay," she says, putting her other hand on mine and giving it a squeeze.

I can see she wants to hug me. Pushing her hands away, I adjust to I can give her a gentle hug. The moment I hug her, she starts to cry and squeeze me tighter.

They are willing to risk their lives for me. I knew they would. That is the reason I didn't tell them. I wasn't going to let anyone else risk their life for me.

Chapter 25: Falling Apart

Mazzy

Harper gets a text from Clay that it's clear to come back to the station.

It's nearly one in the morning when we drive back. Harper is

exhausted, so I drive back for her. It's the least I can do at this

point. My phone goes off, and I glance at the notification as we are

reaching the city line. I take a quick glance at it to see a text

notification.

Message from Verena

Of course, I'm driving and not able to answer that message. *Nice timing V*, I think as I roll my eyes. Not wanting to wake up Harper, I drive the rest of the way to the station before looking at the message. Once I reach the station parking lot and park the SUV, I notice that Clay is outside waiting for us. He gives me a soft smile when he reaches the SUV door as I open it.

"Clay," I whisper as he gestures to me to get out of the SUV and takes my place in the driver's seat.

"It's your fault if I end up divorced, you know," he says in a joking tone.

"What's my fault?" I ask him, utterly confused. He glances over at his sleeping wife and then back at me with a huge smile on his face.

"One quick ride on your bike from the roller park to the station, and I spent the last hour browsing dealerships, trying to find a bike for myself. If Harper leaves my ass 'cause I get a bike, I'm blaming you," he says jokingly. He's trying to lighten the mood. It's not working, but I like that he's trying.

"Get her home, hot rod, and maybe, just maybe, I'll let you borrow the bike every now and then," I say as I start to turn toward the station. Clay slowly leaves the parking lot in the SUV, and I can't help but wonder who else inside the station knows.

I'm not even halfway up the steps of the station when I see Jayce and Zyon heading in my direction. They look utterly defeated. They come and stand on either side of me and escort me into the station. Their glum faces don't give me much hope for Loen or myself. As we enter the lobby, the station is not as quiet as it usually is this early in the morning. The chief is here, and he looks annoyed standing next to Loris's desk.

"Chief," Jayce says as we get closer to the desks. The chief looks at me and points to his office without saying a word. I understand what he is saying, *Go wait in my office.* I'm either in for a long talk, or he is about to tell me bad news. Either way, this isn't a talk I want to do right now. I nod and head down the hall to his office without looking back or saying a word to anyone.

Opening the door to the office, I'm met with a comforting smell. A scent I thought I wouldn't smell again—cinnamon. Knowing who it has to be, I rush into the office. Standing in the middle of the office is a chocolate-skinned, tall, beautiful woman with nearly white hair and crystal-white blue eyes.

"Verena," I say as I walk toward her hesitantly. I want to run to her, but I don't know if she wants to hug me as much as I want to hug her. Before I could reach her, she comes to me, and with no hesitation on her part, she grabs me, pulls me in, and hugs me tightly.

"I have missed you so much, Sister," she says as she squeezes me tighter.

"I have missed you too. I'm so sorr—"

"You have nothing to be sorry for, May. It wasn't your fault," she cuts me off, releasing me from her embrace. "Mom would be so beside herself if she knew you have spent the last ten years hating yourself for what happened to her."

She's right. The woman who took me in and raised me like I was her own flesh and blood would be angry at me for beating myself up over her death, but she died protecting me. How could I not feel guilty for that? I was stupid and got myself into trouble. I had just started shifting and wandered far from where we were staying and found myself face-to-face with a pack of large wolves. I wasn't raised by wolves, so I didn't fully understand why they were upset. I was only fifteen and scared.

"May, I swear if you keep beating yourself up over Mom, she's going to find a way out of the after realm and kick your butt," she jokes with a smile.

"I know. I know. I'm so happy you are here, Verena," I say, giving her another hug before backing away from her. It's been a good seven years since I saw her last, and this girl doesn't look like she's aged a day. "You look stunning as usual, Sis."

"Stop it. You look…exhausted," Verena says with a concerned look on her face. I give her my best *what the fuck* face.

"Nice way of saying I look like hell, V," I sass, but she's probably right. I feel like crap, so I doubt I look much better.

"I didn't say that now, did I?" she jokes. The chief walks into the room and closes the door behind him.

Oh boy, here it comes.

The chief passes us both and heads to his desk chair. After taking a seat, he looks at us both, and we are standing there waiting for him to say something.

"How is the kingdom doing these days?" he asks, addressing Verena. The chief is Verena's uncle, her mother's older half-brother.

"It's doing well, Archer. How is your lovely daughter?" she asks and gives me side-eye.

She doesn't get along with Serafina. They are close to the same age, and that bothers Serafina. Verena's issue is Serafina's princess attitude. She acts more stuck up than a literal fae queen, and that drives Verena nuts. For a fae queen, Verena is down to earth—very chill. Her style is elegant but isn't all fancy all the time.

Oh gods, Serafina.

I have been non-stop avoiding her and hardly talking to her for the last few weeks. It was never her fault. She wouldn't have slept with him if she knew. After the move to the hotel, I didn't make an effort to talk to her. Not even a text. I'm such a horrible friend. I need to talk to her. I'll text her later. She probably thinks I hate her.

Fuck.

After a few more small talk moments, we get into the lecture I expected, but it isn't on the topic I thought it was going to be on. I was expecting it to be about Loen, but it isn't. It is about us keeping our mother's secret, my secret, from him. It is a bit of a shock that he knows, but I guess Loen wasn't the only one who saw the night terrors.

Archer also noticed I seemed more tired and wasn't my normal take-down speed during sparring. When he realized the stars were starting to fade and then the moon was not showing up anymore, he grew concerned. He suspects the Novas are having their magic drained by something or someone. He thinks it's happening to me too. My magic is still connected to them, so I guess it would make sense.

I'm happy someone else noticed the stars leaving the sky, which means I'm not losing my mind. The stars are disappearing. While Archer has a right to be upset that we hid it from him, we were only doing what our mother had asked. Before I can say it Verena jumps in.

"Mother was told by the woman who brought Mazelynn to not tell anyone about her for her own safety," Verena says. "We are sorry, but we were only doing what we were told to do."

The look he is giving us is one of sadness and slight disappointment. I think he's upset because we didn't trust him enough to tell him even after nearly ten years. I'm happy to have Verena here with me right now. We both know we are in for a long lecture, and we deserve it.

***

I left the station feeling defeated, not only from Archer making Verena and me feel like crap for not trusting him with my secret but because that secret has been making me feel weak. Archer decided to cancel the rest of this session's combat seminar. Thirty-six days in, and it's now over.

"Can something please go right?" I ask the sky, but its dark empty response is all I get.

So that's a no?

I figured. Looking around Loen's parking lot, I notice that the twins' car is still there. Once in the elevator, I press the button for our…*his* floor. It's not my place; it's his. When the elevator doors open, I'm surprised by what I see at the end of the hall—moving boxes stacked by the door of Loen's apartment. My keyboard duffle and the rest of my stuff is tossed to the side. The duffle looks like it's been stepped on a few times. My heart sinks. I spent a lot of hours working at a crap coffee shop as a teen to save up for that keyboard. It's important to me. I go over to the duffle bag and unzip it slowly.

Please don't be broken.

My heart shatters when I open the bag and see inside that it's destroyed like they stepped on it a thousand times and then threw it down the hall. What the fuck is wrong with these guys? Why are they packing up their stuff? And why ruin my stuff?

I stand up and head into the apartment, hoping to see familiar faces to chew them out for ruining my stuff. I didn't think they were mad at me. They seemed sad for me. I'm met with three men who don't look familiar to me at all and then finally meet with a face that looks somewhat familiar. Fuck. So much for trying to avoid Alpha Dolton.

"Alpha Dolton, what's going on?" I ask him, and he turns to me.

"What are you doing here?" he snaps at me and that gets the attention of the other three in the room, who stop packing up the stuff and turn to us.

"I was coming to get my stuff. I was hoping—" I start to say.

"Hoping to do nothing. My son got arrested because he was thinking with his dick and not his head," Alpha Dolton snaps.

His tone is angry, and the little wolf inside me, still not used to being around alphas, can feel his alpha energy and wants nothing to do with challenging him. The one time I let myself shift and be around other shifters, I got attacked and then my mother died trying to protect me. I have refused to shift ever since then. Even though that side calls out to me all the time, I ignore it. My magic has always been stronger than the shifter side. The wolf side of me is shy.

Traumatized, dumb ass, not shy, and it's this man's fault. Don't forget that.

Trying not to let that thought take up too much space in my mind, I stand in front of Alpha Dolton not saying a word. Now that Loen is arrested, his father has regained the alpha role until the official ceremony when the alpha of Blackheart happens. Something tells me he isn't actually mad about that. His anger seems almost forced.

"I'm sorry, sir," I say, looking down to the floor. "I didn't mean to cause him trouble."

"Your stuff is in the hall. Can't promise nothing is broken," he says, giving me a dismissive wave. He knows something special to me is broken, and he doesn't give a shit.

"Sir" is all I manage to say as I turn and head back out of the apartment.

"No son of mine will ruin our bloodline by having a broken wolf as a mate," Loen's father says.

I'm not sure if it was to me or not, but it hurts. The girl I was a few weeks ago would be back in that room giving him a piece of my mind, but where there is usually a sassy, standing-up-for-myself mask, there is nothing. No mask, just me. All that's showing is the real vulnerable me that I try to hide from everyone—even myself.

The weak, pathetic, and broken Mazzy.

As I exit into the hall, I get hit with a dizzy feeling. I bring my hand to my head for a second. Shaking my head, I try to gather my thoughts and focus on what needs to be done. I need to get my shit and get the fuck out of here. I pick up some of my stuff, leaving my keyboard on the floor in the hall. There is no point in lugging a keyboard around that can't be fixed—or that I can't afford to fix at this point.

With the seminar shut down and being suspended from fieldwork, I won't be surprised if my pay is cut or Archer fires me for causing so much trouble. I head to the elevator and press the *L* for the lobby. As the doors shut, I can't help but feel like everything is going downhill fast, and I have no way to stop it.

Chapter 26: We Have to Fix This

Zyon

"This wasn't right, Jayce," I say to my twin as we sit in our father's black SUV. I can tell by the way he looks back at me that he agrees. Our father is blaming Mazzy for Loen getting arrested. It's not her fault. It's Loen's own fault.

He lost control of his alpha wolf the moment he heard his mate had been sexually assaulted at the police academy. I don't blame him, not one bit.

This SUV is so silent. I hate it. I keep looking from Jayce to my phone, hoping for a call or text from Loen or something to distract myself. This fucking sucks, and there's nothing we can do about it. Last night after Mazzy went to bed, Loen called us to his room and filled us in on things. Mazzy is his mate. He beat the shit out of Tristen who sexually assaulted Mazzy, Bex, and a few others during his time at the academy almost four years ago. How a human like Tristen has close enough connections with the Blackheart pack to blackmail witches into helping puzzles me.

Leon also explained that no matter what, Mazzy could not to talk to the council. She couldn't tell them he's her mate. We knew what he was going to tell the council. He made sure we agreed to back his story. The sole reason he nearly killed Tristen was because of what he did to Mazzy, that Leon was defending his mate, the mate who doesn't feel the bond because she is a broken wolf.

That's the story, and we were ordered, not asked, with his entire heart and soul to stick to the story, and we plan to do what he asked. Mazzy revealed to us that she's a broken wolf. As far as I knew, Loen thought she was human like we did until she told us that.

"None of this is right, Zyon," Jayce finally says, "but think about what Loen asked of us. We have to protect our luna."

Loen made two calls before he walked in to get himself arrested. One call was to our selfish father, and the other was to me. When we were little, we had code words for things so we could talk about them but not have our parents know. I chuckle to myself thinking about him using our old gibberish when he was talking to me. Whoever was around him probably thought he was a mental case.

"Loen wants us to keep her safe, but does that mean using our selfish father to break her heart more?" I ask, looking out the tinted SUV windows.

Jayce and I were shocked when Mazzy revealed to us that she was a broken wolf, but that was a lie. When Loen reluctantly revealed why we had to keep Mazzy from going to the council, we didn't hesitate to follow his plan. He told Harper, Clay, me, and Jayce her secret. It was clear he didn't want to, but he knew he needed help keeping our stubborn luna from turning herself in to protect him. Her secret is now on us to protect. The council will not find out about the Nova not on our watch. Our brother trusted us.

"I hate it too," he says hanging his head. This is too much. My phone goes off, and that's surprising to me since it's only four in the morning. Looking down, I frown and turn the phone to Jayce so he can see the notification.

Mazelynn:
I'm sorry, so sorry.
I should have stayed away from him like I originally planned.

"What do I say to her, Jayce?" I ask my twin while staring at the screen.

"I don't know. I really don't."

The phone goes off again, and this time I'm done not knowing what to say. I know Loen's plan was to have their father push her away from us so she wouldn't try to seek us out to help her get to him, but after that text, my brother can kiss my ass. Mazzy doesn't deserve this.

Mazelynn:

Tell Loen it wasn't his fault, it was mine.

If I would have pushed him away sooner this wouldn't have happened.

It's my fault, all mine!

She is blaming herself. She is not this Ice Queen everyone sees her as. She's a girl struggling in this world, struggling to belong, struggling to stay alive. It isn't fair that she's now blaming herself for this and who knows what else. Showing Jayce my phone, he is just as over this as I am.

"We are telling her," I say to Jayce and start to open the door of the SUV when he grabs my arm, causing me to pause.

"I agree, but…" Jayce says and sighs.

"But what?" I ask in an impatient tone. This is taking too long.

"Father," Jayce says, and we both sit back in our seats. We can't do anything or say anything with our father running things.

"We need to get Loen out. He's the only one who can stand up to Father," Jayce says, reaching for his phone.

"Who are you calling?" I ask slightly confused about what my twin has planned.

"An old friend," he says with a mischievous smirk. "We could use her magic."

I stare at my twin unsure at first what he is talking about, but then it hits me. Lacey. One of her specialties is mind manipulation. She hates using it, but depending on who he is thinking, this might be helpful.

"Lacey? You want to ask Lacey to help us," I say. It's not a question, but Jayce answers it like it was.

"Yes, if we can have her use her magic to trick the council to let Loen go—" he says

"We can get him out and fix the situation before the spell wears off," I say with a smile. My twin has his brilliant moments, and this is, for sure, one of them. "I'm texting Mazzy. We need her help."

"Agreed. They will take her call because of who her father is. So it's worth a shot," Jayce says. Clearly, we are both thinking the same thing. We are about to break our true alpha's orders and tell someone what's going on, but this needs to happen. Our father has screwed this pack over and over since Mother died, and now that Daren has challenged Loen, he is doing nothing. Unlocking my cell phone, I text Mazzy.

Me:
Hey, black SUV to your left.

I look out the window and see Mazzy walking out of the doors with her phone in her hand. She looks up to her left and sees the SUV. She doesn't look well. While she is normally on the pale side, she looks paler than normal. Dark circles are under her eyes, and her shoulders are slumped forward as she walks.

Mazelynn:
I'm not in the mood, Zyon.

Me:
Mazzy we are getting Loen out of jail but we need to tell you something first.
Please

Looking out the tinted windows again at Mazzy on the sidewalk, she glances from her phone to the sky for a moment, causing me to glance up through the moonroof. The sun is starting to rise, and the night sky is fading away. Where we would normally still see the moon, it's not there.

Huh, that's a little odd.

Mazzy walks over to the SUV slowly. She seems unsure. When she reaches it, Jayce opens the door and motions her to get in. She gives him a skeptical look at first, but maybe she's too tired to fight it. She tosses a couple small backpacks and her bike helmet on the floor of the SUV when she climbs in to sit next to Jayce. Without saying a word, I climb into the front seat and start the SUV. I look back at Jayce once more to make sure we are still on the same page. With a nod from him, I drive off.

An hour out of the city, we finally stop at a gas station. Mazzy hasn't spoken since we got in the SUV. She seems lost in her thoughts. As I head inside to pay for the gas, Jayce texts Lacey, and Mazzy sits in the SUV blankly staring at the floor by her feet. *Something is up with her.*

I scan through the gas station isles, looking for some decent snacks. We still have two more hours to drive before we reach our desired destination, and I'm starting to get hungry. I don't want to go back to that place, but Jayce and I both think it's the only safe—well, safe-ish—place we can go. Father won't go back to that place, or at least he hasn't in a long time. Grabbing the stuff I purchase off the counter, I thank the man at the register and head back to the SUV.

"I got snacks," I say to Jayce as I pass him and head to the driver's seat. He's standing outside the SUV, leaning against the passenger side door.

"Sweet, Lacey says she will do what I asked," he says with a smile. I want to punch that smile off his face. It's his fault Lacey moved away.

"That's great," I say in an annoyed tone. I don't like him talking about her.

"Yup, great," he says and gets back into the SUV, this time in the passenger seat.

"What are—" I start to say but he cuts me off.

"Quiet, dickhead," he whispers and points to the backseat. Mazzy is passed out, stretched out over the backseat. She was awake when I got out of the SUV, but she fell asleep fast. Looking back at Jayce, he nods for me to start driving.

"When did she fall asleep? I wasn't in there that long," I say softly and get into the driver's seat trying not to make too much noise.

"I'm not asleep," she says from the back seat. "I'm just resting my eyes."

Yeah, resting your eyes. Sure!

"Mazzy, we have a good two hours left of the drive. You look tired. Go back to sleep," Jayce says. Mazzy doesn't say anything in response, but we hear her breathing become slower as she falls back asleep.

This ride is boring, and I can only play spot the random out-of-stater plate game for so long before my brain tells me to drive the SUV off the next bridge. I always hated the drive to this place. Even from here, it seems like it's taking forever. Jayce is comfy in the passenger seat, and Mazzy is still asleep in the backseat. We'll be there in maybe another thirty minutes or so.

"Don't look so worried, Brother," Jayce says as he plays on his phone.

"I'm not," I say. It's a lie. I am worried.

"Lacey says she made the call already and used the spell. We have about four days to get everything situated before the spell wears off," Jayce says like it's no big deal. It is a big deal. We have been trying to fix this stupid Blackheart pack challenge situation for years. How does he think we will fix this one in four days?

"How did she cast a spell on all the council members over the phone?" I ask, amazed by her magic.

"Not sure, but all she said when I asked was that's why you don't give the fae your full name," he says with a smirk.

I forgot about that. Fae can bless or curse you with just your name. If it's your first name, they have to be near you, but if they have your full name, you're screwed. *Good job, Lacey*, I think and can't help but picture her face. She's so beautiful. I'm bummed I had to miss our date, but I'll make it up to her if we can get through this mess.

"If you two are done chit-chatting, can you fill me in?" a soft voice asks from the backseat. Shit. We woke Mazzy up.

"Sorry, Mazzy, we didn't mean to wake you up," Jayce says, turning to her.

"All good," she says, sitting up. She slept but looks as pale and tired as she did before she fell asleep. Something is off with her, and it's not good. She looks like she's getting sick or something.

"Hey, Mazzy, are you feeling okay?" I ask while checking back in the mirror.

"Yeah," she says unconvincingly. "I'm…I'm fine."

We all know what "I'm fine" means coming out of the mouth of a woman. She's not fine. She wants to avoid talking about it or is angry. I don't think she's mad. She looks exhausted and sad.

"We are almost there. If you want to go back to sleep, go for it," Jayce says, turning to face the front again.

"Thanks, I'm good," is all she says as she stares out the window. Jayce and I look at each other. Not wanting Mazzy to hear us, we speak to each other through the pack mind link that binds each member of our pack. We can use it as we want, but only if we are somewhat close to each other, like in the same city.

"Somethings wrong with her," Jayce says through the mind link.

"I know. She's not herself at all," I say.

"Should we tell her or wait? I mean if we don't tell her, we end up on her bad side. I don't want my ass handed to me by a five foot three assassin of a woman, but..." Jayce says.

"But she might not be well enough to handle the information. I get it," I say with uncertainty. I don't know what the right or wrong thing is. We both kind of sit there in silence as we think of what to do. We could use Mazzy's help, and I'm sure the rest of the Whitlock Police Department would help us but.

"If you two are done talking in secret, I would like to know what spell and what you two are up to," she says. I take a quick look back, and she's still staring out the window.

"We are getting Loen out with the help of magic and a spell that will last four days," Jayce admits.

"Four days to fix whatever cluster fuck of a mess you guys got yourselves into? Just perfect," she says and grabs her phone out of her pocket.

"Who are you messaging?" Jayce asks.

I hate that I can't focus on the conversation more, but I'm driving.

"No one you need to worry about right this second. We can finish this talk when we get to wherever you are taking me," she says, looking at her phone.

"Okay," Jayce and I say at the same time.

Looks like the rest of the ride is going to be an awkward one.

Chapter 27: The Light Is Dying

Mazzy

"Like hell, I'm going in there," I yell as I walk back to the SUV.

"Mazzy, please," Zyon pleads with me. If he knew what happened there, he would know why I am so against going inside.

"Mazelynn. My name is Mazelynn, you fucker," I yell and get in the SUV, slamming the door behind me. He lost permission to use my nickname.

Overreacting much?

Okay, I might be, but fuck, I don't want to be here. I never wanted to see this place again or be anywhere near it. I don't have the keys, I don't have a plan, and most of all, I don't want to be here. I can see Jayce and Zyon standing in front of this dark grey run-down cottage, and they are looking at each other with pure confusion.

Why here? How do they even know about this place?

I bring my knees to my chest as I sit in the passenger seat of the SUV watching them. I can't focus on anything else. If I do, the emotions I have been trying so hard to hold in will explode out of me, and who knows what magic will follow. I don't feel much of that magic right now. I feel so empty. *The cottage*, I think, *the cottage where my life changed forever.*

Tap, tap, tap.

Looking up, I see Jayce standing next to the door with his hand up to the window. Instead of opening the door, I check that it's locked and then flip him the middle finger. *Come on, V, answer my text will ya? I could use some help here*, I think.

"Mazzy, come on, we need to talk," Jayce says. He never had permission to use my nickname, so I glare at him.

"GO AWAY," I yell and bury my face in my arms. They had been trying to get me into that cottage for the last thirty minutes or so. I'm not going in. I don't even want to be near it. Still sitting with my face in my arms, I can hear Jayce checking each door handle and growling after finding them all locked.

"Fuck it," he yells, followed by a loud smash. It takes me a few seconds to realize what he just did. That crazy fucker broke a window.

Someone has a temper like his older brother.

"Mazzy, get your ass out of the SUV before I climb in there and drag you out," Jayce says, starting to climb his way through the broken back window. "Son of a bitch," he yells as he cuts himself on the glass. Blood fills the air in the SUV, and with how I'm feeling, it makes me sick to my stomach. I unlock the door and get out of the SUV.

"Fine," I say with a snarky tone. "Happy now?" I ask as I hop out of the SUV and walk toward the cottage.

"Yes," Jayce grumbles as he climbs out of the SUV and starts walking toward me. I take my eyes off him and focus ahead of me on Zyon and the building. I walk to Zyon who is now standing a few feet from the steps of the cottage. My stomach is in knots. Jayce walks up next to me and Zyon with a huff. As he goes to say something, all our phones chime with a notification.

Fuck. Talk about timing.

I know what this one is, so I'm not reaching for my phone. Instead, I'm standing frozen in place a few feet away from the entrance to a cottage that haunts my dreams. I didn't even see Zyon or Jayce pull their phones out, but they must have.

"What the fuck? Are you serious?" Zyon asks, catching my attention. I turn to him on my left.

"Sucks, huh?" I ask and turn to the cottage again.

"Why? Mazzy, why would you do that?" Jayce asks with anger in his tone. The mass text went out to everyone involved with the combat seminar.

Chief Archer Whitlock:

Attention everyone, as of this morning the combat seminar is cancelled. An instructor will be contacting all of the participants with future seminar dates.

Well, this is going to go over well. My phone starts chiming over and over as new texts come through from the participants and their chiefs. I roll my eyes and take my phone out of my pocket. I flip the side switch to silence the notifications. I'm not dealing with this right now. Putting my phone back in my pocket, I turn to Jayce and Zyon. It wasn't my choice to shut it down. It was the chief's, and I'm sure I'm removed from the future seminars at this point.

"So how are you getting your brother out?" I ask, crossing my arms and hoping they take this attempt at changing the subject and run with it. I don't feel like talking about the stupid combat seminar.

"He should be released by them soon, I hope," Jayce says, turning to Zyon. "Mazzy, we need to fill you in on what's happening. We could use some help."

"Then start talking," I say as I turn back to the cottage, but I start to feel dizzy again. My vision starts to go black, and I feel myself falling. The last thing I hear before everything goes black is Zyon.

"JAYCE!"

***

A bright light floods my eyes. I open them but I'm not in the cottage. I'm nowhere. I look around confused.

"Hello?" I say into the darkness surrounding me. "Is anyone there?"

I stand and take a few steps forward but stop, realizing I'm surrounded by nothing. It's like a black void. Where there should be light and life, there's nothingness. My heart breaks, and I feel a rush of emotions. But unlike before, not a single star shows up on my skin— no tingle or an ounce of magic coursing through my body.

"The light is dying."

Chapter 28: Together Again

Zyon

"JAYCE," I scream as I run to try and catch Mazzy. I reach her,

holding her in my arms. I'm a little shocked when I see faintly glowing

stars all over her skin, but they are fading so fast. She looks flushed

like she has a fever, so I place the back of my hand on her forehead.

She's burning up. I carry her into the cottage.

If I remember correctly, this place is practically empty with maybe a table and a few chairs. Loen had this place cleared out a while back, but I'm hoping maybe there are a few blankets in there or something to set her on other than the nasty floor.

"Give me your phone," Jayce says walking in close behind me.

"Back pocket." I stop walking so he can get it. He starts to read something on my phone and then glares at me.

"What?" I ask while looking around the living room area of the cottage.

"Lacey. You made plans to see Lacey?" he asks, and I can hear the jealousy in his tone. "How long have you been talking to her behind my back?"

"Not now, Jayce," I snap, still trying to find somewhere to put Mazzy down. I'll have to rest her on the floor.

Shit. Focus, Zyon. Mazzy first, angry twin brother second.

As I bend to put her on the floor, a knock on the cottage door catches our attention. I stand back up with Mazzy in my arms. I'm not putting her down yet. If this is trouble, I'll run with her. Jayce seems to be on the same thought path and heads to the door, nodding at me before opening it. When the door opens, we are both frozen in shock, and neither of us moves or says anything.

"Is she okay?" the female at the door asks as she comes into the cottage.

"She's hot," Jayce says, but as if he realizes that sounds weird, he waves his hands apologetically and corrects himself. "She's burning up. Can we help you?" He sounds panicked. That's new for my brother.

Sensing she isn't here to harm us or Mazzy, I set Mazzy down on the floor. Taking my shirt off and folding it like a pillow, I place it under her head. As I stand, the woman is right next to me.

"She's my…" she starts to say, but her voice cracks as she holds back tears. "She's my sister," the woman says as she lowers herself to the ground by Mazzy. I glance at Jayce, who is likely giving me the same expression I'm giving him.

Sister? How are they sisters?

The only thing they have in common is that their hair is light-colored. Mazzy's hair is silver-white, and this woman is whiter with a hint of blue.

"To answer the question, you two are likely asking yourselves, my mother adopted Mazzy when she was a few days old," she says like she knows what we were both thinking.

"Sorry, Miss, we just, umm… You two are so different, and she doesn't talk about a sister," I say.

The woman has now moved so she has Mazzy's head on her lap, and she is stroking her hair by her face. I can see she cares deeply for Mazzy, but there is something else. She her eyes are welling with tears as she looks at Mazzy on the floor.

"My name is Verena, Queen of the Sagewood Fae. Mazelynn is my sister, not by blood but by choice," she says softly. "I should never have abandoned you, Mazzy." Tears run down her cheeks. "What happened?" Verena asks us after a few minutes.

"We don't know." I explain the past few hours. "I saw stars on her skin, but they faded so fast. We think she is in dire need of help."

I'm not sure I should have told her about the stars, but something tells me Verena knows already.

"Stars? I don't understand," Verena says and looks down at Mazzy. Shit. Did she not know about the stars? Or that Mazzy is a Nova. Did I fuck up again?

"Why would her light be dying so quickly," she says as she smooths the hair on Mazzy's head.

"You knew about her?" Jayce asks.

"Yes, of course, I did. We were raised together in Sagewood until we were fifteen years old. When our mother was killed less than twenty feet from this cottage by the man who lived here," she says and looks at us like she knows who we are. "Your father."

"We didn't—" Jayce and I say at the same time then stop ourselves.

"I know" is all she says, focusing back on Mazzy. Jayce and I take a seat at the only table and chairs left in the cottage. I kind of wish we left stuff in here, but none of us had plans on coming back here— ever. Jayce takes his phone out.

"What are you doing?" I ask him.

"Texting Bex," he says. I give Jayce a look. I'm not sure why he wants to text Bex now.

"I need her to get a hold of her friend in the Blackheart pack."

"Dude, if you tell her about Mazzy, Loen is going to kill you," I say.

"So let him," Verena says. "My sister is dying, and I can't help her. If you think telling this girl about her will help me save my sister then he can take that up with me," she says in a demanding tone like that of a protective sister.

"On it," Jayce says and sends the message to Bex. I completely forgot Bex has a friend in the Blackheart pack. Bex was from Blackheart until she graduated from the academy and pushed to be assigned anywhere else. She doesn't agree with anything the current alpha is trying to do, and like everyone else, she thinks most of the Blackhearts are idiots.

We don't say much. We sit in the cottage, waiting for something to happen—for the council to show at the cottage door or for Mazzy to wake up. As the silence starts to become too much,

Jayce's phone pings with a notification. Jayce scoots close so I can see

the messages.

Bex:

It's a curse.

Me:

What do you mean by a curse?

Bex:

My friend is all about our history and goes through books like crazy, doesn't have much else to do, anyway, she is interested in a marking she saw somewhere as a kid and found in a book in the library.

That book was the prophecy of the moon goddess, the true moon goddess.

Me:

That prophecy is what?

that the soul of the moon goddess is trapped in the moon and has been for 100s of years?

Bex:

no, that she's likely on your floor fighting to stay alive.

Jayce, Mazzy is the moon goddess, she has to be.

Jayce and I look at each other in disbelief and that must have

gotten Verena's attention.

"What did she say?" she asks, still rubbing Mazzy's head in her lap.

"Bex thinks Mazzy is the soul of the moon goddess, and that she's—" I say.

"Cursed," she says and looks down at Mazzy, who is not doing well. "Ask her how to break the curse."

Does she think Mazzy is the moon goddess? Looking at each other again, Jayce messages Bex again, and we wait. It only takes a few minutes for his phone to go off again, this time with a photo message. Jayce reads the text out loud.

"Worried the god's plan to give a chosen soul the magic of the gods would lead to their destruction; the high council members of each tribe came together to find a solution. The high council members worked together with dark witches to make a curse for the soul chosen by the gods that would forever curse her. They named this soul the moon goddess. The soul was forever trapped in the moon never to walk the earthly plane for if she did and found her mate, their bond would drain her light leaving her soul to perish.

"The gods, not agreeing with what had been done to one of their children, cast down their curse to those who had a hand in banishing the soul to the moon. The fae who took part lost their mates, leaving them to never find their true love. The witches involved were cursed that only women in their line would carry magic and that magic would die over time as they partnered with humans. The wolf-shifters involved were cursed to give birth to children who were broken wolves unable to shift or unable to have children at all."

Jayce paused again and looked at Verena. She looked down at Mazzy and then back at us, tears starting to roll down her face. No fae has a mate anymore. That means almost all the fae realm high lords in our world were involved in banishing the moon soul.

"Continue, please," she says, knowing that part of her probably doesn't want this to continue.

Jayce looks back at her and tells her that's it. That's all the text says, and he messages Bex again. It's been a good twenty minutes. She has yet to text back, and we are getting worried. How long are we going to have to wait and hope Mazzy doesn't die? Jayce's phone suddenly goes off. He picks it up and his face shows pure shock.

"It's not Bex. It's…" he says and turns the screen to me.

"No way."

Chapter 29: We Must Save Her

Althea

The moment Bex texted, I went right to the library to find the text I told her about. She was so thankful, but a few moments later, she asked a question I have yet to learn the answer to.

Bex:
How do we save her?

Save who? The moon goddess? She's a myth from hundreds of years ago, but Bex is asking like she's a real person who she knows and cares about. I text her.

> **Me:**
>
> **I don't know the book is 100s of years old**
> **and she's a myth, not a real person**

Bex:

She's real. She's my friend and she's dying.

> **Me:**
>
> **What are you talking about?**

Bex:

My friend from work, she's a Nova.

Not just any Nova

We think she's the moon soul that our stupid ancestors cursed.

> **Me:**
>
> **you're kidding, why do you think that?**

Bex:

she met her mate, and now her lights are dying,

So is the sky, look outside.

I walk to the window of the library and confirm what she has said. The sky is black, solid black, not a star in the sky for miles.

Oh gods.

I rush to the section where I found that book and start searching. If the moon goddess is real and she's dying, I'll do what I can to save her. At least she could live a life with her mate and be free. Trying not to get stuck in my own struggles, I start throwing books that don't fit what I'm looking for. I usually take care of the books but not right now. I toss a book to the side again, and I hear a loud thud followed by "Ouch."

Oh, shit. Please don't be who I think it is.

As I turn around slowly, it's not Daren. It's Soren, my bodyguard. The man trusted by my alpha Daren to keep me locked away in this stupid house.

"Sorry, Soren. I didn't know you were standing there," I say and turn back to the books.

"You're in a hurry," he says and tosses the book on the table next to him.

"Yes, I'm looking up something for Bex. Is that okay with you?" I ask, knowing it should be fine with him. Bex is his little sister after all. That's the only reason I can message her without him telling

Daren. Soren climbs up on the ladder behind me and gets a little too close. Good gods, this man smells like heaven.

"Do you mind?" I say with a sarcastic tone. He needs to back up. I have a hard time being around this man as it is because he looks like a fucking god, but now, he's so close. His scent is invading my nose, and I want more. I don't have a mate, not one that would accept me.

"Not one bit," he says in a gravely tone then backs off the ladder. "Do you need help, Thea?"

Looking down from the ladder, I don't know if I can fully trust him, but screw it, I need help looking for this book.

"Yeah, I'm looking for a book on breaking curses, black magic ones, strong ones," I say as I go back to searching the books. I can't waste time. I need to do this fast. Leaning too far off the ladder in a rush to reach a book, my foot slips off the rung.

"Gotcha," Soren says, catching me in his strong arms.

"Thanks." I try not to make eye contact with him. "I need to keep looking for this book." I wiggle out of his arms and start back up the ladder, but he grabs my arm and turns me around.

"You mean a book like this one?" he asks a little too cocky as he holds up a black leather-bound book with the title *Breaking the Curse*. Snatching it from his hands, I smile at him while skimming through it hoping it has the answers.

"I hope it's the right—"

"Right here. Oh, my gods, it's right here," I interrupt him, practically screaming. I grab the phone and text Bex.

Me:
I found it. I think we can break it.

Bex:
text this number girl they need that info like now.
5556678

I recognize that number. It's my brother Jayce's number. I can't message him. I'm forbidden from reaching out to my family, or they will be killed. Seeing the panic on my face, Soren grabs the phone from my hand and walks away from me.

"Hey, give that back. I have to send a message," I say, trying to chase after him.

"Done," Soren says as he stops and tosses the phone back to me and smirks. "Can we get out of here before Daren wakes up from his sedated nap?"

"What?" I ask.

"He can't have what's not his. Now grab the books you need and your phone, and let's get you out of here," he says as he helps me grab a couple of books.

"Why are you doing this?" I ask.

All he says is that he can. I don't know what Soren did to Daren, but I'm not stopping to ask questions. We make our way through the town, and these people are morons. Half of them think I'm here willingly so none of them are even thinking twice that I'm out in the town right now. The biggest giveaway that I shouldn't be out here is that I'm not out here with Daren.

I have never left the house without him. He made sure that any time he showed off "his luna" he was holding onto me as tightly as he could. I can't wait to get out of here and away from that disgusting alpha. The goal is to reach the Blood River and walk downstream until we can find a safe place to hide. According to Soren, Daren will be out for a few hours, so we don't need to rush all that much. But we do want to get as much space between us and the Blackheart pack as we can.

We finally reach the Blood River, and now it's time for our feet to get wet. I hate wading through this river, knowing all the death that it saw and how much blood ran in its waters. Daren was over the peace of the agreement, so he staged a plan to cause trouble. He figured if he kidnapped me, my father or brothers would react, and they did—but not in the way he thought. So, what does Daren do to frame them? Kills his own man.

"Thea, this way," Soren says as he grabs my hand gently. We would shift into our wolves, but our scents are stronger in that form. We don't want to be found out. Neither of us grabbed extra clothes, and well, shifting means shifting back to a form with no clothes. I do not want Soren to see me naked. I set the phone to vibrate to sneak through the town. The vibration of a new notification in my pocket makes me jump a little.

"What is it?" Soren asks, looking around.

"My phone startled me, sorry," I say, letting go of his hand to get my phone out. It's a text back from Jayce. Soren looks at me confused. I show him the phone.

"That doesn't help me much, Thea," he says.

"The cottage on the opposite side of our territory, bordering the Fae Queen Verena's realm."

"Then we should head there. Let's go," he says as he grabs my hand again, and we start walking through the river again. I can't wait to get out of the water. My feet are starting to get cold. The phone goes off again.

Bex:
Tell my idiot brother to pick
you up and carry you, you'll probably move faster.

I turn and look around. How the heck does she know we are moving slowly? Then a small brown wolf catches my eye as it runs toward us. Tapping Soren on the arm, I point to the small wolf.

"Bex, you pain in the ass, I told you to stay back in the city," Soren says as the brown wolf jumps into the water near us. It tilts its head to the side and does a little playful dance.

"Good to see you too, Bex," I say. She drops her phone from her mouth into my hand. "That's one way to make sure you don't lose your phone in a shift." I laugh. This girl is a goofball, but I love her.

***

Safe and sound in a warm cottage with two of my brothers, the man who saved me, his sister, and two women I have not seen before. I couldn't be happier to be out and away from Daren. My brothers look so different. It's been almost five years, and they have changed so much. I ask about Loen, but they refuse to talk about him.

My brothers hug me for so long when I walk into the cabin, I swear they won't want to let go. Soren helps me with the books I managed to bring with us, and we start reading more about the moon goddess and the curse.

The silver-haired girl on the floor looks ill. She is so pale, and her breathing slower then it probably should be. Zyon told me her name is Mazelynn, and she's a badass fighter for the police department. I hope I can help her. I don't want to see someone die again.

"Are you going to keep avoiding telling me about Loen or are one of you two blockheads going to tell me where our older brother is?" I say and look up through my eyelashes at them. I may be younger than them by like ten minutes, but I'm that doesn't mean they can treat me like a baby. We are triplets after all. They just so happen to be the identical twins of our triplet trio.

"Loen has been arrested for beating the ever-living piss out of a rapist human associated with Daren," Jayce says, and Zyon slaps the back of his head with his hand. "What? It's true"

"Tristen," I say and look down at the book, not wanting to admit how I know about that. Out of the corner of my eye, I check to see if Bex heard me say his name. Bex says she has no memory of

Tristen harming her, but she flinches when someone touches her. And if you say his name, she will shiver. She has the same reaction the other girls have.

"Here is something," Soren says and slides the book over to me.

"*Breaking a curse that is done by many takes many.* That's not super helpful," I say and put my head down on the book. I don't know what to do, and I'm exhausted. Jayce's phone starts to ring, and he grabs it.

"It's Father," he says and answers it.

I roll my eyes. Our father isn't the best dad. His idea of dealing with my kidnapping was to do nothing and let my brothers handle it. I can't help but feel like he is doing that again now.

"Father, you have to listen to me," Jayce tries to say, but I can tell Father cut him off again. He won't let Jayce get a word in, and from the way Jaycees face starts contorting, he's getting angry. His brows furrow, eyes darken, and his jaw clenched. I keep reading the book and wait for the phone call to end when a loud knock scares us all. No one knows we are here. My first thought is they followed our scent. It's Daren coming to take me back.

I won't go back.

Chapter 30: Bring Her Back to Me

Loen

"Open the fucking door," I yell as I bang on the door harder this time. They better open this door before I break it down. Before I pound on the door again, it swings open, and I'm face-to-face with someone I wasn't expecting.

"Loen," she says excitedly and rushes to me, giving me a big hug. I embrace her and thank the gods that she's okay.

"Althea, gods, I'm so happy you're okay, Little Sister," I say and let go of her. "How did you get away from Daren?" I ask as we head into the cottage, but the moment I see what's inside the cottage, I don't care what her answer is.

That might seem cold, but the moment my eyes see Mazzy on the floor with her head resting in the lap of a dark-skinned nearly white-haired fae female, my happiness is shattered. I rush over to Mazzy and drop to the floor by her side.

"What happened?" I ask, and everyone is silent. I turn to my brothers, and they look down. "I asked what happened. Now one of you two answer me," I snap and turn back to Mazzy. "Please," I whisper.

They are not the ones who come up behind me. Althea is. She touches my shoulder and drops down next to me.

"She's, umm…the light she has is dying, Loen," she says softly. "We are looking for ways to help her, I promise, but I'm not sure we will find it in time," she says and stands. I want to hold Mazzy. I want to wrap my arms around her and hold her until she wakes up.

"Hey, can you hold her for a little while?" the fae female asks and gives me a kind look as I reach for Mazzy. "She needs you right now," she says as she watches me lift Mazzy up and into my arms. I sit down and cradle her in my lap. The fae runs her hand over the side of Mazzy's face before walking to a table nearby. Two people are sitting at the table, a male I do not recognize and a small female, Bex. The fae grabs a book and starts flipping through it but keeps looking back at Mazzy in my lap.

"Her name is Verena," Zyon says. He must have noticed me staring at her.

"Verena, as in the fae queen of the realm nearby, Sagewood?" I ask, and he nods. I heard about her. She's a very kind ruler and doesn't like her subjects to play nasty fae tricks on people.

"She's Mazzy's sister," Jayce says, and I look at him confused. "Well, sort of. Verena's mom raised Mazzy until... What did you say, Verena? You guys were fifteen."

Verena nods her head and goes back to looking through the book in her hands. I don't care for this cottage. It was Father's favorite place to take our mother until she died. Then this place became somewhere to beat his rules into our heads. Mother was the only thing standing between us and him.

One particular event sticks out in my mind as I'm sure it does with my siblings. I was seventeen, I think, when Dad took us all out here. There were reports of fae tricking our perimeter patrol, and he was over their games. We were here for a few days with nothing happening, but one night, I went out for a run in wolf form. I wanted to get away from my father and his drunk lecture.

I ran into a snow-white wolf with amazing blue eyes. I could tell she was only a couple years younger than I was at the time. She was surprised to see another wolf at first, but she wasn't threatening me or anything. She came closer. We were just a few feet away from the cottage. I should have done something more to push her away.

I heard Father and the rest of the wolves he brought with him coming out of the cottage. I tried to push the little wolf away, but she wasn't sure why and kind of froze in place. I could hear some fae laughing as my father and his wolves surrounded her. I tried to talk to my father and tell him not to hurt her. She wasn't acting like a typical shifter. She seemed confused, but he wasn't listening and blocked me from mind-linking with him. Like usual, he had his men start going after her, and she could hardly defend herself.

After a few good bites, the little white wolf was now bloodstained and lying on the ground. I wanted no part in hurting her, so I turned my back on them only for my father to grab me by the neck and force me to stay. I remember the fae's laughter stopped, and an older fae woman came in the little wolf's defense.

The little wolf was able to run off, and I thought it was over. But it wasn't. My father said she crossed the territory border, and because she clearly had the intent to hurt us, he ordered the wolves to attack the fae women. I ran back into the cottage when the attack on the fae women started but got a beating for it later in front of my siblings. It was not one of my proudest moments. I was a scared child, and instead of helping to protect the white wolf or the fae who defended her, I ran away.

"My mother told me not to hold what happened to her against you or your siblings," Verena says. I look up at her. "My mother…our mother," she says, nodding to Mazzy before looking back at me. "Our mother wasn't dead when your father and the wolves left her in the woods just outside the cottage. She managed to walk a little way into the woods. Mazzy and I found her and held her hands as she died. One thing she said before she died was one day, I would run into the children of the man who ordered the wolves to attack and that I would not hold anything against the four of you," she says as she walks toward us again.

"My mother knew Mazzy meant something to you, Loen," she says as she sits on the ground in front of me and Mazzy. She reaches her hand to Mazzy's face and moves a strand of silver-white hair from her face. "Wake up, little wolf. Please, wake up."

I can see she's trying hard to hold herself together. The fact that she is here in this cottage and not trying to harm us because of what our father did shows how much she loved her mother and took what she said to heart.

While sitting on the floor, Verena and Althea take turns giving me their theories on what's killing Mazzy. They think she is the moon soul, the one our ancestors cursed. I have a hard time fully believing it. While I see where things kind of fit, there are a few details that don't add up though.

The soul trapped in the moon by dark magic is supposed to have a clear marking of the moon somewhere. Mazzy, as far as I can see, doesn't have a moon marking anywhere. I could see a lot of her body in that tiny black dress she'd wore to sing at the bar a few nights ago. Novas are known for the stars on their body like Mazzy has, but she doesn't have the moon. She has way more stars than the books say a Nova should have, but maybe the books were wrong.

The other difference is the book says the mate to the moon goddess would also have a moon birthmark or something along those lines. The gods gifted the mate of the moon goddess his own magic in an attempt to help break the curse. I definitely don't have any magic or a moon-like birthmark. I want to be hopeful, but I can't help but feel like they are wasting their time looking for a way to break a curse on Mazzy that she doesn't have.

Althea and Soren search the books while Verena and I sit with Mazzy hoping every minute she will wake up. I can see how much this is killing Verena and suggest that she get some rest, but she isn't having it and refuses. Even though they are not blood sisters, she loves Mazzy.

"*HERE*! it's here," Althea screams from across the room, practically leaping into the air. "We found something, but I'm not sure I can read it," Althea says, walking the book over to us.

I'm filled with hope for those few moments, but the moment she bends down and shows us the book, that hope is shattered into pieces like a glass vase hitting the floor. The page is hard to read, like nearly impossible. The smeared words are unreadable. It looks like someone spilled something on it or attempted to intentionally make it hard to read so no one could ever break the curse.

Fuck.

"I'll keep looking for you, Loen. I promise I'll find something. There has to be more than one book with that information in it," Althea says with an apologetic expression before standing and walking back to the table where she starts going through the books again page by page.

Bex looks half asleep at the table, and Soren, the man who rescued my sister from Darren is practically pleading with Althea to take a break for a minute and get some rest. I guess he broke her out, and they traveled quite a ways.

I doubt they will find anything. I shouldn't think that way. I should have hope, but I don't feel much of it right now. This entire situation is chaotic, and watching the girl I have quickly grown to care for, to love, look like she's fading away is making that hope feel so misplaced. Maybe I should be hoping for her to be at peace. Maybe the gods realized that our ancestors were right to banish her soul to the moon, and this is their way of making sure the curse can't be broken.

NO, NO.

She's meant to be here, meant to be mine, meant for something greater than any of us could even begin to imagine. I know it. The light she has isn't meant to die. Not like this. Not right now. I will find a way to bring her back to me. I run my hand through her hair.

"I think I found something here," Soren says a few moments later, putting the book in front of Althea.

The look on my little sister's face as she's reading the page isn't giving away what he might have found. She is so focused. I bet I could yell the silliest sentence, and she wouldn't hear a word of it. She was like that as a kid, her head always in a book reading and learning everything she could about everything. I'm still holding Mazzy in my lap. Verena stands and walks over to the table. When she gets there, she lets out a huge sigh. That was not a good sign.

"She has to accept her fate," Verena says with a discouraged look on her face.

"What does that mean?" Jayce says as he looks around the room from his spot on the floor. He and Zyon are sitting near the table on the floor. They gave up chairs to Verena and Althea.

"No clue," Verena says, looking at Althea.

"It's weird, Loen. The page looks similar to the other one like someone tried to destroy the words on the page. They wanted to hide how to break the curse, but this is clear as day—in a random spot on the page, in ink, like someone wrote it there after someone else tried to destroy it," Althea says.

Can we catch a break? Is that too much to ask for?

"Someone must have written it in there, but who and when? And what the hell does it mean to accept her fate?" Verena nearly yells as she slams her fists into the table. I feel her rage. This is frustrating.

"Hey," Zyon says as he stands up and walks to Verena and places a hand on her shoulder.

"Why don't you get some rest like Loen suggested? We will keep looking," he says, trying to push her away from the table slightly. She doesn't budge at first, but when he tries again, she lets him slowly walk her away from the table.

"I need to get a few things from my realm, and I need air. So…I guess I'll go do that now," she says, heading for the door and dragging her feet. She doesn't want to leave her sister, but I think taking a few minutes is a good idea. I should probably take my own advice and step outside for some fresh hair, but I can't leave Mazzy.

"If we find anything, we will fill you in as soon as you get back, promise," Althea says smiling at Verena and then turning back to the books.

That sister of mine. Even though she went through who knows how many years of being Darren's punching bag, she still has her kind heart. My sister has always been the first to give to anyone even if that meant losing out on something herself. She is our mother through and through. She even looks like her. I'm still skeptical about Mazzy being the moon goddess. I feel like we are looking for the answer in the wrong place.

Trust them.

I'm losing my mind. That sounded almost like my voice, but I wasn't thinking it. Something else or someone else was but in my head. I feel a tight tug in my chest and a warm sensation flows through my body. I normally only feel that warm sensation during a shift when the wolf side is taking over a bit. My wolf. That side of me must know to trust them and trust that this is the right path to be looking for the answers. Fine. I'll trust them, and I'll have to give it more time. Mazzy doesn't have forever. Every time I look at her still body in my lap, my heart breaks more.

"Please, wake up… Please, come back to me," I whisper to Mazzy. I stay on the floor with Mazzy in my lap and embrace her, rubbing her hair with my right hand. My left arm is supporting her neck and head. My hand is near her face, so every now and then, I rub my thumb across her soft cheek. I wish she would have let me in and not pushed me away.

Once she wakes, I won't let her push me away anymore, never again. I fell for her even without the pull of the bond. We are more than fated mates, we are soul bound mates. Our souls cannot be whole without others. Two souls forever bound to one another, no matter what lifetime.

I will not lose her. I can't lose her.

I understand why Verena needed to gather her thoughts, and I think her going back to her realm to get some supplies will help her and all of us. We could use some supplies like food and blankets. It might be summer, but it's windy tonight and this cottage is drafty. I figured she wouldn't be gone too long, so it didn't surprise me when she walked back in less than half an hour later. When she comes back, she has a handful of her fae subjects carrying pillows, blankets, and food with her. She insists two of her guards watch over the cottage for a little while. They will be back every hour or so to do a perimeter check until morning. I'm not about to argue with the fae queen, especially one rumored to be the strongest of the High Fae.

My brothers work together for once to make everyone something to eat with the food the fae brought. They did a good job, considering I'm the one who normally cooks all the meals. Their food is edible.

Bex, Verena, and Althea search the books over and over again, trying to find a way to break the curse. After eating, everyone tries to stay awake, but I tell them it's okay if they need to sleep. I'll stay awake with Mazzy. I couldn't sleep even if I tried. I'm not moving Mazzy to one of the bedrooms.

Hell, the only reason I put her down is because if I didn't eat something I would be useless if someone attacked us. The others decided to stick close to Mazzy, too. They all grabbed blankets and pillows and crashed on the floor in the living room like a giant sleepover party.

It doesn't take long for Althea, Bex, and Verena to fall asleep. They seem to all get along and are determined to help. They have been staring at books for who knows how long, so I'm not surprised they were the first ones asleep. Soren, Bex's older brother, is the next one to fall asleep. He seems like a decent guy, but the big brother in me doesn't like the way he's looking at my little sister. Althea doesn't seem to mind the way he looks at her. I think she likes it. He did rescue her, so he earned brownie points for that.

After helping us clean up the food and checking the perimeter with the fae who left after they returned, Soren took a spot on the floor next to Althea. Maybe they are mates. If my sister is safe and happy, that's all I care about.

The twins are the last to fall asleep, well, besides me, but I have no intention of sleeping. Sitting here in silence while everyone sleeps is going to drive me crazy. It is too quiet. Combine that with the sky looking like someone turned off the stars and moon like a dark TV screen, and it's giving psycho-killer movie vibes.

This cottage creaks with every gust of wind, making it even more creepy, and the memories this place bridging back are ones I never wanted to remember. I will never forgive myself or my father.

Every now and then, I scan the room. I don't need to because the fae queen has a few of her guards watching over us, but I can't help it. After scanning the room again, I focus back on Mazzy who is lying on a handful of blankets in front of me. I want to hold her, but I'm struggling to keep my wolf in control. Ever since I felt like it was that side of me telling me to trust them, I have been feeling a strong pull to shift. One I haven't felt since my first shift. It's intense, and the more I fight to keep control, the harder it pulls. I have been waiting, hoping she would show some sign of waking up, but there has been nothing— not even a whimper or eye flutter. I shift my weight around, so I can try to get comfortable. A small movement catches my eye.

"May?" I say softly. Leaning down to her, I could have sworn I saw her move a little, but maybe I'm seeing things. She's as still as she has been since I got to the cottage.

Need to shift.

Why can't I get control over this? This is getting ridiculous. I shouldn't be losing control over my wolf side. It's not like it's a real being of its own when it's normally more of an instinct. Right now, he feels like another being inside that is ripping away, trying to get free. Resting my eyes for a moment, I try not to focus on how I feel, but a sudden tightness causes me to grab my chest and gasp. I can't ignore this any longer. My wolf knows something I don't. I get the message.

Slowly standing, I take one last glance at Mazzy before walking down the hall into one of the bedrooms. I prefer to have something to change into when I shift back, so I take off my clothes and leave them on the floor.

I don't understand why there was such a pull from my wolf to shift, but now that I have let him out, I feel much better. The tightness in my chest is gone, and I feel relieved, which is odd given my mate is lying in the other room probably dying. Something white passes the window outside, catching my eye, and I'm hit with a strong scent of lilacs and strawberries.

May? Mazzy?

I pad quietly into the living room so I don't wake anyone. I don't need to go all the way in to see that the area I left Mazzy is now empty. She's gone. I hear a loud noise come from the back of the cottage.

The backdoor.

I turn and rush through the rest of the cottage heading to a back door. The door is swinging on its hinges every time the wind blows. It wasn't open earlier. I looked down the hall before shifting and the door was closed.

A blur of white catches my wolf's eye again a few feet ahead. Whatever it is, it's waiting. But the moment I start toward it, it takes off through the woods, and my wolf instinct kicks in, wanting to run after it. So, we do.

As I rush through the forest in my wolf form after what I'm assuming is a ghost, a thought keeps popping into my head. What does the book mean by accepting her fate? How can accepting her fate break a curse? Suddenly, I can finally see what is in front of me. A white wolf. Mazzy's scent is strong, and I know it's her. My mate.

She's awake, and now it's time to make her mine. I won't let her push me away. She must accept me the way I accept her. She's my fate, my mate, the other half of my soul. That's when it hits me. Accepting her fate. What if accepting her fate means accepting me as her mate?

Chapter 31: Awakened

Mazzy

I don't know what happened. I don't even know how I got in the woods or when I shifted. The last thing I remember is getting a text from the twins calling me over to their father's SUV and getting dizzy as I approached the car, then nothing but black. I woke up in my wolf form outside the cottage, a place I never wanted to come back to again. I knew I was close to Verena's realm, so I headed for the forest.

Something made me pause a moment before taking off into the trees, but it was only for a moment.

I'm happy I don't feel weak or dizzy anymore, but I also feel like I don't have full control over my own body. It's like the wolf instinct has more control somehow. As I'm running through the woods, I start to regain more sense of control over my body. Passing a weird-looking tree, I stop. This is the place, the tree where I met a young black wolf who I was instantly drawn to. I wanted to get to know him, but he was pushing me away.

I wish I understood why he was pushing me away back then. It would have changed things. I wouldn't have been attacked by his pack, and my mother wouldn't have had to protect me. She said not to worry and told me to run off to heal, so I did. But when Verena and I got back to the tree, we found our mother. The wolves had attacked her, and she was dying.

Why the hell am I back here? Why did you take me back here? I want to yell at the sky. Looking up, I'm reminded that the sky is dead, the gods everyone asks for help from, and the lights of the

Novas are gone. The moon, the one thing in the world that made me feel at peace and strong, is gone.

I consider lying down for a moment, but out of the corner of my eye, I catch something large coming my way. I take off running. It doesn't take long for the giant thing chasing me to catch up. I'm taken down by it in a matter of seconds.

I always hated trying to fight in wolf form. I'm so clumsy. It's not natural to me, but I'm sure if I had actually spent time practicing and being in this form more I would have gotten better. I refused to shift after my mother was killed because my shift and wandering from home were what got her killed in the first place. I realize what took me down. It's a large black-as-night wolf, reacting instinctively we scramble a bit.

Something smells good.

A deep growl pulls me from my thoughts and back into reality. I go to snap at the legs of the wolf pinning me, and I'm hit with a scent that instantly calms me. I don't like that I'm pinned down, so even though I know this is Loen, I can't help but try a bite to get free. He will hopefully understand. I get lucky and manage to get a good bite into the wolf's front left leg, but I instantly feel strong jaws and sharp teeth latching onto the back of my neck just behind my ears. Letting go of my neck, the large wolf stands there not moving.

I'm small but not small enough to slip out from under him. It smells like Loen, so I'm not afraid this wolf is going to hurt me. The pull to this wolf is like what I felt for Loen before I broke our bond. Did the bond repair itself somehow or am I losing my mind?

I have to admit I'm impressed with the size of this wolf. It's huge. I may be a somewhat small female, but for a male, he is probably the biggest I have ever seen. He has removed his teeth from around my neck, but I still have no desire to move out from under him. It's like I'm frozen, waiting for him to either walk away or permit me to move.

That was a dick alpha move.

I landed a little funny with one of my paws starting to feel weird, so I need to adjust, slightly trying to shift my weight. Risking the move when he didn't give me a sign it was okay might not be good, but I'm uncomfortable. I shift a little turning my wolf hips a tad. I don't think he realizes I'm in an odd position because as I shift my weight to relieve some of the discomfort in my paw, he drops his weight on me.

"OUCH, you Fucker! You know you're like twice my size," I think. He can't hear me, but I wish he could cause he's practically crushing me.

"I know."

"Wait. What?"

He shouldn't be able to hear me, but that was his voice in my head. Well, at least I can tell him to get off me now.

"Loen, you prick, get the fuck off me."

His wolf lets out a sound I can only compare to a cocky laugh. *Is he laughing at me?*

"You're a dick. Get off," I say through our mysterious mind link. This has to be the gods doing.

"Okay, Princess, only if you promise not to run away again," he says. I need to get away from him. I have to stay away. We can't be

together. It's dangerous for him and more so for the innocent shifters in his pack. As much as I want to let myself be with him, I just can't.

A deep growl leaves the back of the black wolf's throat as he nips at my ear teasing me, then moves his body off mine. Still not daring to get up, I wait to see what Loen is going to do. Tilting my head to the side while still lying down, I make eye contact with him. He is now sitting close by waiting.

Letting out a deep breath and shaking my head, I adjust myself as I start to shift back into my human form. It's been a while so it's a little uncomfortable, but nothing like the first shift. One downside to shifting… I'm now completely naked with no extra clothes to cover myself. I try to hide my body with my hair and arms the best I can. *Please don't stare at me.*

I'm sitting on my knees with my arms covering my chest, keeping my head down and letting my hair hide most of my naked body. He knows what Tristen did and that makes me feel ashamed even though I don't have anything to be ashamed of. I had no way of stopping Tristen once the witch's poison took hold of my body.

But the thought of him knowing the truth about that and that I'm a Nova scares me. I sit in silence as I keep my focus on the ground, but a strong hand gently grips my chin, tiling my gaze to his. Loen's amber eyes are seeing right into mine. I try lowering my head more. I want to hide, but his strong hand stops me, gently tightening the grasp on my chin.

"Don't."

Loen gently tilts my face up so my eyes catch his eyes again. With his other hand, Loen moves my hair from my face and tucks it behind my ear. The thumb on the hand holding my chin grazes over my lower lip so softly.

"Loen, please go," I whisper barely loud enough. I almost think I thought it instead. Loen shakes his head for a second then squeezes my chin a little harder.

"Mazelynn, no matter how hard you try, you can't push me away," he says in a deep voice.

The bond might have broken, but it's like the broken fated mate bond woke something else up. The other half of a soul divided.

He is my other half. How can I keep pushing him away when all my soul wants is him?

Accept your fate!

"This can't happen. We can't happen, Loen," I whisper, contradicting my thoughts. My instincts tell me to accept him. I'm trying to turn my head away from him, but he stops me.

"May, I'm in love with you. The moment that bond broke, I felt something different. Like you woke up a side of me that was hidden. A part of my soul that was missing. You. You feel like home," he whispers as his face gets closer to mine. "May, until the last star in the galaxy dies, you have me," he says as his lips crash into mine.

We lose ourselves in the kiss. I don't want it to stop, but he pulls away, allowing me to catch my breath.

"All of me, Princess," he says, looking into my eyes.

Just like that, I'm done for. I'm a puddle for this man, and even with his cocky attitude, at times he can look at me like he sees the real me. He said it perfectly when the bond broke. As much as I wanted to be away from him, I couldn't, and when I was away from him, I felt like a part of me was missing. He gives me the same feeling the moon does when I look at it. I feel whole again, at peace and strong. He leans in, his lips lightly touching mine.

"Please," I say in a whisper.

Like he knows the real meaning behind that, Loen's lips crash into mine again, and the entire world just melts away. All I can focus on is how his lips feel against mine. The kiss starts gently, but there is a fire growing. The kiss deepens until we pull away from each other, gasping for air. At that moment, the hand on my back trails down to my lower back. A shiver runs up my spine, causing me to arch my back.

Before a sound can come out of my mouth, he uses the hand cupping the back of my neck to pull me back to him. His lips are back on mine, catching the soft moan in his mouth. Instead of picking me up, he lowers us both to the ground. He positions himself under me so I'm straddling him. The hand on my jaw is now slightly gripping the hair at the base of my head. He pulls away from the kiss, allowing me to catch my breath.

With a slight tug of my hair, I arch my back and tilt my chin to the black sky. Loen now has a clear view of everything. I close my eyes tightly. I'm overwhelmed with the sensations I'm feeling, trying hard not to think about the last person to see me naked—Tristen.

Like he knows I got lost in my head for a second, he grabs my hip with one hand and my jaw with the other. That pulls me back like he could feel the anxiety rising in me. Instead of grabbing my breasts like I'm sure he wants to, he kisses my jaw, moving a little lower. He's leaving a trail of kisses up and down my neck, nipping it a few times here and there.

"Loen," I moan. "Please, Loen." I get a response I wasn't fully expecting. Moving his hand back away from my hip, he runs his hand up the back of my neck lacing his fingers in my hair with a harder tug causing me to arch more pushing my chest into his.

"Words, Princess. I need you to use your words," he says in a deep voice against my neck as he nips and kisses it again.

"I need you, Loen," I moan, and I can't believe the words I'm saying, but I realize I want this. No, I need this. I need him, and the closer we get, the more whole I feel.

The kisses stop, and his hand leaves my hip and hair. The only parts of him touching me are his legs undermine. In case he didn't hear me, I lower my head when suddenly he embraces and lowers me onto my back on the ground. Loen is now on top of me with the tip of his length at my opening. He is waiting for something.

His hands are roaming my body, and I'm so lost in the feeling. I reach my hand up by his jaw and pull his mouth to mine, making it clear he has my permission. His mouth leaves mine.

"I'm yours. Claim me," I tell him, and he pauses for a second to look into my eyes.

"Good girl," he says in a gravelly voice before his mouth crashes into mine again. Every second, it grows deeper in passion. He releases my mouth and kisses my neck again.

As he starts to enter me, I feel his teeth sink into a spot on my neck. I'm so overwhelmed with sensations that I let out a sound that sounds like a scream and moan. He pulls his teeth from my neck and licks at the mark he left. His body has stilled.

"Are you okay, Princess?" he asks in a deep gravelly voice that makes my core heat.

"Yes," I breathe out. He's larger than my little buzzy friend, so it takes me a second to adjust to the size of him.

Kissing me again, he starts moving in and out slowly at first. I'm consumed in this moment, his body on mine, and how every move he makes my body feel so much pleasure. Every time he moves his hand along my body, I tingle.

Loen starts kissing me again as he pumps in and out of me at a slowly increasing rate. One of his hands is now on my breast, playing with my nipple. He kisses me as he gives it a little squeeze, and I'm moaning into his mouth as I feel my body come undone under his. He pulls away from my mouth and whispers in my ear as he picks up speed with each thrust into my pussy.

"Mine."

"Don't stop," I moan and arch my back again. I may have just come, but I'm so close to coming again. "Loen," I moan as he brings his mouth to my ear and whispers deeply.

"Come for me." Those words send me over the edge as I shatter under him, but this time, he joins me. I feel his dick pulse inside me. His movements start to slow. Breathing heavily, we both look at each other for a moment. My eyes drift to his mouth, and I smile. This gets a handsome smirk from him before he kisses me again. He picks me up off the ground and back onto his lap without pulling away from the kiss. Once I'm straddling him again, he releases my mouth.

"It's your turn to mark me, Princess," he says while putting a strand of my hair behind my ear and tilting his head to the side giving me access to his neck.

Without thinking, I lean in and mark his neck like he just did. Licking the mark, I then move my mouth to his and kiss him. We both let out moans of pleasure. Releasing him from my kiss, he rakes his hands through my hair and down my body. His eyes do the same at first, but something has stopped his eyes from moving further down. His eyes are stuck on my chest. I mean, I know guys like tits but seriously.

"Loen?" I say with a questioning tone, not sure what has caused him to pause, but I get my answer not from him but from my own body.

A tingle has started in my chest, and I can see growing whitish-blue light reflecting off Loen's chest and face. I want to look down, but I can't. The energy makes me throw my head back, so my face is pointed to the sky. I see stars but not in the sky. They are in my eyes, and the light grows brighter and brighter until everything goes black. *What happened?*

***

What is going on?

I ask myself to look around. I'm surrounded by nothing but darkness. I take a few steps forward but then stop. There is no clear separation of the floor and walls. This is a literal black hole of a room. I can't tell if I'm outside or inside.

"Hello, is anyone there? Loen? Where are you?" I call out in the void.

"Welcome goddess," many voices say.

"What?" I ask still so confused.

Turning around, I try to see if I'm missing something, but there's nothing here but darkness as I spin around again. I hear the voices again—this time a little louder. The voices are coming from all directions.

"The moon goddess has awakened." It sounds like an entire stadium full of people talking at once.

Accepted your fate.

A glowing light grows brighter around me. Looking down, the glow is coming from me. There are three times as many stars on my skin as there normally are. I'm wearing a whitish-blue dress with sheer swoop straps. It's Greek goddess-looking. I have what looks like a moon necklace on, but after a second, I realize it's not a necklace. It's a glowing marking on my skin.

In the center of my chest below my collar bone is a glowing symbol. I recognize this symbol from the history books in school. A full moon is at its center just above, and below the full moon is another moon not as full, and then on top and bottom is a crescent moon. There are stars throughout this design. This is the moon goddess marking.

The one the history books said the moon goddess would display on her body, revealing her to the world.

This must have been what Loen was looking at.

"You accepted your fate. You have awakened your true self, Goddess," the voices all say.

***

Blinking my eyes, I wake up, feeling rather warm. I have no idea what that dream was, but what I do know is I have the moon goddess markings. I'm the soul those of this world tried to banish to the moon forever. How am I just now realizing who I am? Did my mother know?

Feeling around, I realize I'm very much naked, but I'm covered by something warm and fluffy. The floor under me is a little cold. It feels like stone. I can only assume we are in some kind of cave near the cottage. We were in the woods. Maybe Loen carried me to a nearby cave.

I open my eyes more, and all I see is black fur surrounding me. I try to move a little, but I'm being cocooned by a large sleeping black wolf. A wolf that is keeping me safe. He is wrapped around me as the night sky wraps around the moon.

"Loen," I think, trying to wake him without actually talking. He doesn't move. I feel different this morning. Like I have more energy and more magic flowing through me than I did even before all of this. I feel whole which is weird, but I don't feel like there's a part of me hiding or missing anymore. I remember something, not from a history book, but my adoptive mother's journal I found it after she died. There was a page with a similar symbol on the top of it and a note under it.

"The moon goddess will have to choose.

Accept fate or keep hidden,

Accepting her fate will free us all."

That note didn't make sense until now. I was never meant to choose the Novas, never meant to hide myself from this world. The gods knew how to break the curse. They found a way around the rules of the curse by giving that note to the woman who raised me like her own.

If I choose to keep myself hidden, thinking it's what's best for everyone and the Novas, I will doom my soul to the void, to be gone forever. The ancestors who banished my soul thought I would choose the Novas, and that would be the end of their rule—their way of life. The Novas would rule and see them as weaker beings.

Idiots.

I was always meant to pick my mate, to pick those of this world, to stay here, and to live a life. To make a change for the better for all of our species. I'm sure the gods want the Novas to walk this earth, but when they do, they want a soul here who could keep them in check. The ancestors had it all wrong. The Novas are not something to be feared. We are one of everything in this world connecting us to them all. All the magic hidden within every inch of my being is free, including the souls I am in charge of—the Novas.

Accepting my mate freed me, and it freed them too.

I smile at that thought, realizing I was wrong for pushing him away. Thinking I was doing what was best for him, but I was doing the opposite. I hope he truly does forgive me for trying to push him away.

"Okay, handsome, time to wake up," I say, and I shift into my white wolf under him. Even small, I manage to almost flip him over during the shift. He jumps up and gets into a defensive posture, and I lazily stretch like downward dog. I'm a dork, I know. This man sleeps like a rock. I couldn't wake him until I literally shifted into my wolf under him.

"About time you woke up. You were about to suffocate me," I joke through the bond.

He doesn't respond, but I can tell he wants to. His big bad black wolf head tilts to the side, and his eyes darken. I feel the urge to run not because he is going to hurt me but because I want him to chase me.

Turns out, I like to push his buttons, and he pushes mine. It's kind of fun. I wouldn't admit it before, but gosh, his face when he's trying not to smile is so handsome. It also helps that he looks hot as hell when he's trying to be all big and bad. I stand and start to pad to the opening of the cave we apparently slept in last night. The sun is shining like a good morning for a nice run.

"Don't even think about it," Loen says.

"Think about what, Loen?" I joke and start slowly walking out of the cave.

"Princess," he warns.

Turning around so I can look at him, I tilt my head and let out a small growl. The wolf side of me desperately wants to play this game, and I'm tempted to let it.

"Princess, I'm warning you. Take it easy. You were just on death's doorstep not even twelve hours ago," he says, and I have no idea what he is talking about. I feel fine, fantastic even.

Then I remember I passed out walking to the cottage with his brothers. How long was I out for and what happened during that time? I stop at the mouth of the cave and wait for Loen to join me.

"We should head back to the cottage, May," Loen says through the mind link while he rubs his body against mine.

"I don't want to go back there," I admit. I don't like that place. I wish I had never found it.

"I tried to push you away, tried to tell you to leave, but you didn't understand. I should have tried harder to make you leave before they showed up, little wolf. I'm sorry," he says.

Oh gods.

He was the young black wolf I wanted to play with all those years ago? The one that drew me to that cottage in the woods in the first place. I felt drawn to him, and when I was finally near him, I felt safe. I wanted to be near him. He pushed me away, and I didn't get it then. But I do now. He was trying to protect me from his father because he knew he would harm me.

"I should have stopped him, May. I was young and too afraid of him," Loen says. I can tell he feels remorse for the attack. It wasn't his fault. It was his father's, but there's something I know that Loen doesn't. I have never held what happened to me or my mother against the young wolf. Hell, I didn't even hold it against his father, the one who ordered the attack. I blamed myself, always.

"I was a lone wolf pup trespassing. Even though I had no idea I was in the wrong. You were a kid. I don't blame you. Never have." I pause and turn to him, rubbing my head against his trying to show him

it's okay. *"I blame myself and always have. Loen, you ran inside while they attacked my mother. You didn't see the attack, did you?"* I ask. We start a slow track out of the cave, heading toward the cottage.

"No, I didn't," he admits.

"My mother cursed the firstborn son of your father to lose his wolf. He would have lost his ability to shift in an instant. You would have lost it, but you didn't," I hinted at him while we traveled down the tiny mountain. I'm shocked he carried me this far cause. We are high up on Sagepeak, the tallest mountain in the Sagewood Forest.

"That's impossible," he says, and his tone is defensive. I didn't mean to upset him.

"It's not Loen, not when your father cares only about himself," I say, trying to lessen the blow a little. He isn't going to like this one bit.

"Mazzy what are you saying?" he asks as he passes me in his wolf form turning and stops nose to nose with me. Not going to lie, I completely lost my train of thought when he did that. It's hard not to get distracted by the size of his wolf, and those fucking eyes. *"May"*

Shit, what were we talking about? Oh yeah…

"You have an older brother, Loen. One who was there in wolf form during the attack, but after that, lost it. Do you remember anyone like that during that trip?" I ask him, trying to let him come up with the name on his own.

Come on, Loen. It will tell you so much about what is happening with you and your pack. I could tell him, but I also don't want to be the one to reveal a horrible secret about his father.

"Only Daren Blackheart. He was supposed to be there working with my father on revising the peace treaty," he says.

Yes, finally.

Finally, he's got it. My mother told us about the curse before she died. It took Verena and me a few years to put the pieces together—well, as far as Loen not being the oldest child of Alpha Dolton. It took Tristen's assault on me to figure out it was Daren.

Want some tea? Tristen's father knew Daren was not Alpha Blackheart's child. He knew that Daren was a broken wolf conceived when Alpha Dolton kidnapped, drugged, and assaulted Daren's mother in an attempt to gain the territory by having her give birth to his child. The witches spelled the woman similar to the spell Tristen had them use on his victims.

Only after Daren was born did she remember, and that memory was why she took her own life. Alpha Blackheart took a new mate shortly after that, having another child, Soren Collins. He's a nice guy. He's Bex's brother. She talks so highly of him.

"DAREN, that son of a bitch," Loen says loudly in my head causing me to wince a little. *"Sorry, May, that was loud. I'm just— There is no way Daren is my half brother. If he is, that means he kidnapped my— No, his own half sister and forced her to be his mate. Fuck, I'm going to kill him."*

Loen is getting worked up. That isn't what I'd intended. It was bound to happen, but I need him to calm down. He doesn't realize what he is losing control of.

"LOEN, breathe, calm down," I try to say to him, but he isn't responding.

The once-sunlit forest around us is starting to look like a dark black fog has rolled through it, taking every inch of light and snuffing it out. The trees, grass, and other living things within the darkness are being drained of life. The shadow magic of the moon goddess's mate, the darkness that comes with the light she holds. If only I remembered that part of the story before I told him.

Fuck. Fuck. Fuck.

"LOEN, STOP and look around," I scream at him through the mind link, and his wolf eyes widen as he looks around us. *"It's okay. Just breathe and come closer to me."*

He takes a few steps closer to me, and when our wolf forms touch, the rage in his body drains. The light that was going out because of him is now coming back. He is the darkness to the uncontrollable light I try to hide from, and I am the light to the darkness he feels within but keeps hidden. Okay, Fate, I get it. Fate bound eternal souls. I was never going to be able to push him away no matter how hard I tried. I get that now.

Are you happy now? I ask the Goddess of Fate in my mind as I look to the sky for a second.

To my surprise, she fucking answers, *"YES."*

Well, that's a new one.

I have a feeling there are going to be a lot of new things coming my way now. Let's hope that it's good things and not more of the dumpster fire my life has been until this point.

"May, are you okay?" Loen asks through the link, and without responding, I nip at him and take off running. It's time for a little distraction. It doesn't take him long for him to be right behind me. I doubt he is trying too hard. I'm slower than I should be.

The cave wasn't that far from the cottage. It shouldn't have taken us as long as it did to get back this way, but we may have gotten a little sidetracked halfway back. I'm not even the slightest bit upset about that either. It turns out he likes the little push-and-pull game we do, too, and it doesn't take much for either of us to get lost in each other.

I think I understand why Harper and Clay don't even seem to realize Serafina and I are around or notice when we come into the apartment when they are together. If they get lost in each other like I do with Loen, I get it and will never tease them about it again. That's a lie. I like teasing them, and they give it right back.

"Hey, if you keep putting your ass in my face, I'll have to pin you to the ground again," he says, causing me to stumble.

Oh gods.

I lose my focus and trip over a log I was about to jump over. Fucking hell. I kind of flip and roll a bit before regaining my balance. Shaking my body from head to tail, I turn and glare at Loen who is now standing on the log I managed to clumsily trip over. If a wolf could smirk, I'm pretty sure he would be. That was super embarrassing.

"How do you expect me to focus on not falling on my face when you say stuff like that?" I ask, and he jumps down and stalks toward me.

"You should know how to move without having to focus that much. How many times have you let yourself be in this form?" he asks, and I ignore him and start walking toward the cottage.

I twisted something in that little show of how clumsy I am. I know it will heal. It was a little strain, but I'm still super embarrassed.

He's so steady on his four legs, and I'm like a new pup learning how to work her paws.

"It's okay, May," he says. I can tell he's trying to make it sound comforting.

"I know," I say but keep walking. The pain fades as I walk it off. Instead of pushing me, Loen slowly walks behind me.

A loud scream echoes through the forest, and it catches both of us off guard. My ears perk, and I try to focus on where that scream came from. It was definitely a female, and she sounded terrified. It sounds like it came from the same direction as the cottage.

Loen takes off, and I know that means trouble. I follow as closely as I can, trying to keep up with his giant gate. But it's hard. I need to spend more time in this form. I trip again but catch myself before fully falling. I can see the cottage, and something looks off to me and that's when my eye catches something to the left side of the cottage.

"LOEN, STOP," I try to yell through the bond. Something is wrong. My gut says he is in danger if he goes in blind like he's about to do.

"Loen, please stop. Something isn't right," I yell again.

He still doesn't stop, and I decide I need to use my magic to stop him before he gets his ass killed. Looking around as I'm running, I dart to my right. A downed tree is angled just right so that if I can run up it fast I could jump off it, and I should land close enough to him to get his attention or get a barrier around him to stop him. Running up the tree, I shift back into my human form.

That was smooth.

Thank gods my magic is stronger. I shift and create a simple outfit, a tank top and a pair of simple black bike shorts. This was one of the tricks my mother tried to teach me before she died. I'm happy I remembered the spell. I look to my left as I race up the down tree and spot Loen, who is more focused on the cottage than where I am. I'm not taking that personally right now. He makes a turn my way, and I'm in the perfect spot to drop down almost directly in front of him.

I look down at my hands to see the stars glowing. I summon my magic, collecting the energy to make the barrier spell. Not ideal but I doubt landing in front of him will break that hyperfocus he has.

"Last chance, Loen. You need to stop and listen to me," I say through the bond one more time.

Nothing.

I jump from the tree and land on my feet, bending my knees and helping my body absorb the impact, landing only a few feet from Loen. I outstretch my arms in front of my body, palms facing Loen, and spread them apart quickly. A soft white glowing barrier resembling a bubble forms around him. The glow fades, making the barrier nearly invisible. If he doesn't slow down, he's going to hurt himself when he runs into it.

"Loen, stop," I yell but not so loud that whoever is at the cottage can hear.

I stand up as he slams nose-first into the barrier and try not to laugh. His impact sends a bright white magic ripple through the barrier that looks a lot like a ripple on a still pond. I'm now standing with my arms crossed and looking down at him. I bet that hurt a little, and he's probably going to be pissed off. He stands a little wobbly on his four legs at first, growling as he glares at me and then gives a little head shake.

"Did you rattle your brains loose?" I ask with a little cockiness. On two feet, I was faster than him on four. I'm slightly impressed with myself. I can tell he isn't happy with me at all, but I need him to focus on me, not the cottage for like two minutes.

"Don't give me that look. You were running into a dangerous situation blind. Did you learn nothing at the academy?" I ask, and his wolf growls again.

Rolling my eyes, I turn to face the cottage. We are far enough away that I don't think we were seen, but to play it safe, I release the barrier around Loen and point to under the tree I jumped from. Hoping he will follow me, I head to the tree and move some branches out of the way. There's a perfect little hiding hole here.

"Are you coming or not?" I ask. It's probably best to still communicate this way, just in case.

Without responding, he slowly walks under the tree. I reposition the branches, so we are hidden again. I feel the heavy breathing and hot breath of a giant pissed-off wolf breathing on the back of my neck.

"Your breath stinks," I joke and turn and push his chest backward a little. *"You didn't notice the cottage window, did you?"* I ask and wait.

"What window?" he asks, still huffing and puffing like a big bad wolf.

Eye roll.

I move a few branches out of the way so he can see and point to the window on the far left of the door. His wolf ears go back, and he lowers himself to the ground.

"Verena is being forced to glamourize something. I'm guessing there are wolves we can't see," I say.

Gesturing to the house, the left window has been smashed to pieces. The frame is still somewhat intact, but the little squares are missing the glass. The rest of the cottage looks perfect, picture-perfect even. The other thing that caught my eye was a hanging flower pot on the front porch. Those are not flowers you see every day. They are fae flowers, and the vines are moving oddly.

"How do you know that?" he asks, and I glare at him

"Why do you always second guess what I'm saying? Verena glamoured the cottage but left a window smashed out. She also put the illusion of a flowerpot on the porch with flowers you only find in the fae realms. It's a warning. She knows I'm okay and that I'll recognize it."

He shifts down. We need to make a plan, and with my magic feeling better than ever, this should be fun.

Chapter 32: Our New Beginning

Verena

I promised my mother I would protect Mazzy. I failed her when I abandoned Mazzy to rule Sagewood, but part of me was running away from myself. I blamed her. I didn't want to admit it, so I ran away. I should never have left her.

I will not make that mistake again. I will do what I promised our mother I will keep her safe. When we were children, our mother showed us different ways to use our magic. Mazzy was a quick learner. She picked up on spells better than I did, and I was a little jealous of that. But our mother reminded us that we are strong in our own ways.

One spell I mastered before Mazzy was a shared energy connection spell. This spell allows the giver to connect his or her magic energy to another in their time of need. I used that spell on Mazzy the moment I held her in my arms in the cottage. I thought it would help her, but when it didn't do anything, I thought for sure she was going to die.

The moment that connection breaks, I feel a rush of my magic energy come rushing back, waking me up. I think for sure that I am about to look over and see my sister's lifeless body, and I didn't want to look. When I finally look, I'm so relieved to see her spot on the floor empty.

Loen is gone as well, and in my heart, that means she is alive. I step around everyone sleeping on the floor and look out the window as the stars and moon start coming back into the sky. The moon shines brighter than it has in a while.

Mazzy is alive, and her true self has finally awoken along with the magic of her mate, Loen. The true moon goddess is awake. My job now is to keep her that way.

Turning back away from the window, I go back to my spot on the floor. I try to go back to sleep, but my mind keeps me awake. Our ancestors fucked up all those years ago. They never should have locked her soul away on the moon. She was never going to hurt any of us. She was chosen to protect us, all of us.

My heart is so happy my sister is alive, but it sinks the moment I realize this fight is nowhere near over. The others will now know of her existence, and now, she'll be hunted by anyone who feels she is a threat to their power. I will do everything in my power to keep this world's true luna, the moon goddess alive.

Sitting up, I fiddle with some strings on the blanket I have on my lap. I don't know how long I'm zoning out, pulling the strings on the blanket, but it's long enough that I don't hear or sense anyone coming near the cottage.

Out of nowhere, the cottage door opens, and a pack of wolves rush in, overpowering us all. No one is ready for this sneak attack. For shifters known to be idiots, they do a good job sneaking up on us. We try to fight them off, but they have a witch on their side, who enchanted ropes to tie us up.

I hate witches. When they feel they are stuck, they will do whatever is asked of them to get out of debt, like help people do terrible things. The male witches are usually the ones telling off the females to get blackmailed. They are pissed they were stripped of their powers after the gods found out they helped curse the moon goddess.

Tied up on the floor of the cottage, I need to find a way to signal Mazzy and Loen—ideally without the attacking shifters noticing. It's the middle of the night, and I'm sure Mazzy and Loen won't be returning here until after the daybreak. The amount of magic that awoke in her will knock her out for a few hours while her body adjusts to it. We will have to play captive for a little while.

"Althea, it's okay. It will all be okay," I whisper to her. We are tied up and placed near the center of the room. We are far enough away from each other that we can't untie one another without one of our lovely captors noticing. Althea doesn't respond, only a small whimper escapes her mouth. Soren is tied up adjacent to us with a look of pure rage on his face. Althea must mean a lot to him.

I'm slightly impressed with the witch who enchanted the ropes. Her charm on them is actually quite good. She made sure none of the shifters could use their abilities and blocked me from using any magic to untie them. She probably should have thought about a different enchantment because while I can't untie the ropes, I can still do other things like place a few little tricks for them to stumble on. I'll have to make them count and not be a risk for one of us to get caught in.

"Alpha," a male voice says to my left. A tall dark-skinned man is standing at the door, wearing what looks to be a rather old leather jacket and jeans, but they are both so dirty that they are almost more dirt than clothing. Yuck, no wonder it smells in here now. These guys need to take a bath.

"Is she here?" a deep voice asks as a large man who looks somewhat similar to the twins walks through the door.

"She is, sir," the filthy man says as he moves out of the alpha's way. Althea tries to shrink herself like if she curled up small enough, she would disappear into the floor unable to be seen.

Poor girl.

"Breath, darling girl. It will be okay," I whisper, trying to calm her, but I can tell my words mean nothing.

The alpha walks over to us trying too hard to make himself seem powerful by stomping dramatically each step. When he reaches in front of Althea, he squats down and reaches for Althea's face.

"Touch her, Daren, and I promise I will take your head off," Soren yells from across the room.

All that gets out of Daren is a gravelly menacing laugh as he stands back up and turns around to face Soren. Althea keeps her head hung low, trying to hide her face with her hair. Daren stalks toward Soren, who isn't showing an ounce of fear.

"I trusted you, Soren, Brother," Darren says, stopping in front of Soren.

"Go to hell, Brother," spits Soren.

"After you, Little Brother," Daren says as he takes a blade out from his belt. He's going to kill him. I need to do something.

Think of something, Verena, come on. You can't use magic to get out of the ropes, but you can use magic to stop him from killing anyone.

"Our mother treated you like a prince and treated me like trash," Daren says as he squats down in front of Soren, blade in hand. "She should have loved me as she loved you. Then maybe I would feel some remorse for ending her favorite son's life." He raises his arm.

There is no way Daren doesn't know that Soren's mother is not his biological mother. He has to know. That information wasn't super hard for Mazzy and me to figure out. Okay, it helped that we could use magic...so maybe he doesn't know.

"Daren, you may not hurt any of your captives in this cottage," I say using my fae magic to place a mini curse on him. If I knew his full name, I could curse him for life or worse, but knowing his first name will have to do for now. "I claimed this cottage as part of my realm years ago. You are on my land. You will not harm anyone." That's a lie, but it's worth a try.

Daren laughs, making me feel slightly unsettled. He should not be laughing at me like that unless he knows I am lying.

"Fae Queen, I am not in your realm. You will not claim this land even if you wanted to," Daren says and turns to me. "You look a lot like your mother, you know that? I remember her face. I will always remember the face of the fae bitch who cursed me to lose my wolf," he snaps.

My eyes go wide. Shit, I was hoping he didn't remember what my mother looked like.

"You are Colak Dolton's firstborn child, the true firstborn," I say with anger. "You were ordered by your bastard father to attack my sister and kill my mother."

Daren has taken his sights off Althea and Soren and is now focused on me. This isn't good, but at least, he isn't a threat to Althea or Soren for the moment. I can see the faces of the twins off to my right. They are shocked by what I said. They had no clue their father had another child and definitely not that it was Daren, the alpha of Blackheart pack.

"Your bitch of a mother took my wolf," Darren says, reaching for me and picking me up by my throat "You will give it back to me." He presses his blade against my neck.

"I will do no such thing. My mother's curses are permanent, so I couldn't even if I wanted to," I say with a blank expression. I will not show this man any emotion. He will not have the satisfaction of scaring me.

The cold blade cuts into my flesh, but as he starts to cut, the cottage fills with the sound of breaking glass. He drops me, and I fall to the floor onto my knees. A few drops of blood from the small slash on my neck drip down my chest, staining my skin and tank top.

"What the fuck was that?" Daren yells. "Find out." He points to his pack. A few start searching around the inside of the cottage and a few head out to search outside. Darren heads toward the backdoor of the cottage. Letting a shaky breath out, I try to compose myself before Daren comes back over.

"The less you say to him the less he will hurt you," Althea whispers so softly I barely hear her.

"Althea, did he hurt you?" I ask her.

"He told me who he was, that he was my older half brother, and even though he was twisted in the head, he wouldn't mate claim his own blood," she says. I'm relieved by this, but the way she says it makes me worry there's more. "He let others hurt me, a friend of his, Tristen, a cop he sent to track down Loen after his bounty hunters never came back," she says, and my heart sinks.

Tristen is the one who hurt Bex, Mazzy, and who knows how many other women. Fucking monster. He wouldn't hurt her in that way but would hand her over to a man who would. How could he hand over his own sister like that?

"Daren beat me daily. He only stopped when Soren became my bodyguard. About two years later, Soren convinced Daren that if he was trying to pass me as his mate then having a mate battered and bruised would give the pack the wrong view," she admits.

"So he started hitting me in less visible places and eventually stopped beating me." She looks up at Soren who is looking at her with sadness in his eyes.

You can tell his heart is breaking, knowing what Daren has done to her and what he let Tristen do to her. Both of those men deserve a curse worse than death itself. I'll give it to them if I get the chance.

The loud sound of a knife stabbing into wood echoes through the cottage, causing us all to look up. Daren is back, standing at the table in the open-concept kitchen area stabbing the table over and over again with the knife he held to my neck. He has an evil smile on his face.

"Nice try, Fae. Your men should have been stealthier about their attempt to rescue you," Darren says. I completely forgot I had two fae checking on the cottage. I hope he didn't kill my men. If he did, I get to choose what happens to him.

"Alpha, the two fae guards are dead, but they caused a mess out front. It looks very obvious that the cottage was attacked. I think it will stop Loen from getting too close," one of the wolves says.

"Well then, we should find a way to fix that, shouldn't we," he says, turning his head to me.

I know where this is going, and I'll absolutely take advantage of that. Darren gets up and walks in my direction again, stopping in front of me he brings the blade to my face.

"Glamour the cottage, fae, unless you want to lose one of those pretty eyes of yours," he says, bringing the blade closer to my eye.

Glady, you dickhead, I think.

"Okay" is all I whisper out. Let him think this will go his way. It won't. I'll put clues into the glamour for Mazzy to see. Let's hope she picks up on them.

***

A little after sunrise

The attack happened a little after midnight, and it's now sometime after 9 a.m. The sun has been up for a little bit and so has my glamour spell. Daren is sitting at the table. He is clueless to the warning in the glamour and so is the witch. Turns out, she is good at enchanting things to keep people prisoner but not much more than that. I thought I heard a wolf howl a few minutes ago, and I swear if Loen gets my sister hurt or killed by coming in here raging and blind, I'll make his afterlife hell.

"Hey, he isn't that dumb, Sister," Mazzy says in my head. As much as her smart-ass attitude gets on my nerves at times, I'm so grateful to be hearing it. Thank gods, she is talking to me.

"Mazzy, fucking hell. Thank gods you're okay. Also, he is that dumb," I say. Only she has the magic to allow me to talk to her like this. Talk about a nice power, huh?

"Better than okay. Got any tricks up your sleeve? Or do I need to do all the work, like always?" Mazzy asks. Gosh, I love my sister.

"Just one, but I need a distraction, love," I say. I do have a trick up my sleeve, but I have a feeling I won't need it.

"You got it!" she says in excitement. I should probably be slightly afraid of the way she said that. A loud cracking noise like a bat breaking causes everyone to jump to their feet. It's quickly followed by a loud thud and the ground shaking under us. *"A tree? Mazzy? A tree is the best you've got?"*

"Not even close," she says in my head again. What is she up to?

The sky goes black as night, and so does the inside of the cottage. It's like a blanket of solid black has surrounded the cottage.

"How did you do that?" I say.

"It's a secret," she says.

There's my sister, the girl not afraid to let her sassy side shine. The doors of the cottage open as the alpha sends his men to check it out, but as soon as they exit, it gets quiet, too quiet. I feel the ropes around my wrist drain of magic and use my own to untie all of our bindings.

Soren takes that chance to shift and heads right for Darren. He tackles the alpha out the door of the cottage. The twins are on his heels, wanting a piece of the man who kidnapped their sister and held us hostage.

We walk out to a sight I wish everyone could see. Standing in the middle of a pack of wolves, Mazzy bows down with her stars and moon markings on full display. Her eyes are white as she lets the magic inside her show. The alpha wolves are not his anymore. They are hers. They have no choice but to follow her directions.

Soren has the alpha pinned to the ground with his teeth at the alpha's neck when the darkness surrounding us starts to fade and the bright sun of the warm summer day returns. The trees and grass surrounding the cottage are dead like the forest surrounding it was drained of life in seconds. Loen's magic. Yikes, the gods packed one hell of a kick with that gift. Soren still has his teeth on Daren's neck, raising his eyes to Mazzy and not letting go of his prey.

"Soren, do not kill him," she says in a stern but soft voice. She knows why he wants to hurt him, but something tells me she has far worse planned for him than a quick death. Mazzy looks around. The wolves around her don't move a muscle.

"Loen," she says, looking over her left shoulder as the rest of the blackened sky lets the light back in, and out of the shadows of the trees, a giant black-as-night giant wolf appears. The wolf walks right past Mazzy heading in Daren and Soren's direction. She tilts her head watching him walk by her. She lets a small smile form but only for a moment.

"Loen…the same goes for you," she says, and the black wolf lets out a growl but stops in his tracks only a few feet away from Daren.

"Hello, little wolf… I'm so happy you are awake, Goddess," I say to her, looking up and smiling. The power she has is overwhelming.

"Goddess? Not possible," the pinned alpha says through gritted teeth. Something tells me the wolf on his back is biting down just hard enough to make it hurt but not kill him. Good. He deserves that, at least.

"Soren, please let Daren go," Mazzy says. I can see Althea's eyes go wide as she stands next to me, and I nudge her with my arm.

"Don't worry. She isn't going to hurt Soren, she knows," I whisper to Althea, who looks at me in a slight panic but then relaxes.

Soren reluctantly gets off Darren, who sits up holding his bleeding neck. He looks pissed. I look from Darren to Mazzy who has let some of her light dim a little. She showed her power. She doesn't need to show that much anymore.

"Bitch," Darren snaps.

Oh, snap. That was the wrong thing to say, dumbass.

In seconds, the black wolf is on him, baring his teeth and growing in Darren's face. The alpha looks absolutely terrified. Loen in his wolf form is impressive. He is twice as big as an average male wolf and so black in color that only his eyes would be visible if he were in the shadows. He is showing a great deal of self-control because something tells me he wants to rip Darren's head off, literally.

"Althea?" Mazzy asks, startling Althea when she realizes Mazzy addressed her.

"Yes, ma'am," she says with a shaky voice. *There's no need to be scared, sweet girl*, I think. Knowing Mazzy is trying to get information from Althea, I step forward.

"Mazzy, the man deserves a curse worse than death. Not only is he one of the men who took our mother from us, but he allowed Tristen to use Althea's body how he saw fit. When that wasn't happening, he was beating her."

Soren moves away from Daren, who is still pinned by Loen and surrounded by the other two, Jayce and Zyon. Soren nudges his wolf nose against Althea's arm, and she collapses, hugging him. Bex moves next to Althea and Soren, watching over her brother and friend.

"A curse worse than death, Sister?" she asks, and I nod.

"Loen, let him up. I have something I need to ask him," she says as she walks toward

Loen and Darren. With some hesitation, Loen backs off Daren but stays in between him and Mazzy.

"This was not your plan, and you are not fully to blame for this, are you, Darren?" Mazzy asks. He is still terrified, lying down where Loen had him pinned. He doesn't even try to sit up. "Are you fully to blame for this?" she asks again, squatting down near his head.

"No," he stutters. "My father, my biological father, he said the territory is rightfully mine. Both are since I was the son of the luna of Blackheart and the alpha of Crestwood." He doesn't move from the ground. Loen backs away from him and looks at Mazzy. She stands and goes over to a second SUV I hadn't noticed before.

"Is that enough for you, council members?" she asks, facing the SUV.

What is she talking about? I think as the passenger door of the second SUV opens and a man in a black suit gets out of it. I recognize him the moment I get a good look at his face. He is the fae head council member for the southern territories.

"It is enough. He will be dealt with accordingly as well as Colak Dolton, former alpha of Crestwood," he says as he walks to Darren. "Loen, both territories are yours to do whatever you wish with. Your father and your half brother are going to be handled by the council." He reaches down and helps Darren to his feet. It's not gentle. He bends Daren's hands behind his back and cuffs him with silver cuffs, causing Darren to hiss in pain. Hold up? He shouldn't be in pain because his wolf was taken from him a long time ago. I turn to Mazzy with a puzzled look. Mother's spell was permanent. Only she or someone nearly as powerful could... Oh.

"I'll explain later," she says. I hope she didn't give his wolf back to him after what he did to us and Althea, but I can't worry about that right now. Right now, my heart is bounding thinking about this

council member. He could have Mazzy killed, but she's standing there like she knows he won't hurt her. As the man puts Darren into the back of the second SUV, he turns to Mazzy and bows his head.

"Luna, please stay safe. Anything you need, please reach out. For now, I would suggest you all get out of here before the rest of the council shows up," he says, opening the driver's side door and looking into the backseat. "And if you say anything about the goddess here to anyone, I'll gladly feed you to her mate, who looks like he very much wants to make you bleed," he snaps at Darren in the backseat.

After hugging Mazzy tightly, I apologize for leaving her for so long. She doesn't blame me, and I think she has learned to finally stop blaming herself. I'm headed to my realm to inform my people of the death of two of our own at the hands of the wolf shifter Darren. We will see justice for our loss. As I walk to my realm, I am passed by two wolves running together, a snow-white wolf with piercing blue eyes and a giant black-as-night wolf with eyes of amber. I smile and look at the sky for a moment.

The moon goddess has awakened. As I reach my kingdom, I take a deep breath before passing through the portal. All I can think about is how much this world is about to change. One curse is broken.

This is our chance to right the wrongs of the past and…start our new beginning one story at a time.

Epilogue

Few months later

Loen

"Princess? Are you okay in there?" I ask May. She's been in the ladies' locker room for the last two hours.

"I'm fine," she yells through the door.

She's not fine. I can feel it. But I will let her come out when she is ready, or until we are insanely late. Then I'll break down the door and carry her out.

"You better not or you won't get laid for a month," she yells.

Fucking mate bond. Sometimes, I forget she can pick up on some of my thoughts if they are about her. I don't always mean to share them, but sometimes I do. Like now, I laugh to myself.

"Mind out of the gutter, Loen. I don't need to be horny and anxious at the same time thank you very much," she says through the door.

"How about you come out here or let me in and I can take care of one of those two issues?" I tease. The dress she has on is stunning and shows off her amazing curves so well. I couldn't stop looking at her. Until of course, she turned and ran for the hills—or in this case the locker room.

"Seriously, Loen. You need to stop. I'm fine," she lies. I can feel her anxiety.

Thank you, mate bond.

"Is she still hiding?" Zyon asks from behind me.

Turning around, I come face-to-face with my younger brothers Jayce, Zyon, and our sister Althea. They are all dressed in what is supposed to be formal attire. If we don't get going, there will be no event to go to.

"Zyon, how many outfits did you bring to try on?" I asked.

He was in a green suit, but now, he has on dark blue jeans with a white button-up shirt, a brown suede vest, a dark blue jacket to match the jeans, a blue tie, and brown dress shoes. Won't lie. This outfit is probably the one I like the most. The one before the green one was tan. It didn't look good on him at all. This one, however, looks nice. He also kind of matches with Jayce a little. Jayce has on a brown pants and vest suit with a baby blue button-up shirt, a light brown tie, and similar brown shoes as Zyon. Identical twins wearing similar but still different-looking outfits.

"Hey, now, Althea has changed like four or five times at this point, so why aren't you picking on her?" he asks with a pout.

Why? Because she spent five years being assaulted by Tristen whenever he wanted and beaten by our asshole half brother, that's why.

"You can't tell her that," May says through the bond.

"I know, but it's true," I say. She's right, though. I can't tell them that. She hates it when we treat her like she's fragile.

"I hate it too," May says. Okay, okay, I get it.

"I'm sorry, love," I say. I don't mean to treat either of them like they are fragile, but they kind of are.

"Zyon, if she wants to try on a bunch of outfits, let her. I'm just picking on you," I white lie. Althea is so strong, but I know she hates it when we treat her too gently.

"You don't have to hide it, guys. I know you don't say anything 'cause you think I'm fragile or breakable," Althea says. Her expression is half sad, half pissed.

"No, we don't, Thea," Jayce, Zyon, and I all say at the same time.

Yeah, that wasn't convincing, boys. We need to work on that.

"I don't think she's breakable one bit," Soren says as he comes down the hallway and grabs hold of Althea's waist, bringing her tightly into him.

"Get a room, you two," Jayce teases.

"Think there's time? How much longer is the new luna going to hide in the locker room? I can make it quick," Soren says teasingly but also probably half wanting to know if he does have time to take Althea somewhere for a quick trip to Pound Town. That's my sister… Nope, not going there.

"Soren, stop," Althea says as she wiggles free of Soren's arms and swats at his upper arm. "Let me see if Mazzy will let me in." She walks to the locker room door.

I hope she lets her in. I know she's anxious, but none of us are going to let anything happen to her. As Althea passes me, I get a better look at her in this dress. I think this final dress suits her. The other two were more modest and dull. This one is a red corset floor-length dress with sheer off-the-shoulder straps and a flowy sheer layered skirt. There's a high slip up one side, and the big brother in me wants to safety pin that slit so it's not so high up her leg. But honestly, she looks amazing. She matches it with gold jewelry and shoes, and her jet-black hair is in long curls.

Soren is literally drooling over her. This dress shows the fire this girl has inside her, and I'm proud of her for showing how brave she is. Let's hope my mate doesn't destroy that in like two seconds.

"That's fucking rude," she says through the mate bond.

"Sorry, Princess," I respond. I need to work on that.

Althea walks up to the locker room door and knocks on it twice. The doors open for her and shuts the moment she gets inside. Before I can get to the door, I hear a click. The door is locked, again. Ugh, I wish she would let me in.

Mazzy

After letting Althea into the locker room, I sit back down on the bench. She is standing at the door with her eyes wide and a look on her face like she wants to say something but isn't sure what to say.

"You can just say it, Thea," I say.

"Umm, you look stunning Mazzy, but umm…" she trails off, standing silent again.

"I know, I'm glowing, right? Like literally. I felt the tingle which is the sign my anxiety has taken over and my magic is starting to spiral out of control, and now, I can't calm down. None of the stars will fade, and the more I think about it, the more anxious I get and the brighter the glow becomes," I ramble on and on. I'm so anxious I feel like I'm going to throw up.

I can't show this yet. I'm the moon goddess, the soul chosen to protect all life and magic. This also means I'm being hunted by a lot of people who fear my abilities. Luckily, they don't know exactly who I am yet.

Everyone who knows is keeping me safe and keeping my secret. But it won't be a secret for long if I can't get control over my fucking magic. As I think that last thing, the lights glow so much brighter than they were before, and the locker room lights flicker then go out. Fuck my life.

"Ahh," Althea screams. "Mazzy, are you okay?" she asks, staring at me. I look like a giant glow stick at this point.

"Yeah, Thea, I'm okay. Just feeling defeated," I say. Looking down, the glow has started to fade, but it's still there. I'm lighting the room now. My magic surge has blown out all the lights in the locker room.

"Hey, is everything okay in there?" Loen yells through the door.

"Everything is fine," I snap back to him.

Fuck.

What am I going to do if I can't calm down? How am I supposed to go to this stupid luna ceremony and make it through it? I'm not ready to be a luna.

"You are ready," Loen says through the mate bond and that makes me smile.

"I'm not but thank you for trying," I say back to him. He's trying so hard, and yet, I'm still a giant mess.

Loen looks so handsome in his suit. He's keeping it classy in all black, and I think he looks sexy, especially with the top few buttons of his shirt unbuttoned.

Sexy.

Nope, not going there. I need to focus and thinking about sex is not going to help that. But oh, it would be such a good distraction right now, and Loen always makes me feel so good.

Shit, shit, shit. Get your head out of your pussy, Mazzy.

"I'll put my head there instead," Loen says to me through the bond. Fuck, nope. No, not right now. Fuck it.

"Hey, can you switch with Loen? And take Thea and the twins for a nice long walk?" I ask her.

"I'm picking up what you're putting down. I have sex on the brain, too. I think I can throw a stick and the twins will chase it for like twenty minutes," she says, and we both start laughing. The stars on my skin fade more, and the room is getting darker.

Finally calming down some.

Althea unlocks the door and opens it with a smile.

"Oh, Loen, your mate needs your undivided attention," she teases as she walks out the door.

Rolling my eyes, I wait for Loen to come in. This is a bad idea. We have to go. We are going to be so late, and the ceremony is for me. I can feel the anxiety start to bubble up again, but before it can take hold more, I'm grabbed by two strong arms and pinned up to the locker room wall behind me. Loen's scent fills the air, and I'm instantly calmed.

His mouth finds mine in the dark, and I can't get enough of the way his mouth feels on mine. My hands wrap around his neck as his hands reach under my black dress, finding my ass. He gives me a gentle squeeze, lifting me so I can wrap my legs around his waist. I can feel the heat starting to run through my body. He breaks away from the kiss, and I gasp for air but miss his mouth on mine.

"What?" I ask, looking at his eyes and then at his mouth. I want to kiss him again.

"You look stunning, Princess," he says and then crashes his mouth back on mine. This time, he deepens the kiss, slightly moving his body into mine. I can feel his erection in this position, so I grind my hips a little. He must like that because he lets out a low growl-like moan into my mouth and then releases the kiss again.

"We are going to be late, Princess, but I know one way to remove that anxiety at least for a little while," he says with a smirk.

He carries me over to the bench in front of the lockers. Straddling the bench, he sits down while kissing me and then leans me back, so my back is resting on the bench with him on top of me. His hands wander under the dress, and I'm waiting for him to realize I have nothing on underneath. He should have noticed when he picked me up but if he did his face didn't show it. Moving the long fabric of the dress up more, he slides his hands up like he's going to remove my panties then pauses. Pulling away from the kiss, the look in his eyes is that of excitement and a little bit of shock.

"Love, were you planning on going to the ceremony like this?" he says as he flips the dress up revealing my lack of undergarments.

I smile and the glow of the stars starts again, but this time, it's not out of anxiety.

"I was. Is that a problem?" I tease.

"Yes, 'cause now I won't be able to focus on the ceremony because I'll be thinking about your bare pussy," he says and lowers himself to me. Instead of kissing me, he kisses my jaw and then down my neck. This dress doesn't give him access to my breasts which is a bummer because I love it when he plays with them.

"I'll play with them later, love, after the ceremony," he says.

I roll my eyes. I forget about the mate bond sometimes. It's heightened when we are connected. I can see a few stars on his skin, and the marking of a moon on his neck starts to glow too. His markings showed up after we claimed each other six months ago.

"Loen," I moan as he keeps kissing my neck, nipping at it gently a few times as his hands roam my body. One hand reaches between my legs, his thumb finding my clit. He starts gently moving his thumb.

"Loen, please," I moan, and he brings his mouth to my ear.

"Those aren't words, Princess. We talked about this," he says in a deep voice into my ear. "Tell me what you want."

"I want," I pant and stop talking. I can't focus on talking at the same time he's playing with my clit. It feels too good. My brain kind of shuts off.

"Come on, love. What do you want from me?" he demands again. This time, his other hand is now at the base of my neck, weaving through my hair. He gives it a slight tug.

"Loen, I-I want to come," I moan louder. Gods, I hope Althea got the four of them out of there fast because I cannot be quiet anymore. The locker room doors aren't that thick.

"Anything for you," Loen says as he kisses me quickly then pulls away, removing his hands from my hair and clit as well.

"Hey," I say starting to sit up, but he leans back into me

"Did I say you could get up?" he asks in a deep voice that turns me into a puddle.

"No," I said meekly.

"Good girl," he says and moves his body down mine until his head is between my legs. The way he says "good girl" sends tingles down my spine.

"I told you I will put my head here, and that's exactly what I plan to do," he says as he puts his mouth on my clit, moving his tongue around it and sucking on it now.

"Yes, yes," I moan and grab his hair with one of my hands. He lets out a growl but continues licking my clit. I start to grind my hips, chasing my own pleasure. Loen lets go for a moment to catch his breath then dives right back, assaulting my pussy with his tongue.

"Yes, fuck, yes, yes," I moan louder. As I get the last "yes" out, Loen shoves a finger inside me, and I gasp in pleasure. "Oh, gods, yes," I scream.

"Like that, Princess?" He goes back to my pussy before I get a chance to answer him.

"YES, don't stop… Please, don't stop," I moan. I'm getting close to the edge, and I want to go over it. Loen pushes another finger inside me, moving them in and out of me at an increasing rate as he sucks and licks at my clit.

"Faster, Loen, faster," I plead, and he does as I ask, moving his fingers out of me faster and pushing them deeper. "Loen, I'm going to come," I moan as he doesn't slow down his movements.

"I'm coming," I scream out as my body shakes and my pussy clenched around his fingers. After a few seconds, he slows his movements and stops altogether. Bringing his face to mine, he kisses me deeply, and I can taste myself in his mouth.

"Good girl," he says when he releases me from our kiss. "Now let's get you cleaned up. We have somewhere to be," he says.

"But—"

"But nothing, Princess. This was about you right now. Though I can't promise I won't try sneaking a few fingers inside you whenever I get a chance while we are at this party." He smirks and heads to the sink.

Okay, I think I'm ready now. If not, I'll make him do that again.

Loen

Fucking hell.

I knew this girl was going to be the death of me. I can't get enough of her. I want to be touching her, kissing her, and pleasuring her every chance I can. If we didn't have a ceremony and a party to go to, I would have ripped that dress off her and fucked her right in the locker room. I'm pretty sure that's what she wanted me to do, but I like the idea of teasing her during the party. A little payback for trying to tease me with having nothing on under her dress.

After cleaning us both up and fixing our clothes, we left for the ceremony. I can't wait for everyone to see how stunning she looks in this dress. My Mazelynn, my beautiful May, is in a black off-the-shoulder floor-length dress. The skirt is layered similar to Althea's, but the slit up the leg goes a little higher which I love. There is a black sheer layer over-the-top that has embroidered silver stars all over it. Her dress looks like the starry night sky. Her silver hair is half up and half down with star-like glitter in it. She looks like a vision to me, and I can't wait for everyone to see her.

The goal is to get to the ceremony location without any detours or distractions, but I have a feeling with the way May is looking at me in the passenger seat of the SUV that we are going to hit a detour—and soon. The look in her eyes is intense. When she licks her lips, my cock twitches. I want this girl so badly, and damn it, I don't think I'll be able to wait until after.

"Hey," May says in a soft voice. I let go of the steering wheel with my right hand and reach over to touch her face.

"Yes, Princess?" I ask her, keeping my eyes on the road but wanting to be looking into her eyes.

"Pull over please," she asks. Her tone sounds a little off, so I move my hand back to the steering wheel and look for a place to pull over. After finding a little turnaround, I park the SUV and turn to May

"Is everything okay, love?" I ask, but I don't get an answer from her. What I get is her mouth on mine, her arms around my neck.

Pulling away from the kiss, she looks at me with her amazing blue eyes, and I'm a goner.

"Backseat, NOW," I demand, and she hops in the back without hesitation. I unbuckle and climb back there with her. After I'm sitting in the backseat next to her, I go to grab her, but she stops me.

"Wait," she says and crawls across the seat toward me. Gods, she's hot as fuck.

"You got to taste me. It's only fair I get to taste you," she says, and I recognize that look in her eyes. That little devil is right there.

"Princess," I warn her. "Once you start, we won't be stopping," I say, and she reaches for the belt buckle of my pants, undoing it as she nods her head.

Assisting her, I help her free my cock from my pants, and she instantly grabs it. My eyes close, and I tilt my head back, letting out a low moan. Anytime she's touching me, I'm a happy man. Before I open my eyes, I feel her tongue lick the tip of my cock. I fist her hair giving it a slight tug as a reminder of what I said. She lets out a moan.

"Open your mouth," I demand, and she instantly opens her mouth. Moving her mouth over my cock, she slowly takes me in her mouth coming up and going further down with each bob of her head. She bottoms out my entire cock in her mouth.

"Fuck, your mouth feels so good," I say as she starts to bob her head up and down faster. "Princess, fuck this feels amazing. Keep going." I reach my hands up the back of her dress and find her pussy. She's soaking wet when I push my fingers inside of her. She lets out a moan but keeps sucking on my cock.

"Oh, Princess, you are incredible taking my cock in your mouth, but I need to be inside you. Get up here," I say as I grab her ass with one hand and use the other to grab her face and bring her mouth to mine.

She follows my movements, so she is straddling me and lowers herself onto my cock. Her wet pussy takes every inch of me.

"Ride my cock, baby," I say as she starts moving her hips and working my cock.

Her moans and sounds are pushing me closer and closer to my release, but I want her to get one first. I grab the back of her dress and give it a tug, popping the top button off the back of the dress. She reaches her arms back and undoes a couple more of the buttons all while grinding on my cock. Once her breasts are free of her dress, I pull one to my mouth and start sucking and nibbling on it. That seems to be enough that her moans are now higher pitched, her movements picking up pace.

"Baby, you need to come for me," I say to her. She moans, throwing her head back and moving her hips faster and faster.

"I'm coming," she screams, and I pull her mouth to mine as I fill her pussy with my release, kissing her deeper. I kiss her until we both can't breathe. When we pull away, we are both panting.

"I love you, Loen," she says. I smile at her. "What?"

"Nothing, this is the first time you said it first. Normally, I say it first, and you say 'I love you too,'" I say and smile at her again.

"I love you, Loen. Until the last star in the galaxy dies, you have me, all of me," she says as she pulls my mouth to hers again.

She used my line on me. I love this woman.

My luna.

Lost in her eyes and touch, I don't care to move, but a chime on a phone pulls her attention away. Jumping off me and practically flying into the front seat, she grabs her phone.

"She finally messaged," she screeches as she comes back into the backseat with her phone in hand and a huge smile on her face.

"Serafina finally messaged me," she says with a smile, but that smile fades but not to one of sadness.

Serafina left for a modeling gig a few days before the May almost-dying thing. She refused to answer any calls or texts from May, Harper, or Clay. She only messaged her father, Archer, who kept telling May to give her space.

May worries she took the job to get away from her, and she might be right. In her defense, the mate bond makes shifters super possessive, so I get it. But Serafina didn't and still doesn't. Archer says May has to be the one to explain the situation to Serafina, but Serafina isn't giving May the chance.

"May? Is everything okay?" I ask.

"She says wants me to leave her alone. No matter the explanation, she never wants to see me again. That I'll never find her because she glamoured herself from me," she says, and now I understand the look.

Serafina can't glamour herself. May told me about the glitter bomb thing and how Serafina's magic can't hold spells for more than a few minutes.

"She's in trouble," I say, and all May does is nod her head. "We will figure it out, Princess," I say, pulling her face to mine kissing her softly then letting her go. "I promise."

Thank you.

Thank you so much for taking the time to read my book. I have always loved creating stories and had an absolute blast writing this one. Thank you to my husband for pushing me to keep going. Thank you to all my new book and author besties for all the support and advice along the way. I couldn't have done this without all the support.